HIKING IN

BILLIJO LINK

BONETRAIL MEDIA

For more information contact,
Bonetrail Media
www.bonetrailmedia.com

Cover design by Books Covered

ISBN 9781734287004 (paperback) | ISBN 9781734287011 (ebook)

*"Sometimes, you have to explore outside
to discover what's inside."*

CHAPTER ONE

April's smartphone showed 12:55 a.m. Forty minutes had passed since she had last checked. She decided that this Saturday night was a bust. Maybe if she got up and made a cup of tea, she'd feel better.

In her kitchen, the idea of turning on the ceiling light felt too bright. She opted for the nightlight cast of the stove light. It helped her pretend that this was a short intermission and not an entire night of lost sleep.

April looked through her tea boxes. What flavor did she want? Impatience had her hands knocking over traditional standby boxes like dominoes. Standing on tiptoes, she dug deeper into the cabinet. Then April saw the old box of spearmint. It was Justin's.

He missed this box. It had been almost three months.

She withdrew the package and stared at the tea bags as if they would reveal answers. Closing her eyes, she inhaled the dried mint. The smell brought up a memory of her ex-husband sitting at the kitchen table after an afternoon ski. One hand cupped around a mug of tea and the other hand holding his phone while he read sports scores. The beginning of a work-induced stomach ulcer had motivated him to switch from coffee to tea.

His transition month swapped Justin's affability for a sulky, grump who had headache complaints, sharp responses, and moaning about the absence of his favorite drink. When April pointed out his favorite beverage was beer, he bleated, "You know what I mean."

To be a good sport, April had switched to tea in the morning. After a week, she began to leave the house thirty minutes earlier so she could purchase a to-go coffee on her way to work.

April dropped the tea box and stomped on it. It felt good. She stomped again and growled, "Things were supposed to be different."

Then she ground the box into the wood flooring.

She thought about that day and the events that followed. It had been an ordinary spent-at-home mid-summer Sunday afternoon. Justin had been watching the end of a ballgame when April sat down on the other side of the speckled cement-colored couch. He didn't acknowledge her and kept his attention on the last minutes of the game clock. The time ran out.

Justin leaned back into the deep seats. He tipped the last of the beer bottle back into his mouth. "Man, can't beat that last play. Seriously, so good."

"We have to talk," April said. She gave Justin credit as he hadn't groaned aloud. He put his empty beer bottle on the coffee table and swiveled to look at her.

"What's up?" Justin asked.

"Are you happy?"

"Ya."

April tried again. "Are you happy in our marriage?"

"Happy enough."

April rubbed her eyes. "Is it enough? Justin, you're a good man, but I'm not sure we're right for each other."

"What do you mean? I asked you to marry me. We got married. Is this about having a kid? Do you want to have a baby?"

"This isn't about having a baby."

Justin rubbed his eyes. "What do you want?"

April had been asking herself that question since last winter. The desire for answers rolled around her heart. She was attempting to discover them. "I want to be happy."

"I thought we were." His bewildered expression reflected April's heart.

"Are we?" April asked.

"Yes. We're not the happiest couple, but marriages have their dips."

"I think this is more than a dip. It's like were two friends living together." They had met their senior year in college, fallen in love, and together had matriculated into tax-paying and lawn-mowing adults who shared each other's lives and a house.

"April, we're just going through a phase."

"I don't think it's a phase."

"What do you want?" Justin repeated. April said nothing. "If you're going the direction I think you are, then you have to say the words out loud. I'm not doing it for you."

"We don't act like a couple in love. When was the last time we went on a real date? Not just grabbing dinner so we could sit on the couch and watch TV while we eat. You don't hold my hand anymore," April said.

"We had sex a couple of days ago."

"That's it. You said having sex. It wasn't making love."

"Fine. I'll call it whatever you want," Justin said.

"I don't want you to call it what I want. I want you to name it for what it is."

"I don't get you. We have a good life together. It's not perfect, but what relationship is? You're willing to walk away from our marriage because you're upset I don't hold your hand? Grow up, April."

"We've grown apart."

"Cut the crap. You've got some idealistic fantasy in your head. Marriage takes work."

"You think I haven't been working at our marriage?" April asked.

"You're ready to walk because you're in a rough patch. I'm happy. Why can't you be happy? Why aren't you satisfied?"

She wanted to be. "I want a divorce," April said.

Justin's chin drew back, and his eyes narrowed. Squeezing the bridge of his nose, he then said, "If this is what you want, I'll get my stuff out of the master bedroom and move into the spare. *You* set this into motion."

Her soon-to-be-ex-husband left the room, the TV on, and the empty amber bottle on the coffee table. They continued living together. To April, Justin moving into the spare bedroom felt of little difference to the rhythm they had lived together before the divorce talk. The worst of their tussles involved sharp words of painful dismay and detachment. They began to separate their lives and the food in the fridge.

Two weeks later, on a Saturday afternoon minus any explosive outbursts or harangues, they divided their joint assets and debts with efficiency and quickness. April bought Justin out of the house, and they each kept their individual retirements. There had been no war with Justin, yet they surrendered their marriage vows.

April mentally reversed out of her recent past. Several of the tea bags had burst open. Mint flakes stuck to her foot. She didn't bother dusting them off and tracked the scent to her bed.

Next, when April awoke on her high-thread-count marriage sheets, the time was 7:55 a.m. She stared at her blank white ceiling as the fall morning's sun rays slipped into the room.

Divorcing Justin was supposed to have moved her life forward in a happier direction. Rejuvenate her. Why did she feel so bad he was gone? This was the change she wanted, she asked for, and was given. He didn't even fight for the house. Had she wanted him to fight for the house? Was she upset because Justin didn't put up a fight for her? The last question made April's breath stall.

Why should he fight for her? She gave him his walking papers. It was insane ego to want a divorce *and* have Justin pine for her. April rolled over and pressed her cheek into her pillow.

What did she think would happen? That exiting her relationship with Justin would be like turning off a faucet of dissatisfaction? Maybe April should have stayed in the marriage longer? Maybe their relationship would have improved?

April kept second-guessing. Maybe she should have tried harder. Justin should have tried harder. They could have tried harder. She did try, and her marriage still failed. Was that the saddest part or her absolution? More 'maybes' spooled around her head and heart, wrapping tighter. Her shoulder-length brown hair soaked up her tears.

She had known there would be sadness with her divorce, but April was surprised by the sorrow she was caught in. Her new freedom was supposed to bring in more happiness and contentment. *Was she in a cage of her own making?*

April laid in the memories of her past, the rubble of her present, and wondered what to do next.

CHAPTER TWO

At mid-day, April returned to the kitchen. Thirsty and exhausted, she walked around the mashed tea mess on the floor.

She opened the kitchen cabinet and withdrew a coffee mug. Earlier that spring, she and Justin had discussed upgrading the 1980s chipboard cabinets or at least replacing the scroll hand pulls he sometimes jammed his fingers on. Those conversations felt like a lifetime ago.

April could update and switch out the hardware on her own. What style and design did she want? Before the divorce, they would have discussed the choices and decided together. She liked making her own decisions, but she missed his input and knowing there was another person to depend on. Breaking the habit of including Justin in her plans was more tangled than she had previously understood.

Skipping water and coffee, April opened a bottle of red wine and poured herself a full mug. Seated at the kitchen table, she sipped but did not taste.

April started thinking about Justin's new life. It had only been a few months since their breakup.

Had he already found someone new? April's stomach tightened. She wondered why that thought felt sharp.

Justin was free to date anyone he wanted. Was it because April hadn't wanted him to replace her so soon? She was the one who let him go.

Knocking back the wine like water, April scowled. Somewhere in her subconscious, she had forecasted she would be the first to find someone. It was a nutty prediction. Their divorce was not the starting pistol for a replacement race. It would be better if Justin were so devastated it took him a long time to find someone. This convoluted pathos whirled in her mind.

April wondered where he was living. She hadn't asked where he was moving to. His choices weren't her business anymore. April lashed herself with the thought that she should have cared enough to inquire what his plans were. Being honest with herself, she acknowledged she hadn't wanted to know.

She moved the empty breakfast mug in circles across the cherry butcher block tabletop. April recalled her surreal evening a month ago. That Friday in early September, the St. Paul, Minnesota sunset had been rich bands of dusky coral, peach, and canary yellow with a topping of sea blue.

April had entered the house and stood in the entryway. Something felt different. She walked to her bedroom to change out of her work clothes. A chrome floor lamp was gone. Her sweeping gaze noted a sloped-back Scandinavian chair, a shelf of books, and a Montana mountain vista photographic print, a wedding present from Justin's parents, were missing.

To confirm her theory that Justin was moving out, she went to the guest bedroom. The door was swung open all the way. The bedroom suite was gone. April stood still in shock.

A framed seaside landscape he had disliked, and a wastepaper basket remained. Justin had emptied the trash. The courtesy and finality of the action bothered her.

April barreled into the guest bathroom and yanked open the vanity drawers. The pulls gave easily as no weight impeded them. All were empty except for old hairs and lint. Next, she looked in the shower. He had removed his shampoo and plain, unscented soap.

Back in the bedroom, April stared at the carpet imprints from the former furniture. Then she leaned on the doorframe, and the tears began a slow slide down her cheeks, eventually accelerating into sobs.

He was gone. The divorce had become real.

When she woke the next day, April felt discombobulated. During sleep, the iron-gray sheets had twisted around her legs. She untangled herself and went into the master bathroom. In the mirror, she saw matted hair, puffy cheeks, and a blinking, bloodshot-eyed thirty-two-year-old woman trying to remember the new reality she had faintly envisioned.

April shucked off yesterday's work clothes then turned on the shower. She leaned under the direct water spray and pressed her forehead into the white subway tiles.

"Wash your hair. The shampoo suds can run over you," April told herself. Her voice echoed loud, making her wince.

Exiting the shower after the hot water tank's gallons had wrinkled her skin, April stood on the bathroom rug wrapped in a bath towel, wrestling with what to do next. No immediate decision came, and she continued to grasp at ordinary tasks. Eat something?

It was something she could do. Once in the kitchen, she couldn't decide what to eat. April recognized the ridiculousness of her inability to choose. The realization wasn't strong enough to shake off her dazed state. She wanted something easy, like crackers and peanut butter.

With a decision pinned to the top of her brain, April opened a cabinet. She saw crackers but no peanut butter. Confused,

April's eyes and hands skittered over groceries trying to find the jar. It wasn't there.

"That son of a gun took the peanut butter!" April yelled.

That's when April noticed several other food staples were missing. She struggled to comprehend: that not only had Justin moved out without telling her, but he had also taken the *peanut butter?* She wanted to throw something but instead chewed and ground the brittle, salty crackers.

April's silent diatribe raged at Justin. He just had to take the peanut butter. He couldn't have bought another jar? She was the one who bought it. That man is a jerk. Next time April was at the store, she'd buy the boutique, organic kind.

A decision made. April continued eating to dissolve hunger pain. She wondered what else her ex-husband had taken. Leaving crackers and crumbs scattered on the countertop, April, still wrapped in a towel, rushed and dove into every room, closet, and cabinet, adding recriminations for her ex-husband's actions of doing the deed while she had been at work.

What movies did he take? She was sure he took all the good booze too. It'd be just like him. What about the personal pictures?

April found several of his books, a worn-out pair of running shoes he used for yard work, and their wedding pictures. Exhausted by her angry scavenger hunt, April returned to bed.

It was late afternoon when a knocking cut through her drowsiness. April ignored it. The sound increased to a pounding. She pulled a pillow over her head. It went on a few more minutes, and then stopped.

Then April heard her name called. Like a confused search and rescue pointer dog, she held her head up and listened.

It was Lauren. She and Lauren had been friends since their first post-university corporate jobs.

April croaked, "Up here."

"There you are. Thanks for not answering the door," Lauren said.

Too weary to defend herself April shrugged.

Lauren looked April over. "How are you?"

"What do you think? I'm upset."

Lauren lifted her eyebrows and then lounged beside April on the bed, arm propping up her head.

April sat up. "Sorry, I'm a jerk and a basket case. This divorce was supposed to be easier. It was supposed to make me happier. I thought I was ready. I had saved money to buy Justin out of the house when the time came. I tell him, and he's crushed. The crazy thing is that he didn't stay mad. Nope. After a few weeks of my divorce demand, he starts a new life."

"How long did you expect him to hang onto the marriage?" Lauren asked.

"Not forever, but the guy moved on fast."

"Would you have preferred him to drag his feet and make a stink about divorcing?"

"No. I don't know. His anger should have lasted at least six months."

"April, that's crazy. He gave you what you wanted."

"I know. I expected this all to be easier. In a way, I had already started to emotionally leave my marriage before even talking to Justin. I'm surprised at how sad and unsteady I feel."

"Maybe before it wasn't real enough?" Lauren offered. "Just because you're the one who wanted the divorce doesn't mean there wouldn't be grief and loss when it ended."

"I want to get through this and feel better."

Lauren patted April's shin. "Give yourself time. That will happen."

"I hope so because my heart hurts." April's heart squeezed in response. There was a helplessness tied to the idea of staying in the emotional hole she was in.

Lauren stood up. "Get dressed. We're going to the movies."

"I'm not going to the movies."

"Yes, you are. Hurry up. The movie starts in half an hour."

Avoiding arrest for indecent exposure was a substantial detriment, so April dressed in yoga pants and a sweatshirt. Wearing underwear and socks demanded too much and was skipped. She didn't remember much of the movie and was glad the darkness and the surround sound hid her.

On the way back to April's house, Lauren asked, "What food do you have at your place?"

"Crackers. There are frozen meals in the freezer."

"Do you have any pasta?" Lauren asked.

"Maybe." April couldn't recall if Justin took it all.

"We're stopping at the grocery store."

"Lauren, I don't want to go to the store." April paused, then added, "I don't want to go to work on Monday."

"Ask to take a mental health day," Lauren suggested.

"I could be sick all week."

"Take a day or two off. I know you're still processing your divorce, but you can't hide from the world."

"Says someone who's never gone through a divorce," April said.

"Low blow. I'm trying to help. You think hiding at home is going to make the situation better?"

April pulled her hand across her eyes before any tears fell. "Maybe?"

Lauren gave April the stern look she used on her young children. "You're coming inside the store."

April followed Lauren around the store. They didn't converse so much as have a question and answer dialogue.

"Do you want spaghetti or penne?" Lauren asked.

"I don't care."

"Penne, it is. Should we top it with grape tomatoes and basil or sauce?"

April muttered, "Whatever."

She knew she frustrated Lauren. A part of her wished she cared about the answers with an eagerness indicative of their friendship. The other part wanted to crawl back under her gray and white duvet.

"Dessert?" Lauren asked.

April didn't want to pick. She wanted to sleep until she felt normal again. Was that what she wanted? To feel like she felt before?

"Shut up," April moaned.

"What did you say?" Lauren asked.

"Sorry, I'm having a little psychological break."

"It's temporary," Lauren said as she picked up a slice of double chocolate cake.

April found the dinner with Lauren lasting forever. She wanted Lauren to leave. An element of rationality kept her in check. She knew Lauren watched the amount of food she ate and her behavior. If April didn't pretend to behave somewhat normally, Lauren would not leave.

"How'd you know to come over today?" April asked.

"You didn't answer any of my texts or phone calls."

"Sorry," April whispered.

"Plus, Justin called and told me he moved out."

April's chin jerked up. Her eyes bore into Lauren.

Lauren kept speaking. "He wanted to move out by himself. He thought you might be upset by that."

Some of April's hurt lessened at the idea that he needed his own space to move from the house that had been his home for five years.

"Justin is a good guy. I just wasn't in love with him anymore. Our marriage faded for me. I wasn't happy."

Lauren squeezed April's hand. "I know."

When the meal was over, April grabbed Lauren's plate. "I'll clean up. It's getting late. I bet you need to get home."

"I'll help."

"No, you cooked. My turn. Do you have a busy week ahead?" April asked.

"My presentation for the board is Wednesday. The kids have their swimming lessons on Thursday. We're going to the zoo this coming weekend. Come with us. We'll make a day of it."

Panic clenched April's throat. She appreciated Lauren's invitation. The idea of spending the day at the zoo with Lauren and her family, and all the happy people, felt exhausting.

"We'll see. If I take any days off this week, I might have catchup work this weekend," April said.

Lauren long hugged April. April had seen her friend embrace her children this way after seeing crocodile tears and hearing about hurt feelings. "We'll play it by ear. I'd better get home. I'll call you tomorrow. If you don't answer, I'll come looking for you."

"I'll answer."

Lauren patted April's back. "I know all this will take some time to get used to. Tomorrow, get up and take a shower. Just start there."

CHAPTER THREE

After Lauren left, April was alone again in her home and mind. The day spent with her friend had wrung her out. Leaving the kitchen lights on, she went to the couch and fell into an out-cold sleep.

April, still in her movie clothes, camped on her couch. She called in sick on Monday and Tuesday. If she stayed home a third day, her employer would require a doctor's note.

She could go to the doctor. Tell her the truth. April ached.

Calling her doctor felt arduous and shameful. She returned to work on Wednesday. April was grateful to bury herself in the distractions of her job. After the workday, she didn't rush out of the building. There was nothing on her calendar. No one waiting at home.

Later at home, she dropped her jacket and brown canvas messenger bag on the floor by the door. Again, she parked in front of the living room television and switched channels at footage of happy couples. Crime dramas kept her attention.

For the remainder of September, April continued this pattern and gave the minimum social participation with Lauren and her parents. After telling her family about the impending divorce, they had extended support and asked if she needed anything. The subsequent weekend following Justin's moving out, her parents, Sue and Duane invited April, her older brother Kevin, and sister-in-law Natalie to Sunday brunch.

When April arrived at the restaurant, her family sat underneath patio umbrellas sipping from their 'build your own' Bloody Marys. She watched her uncertain family examine her pale face, comfortable clothing of blue jeans, a striped shirt, and slip-on shoes, and her greeting for nuances to help direct them.

Safe topics of weather, work, and wayward relatives dominated until the end of the meal when her Mother's wellbeing questions poked, "April, are you taking care of yourself? Getting enough sleep?"

The familial looks of concentrated concern pushed into April's depression and ignited a wave of slow-burn anger. She knew they wanted the best for her, and that concern made her feel embarrassed. "Some nights are better than others."

"I was reading that ... when ... a marriage falls apart ... divorce ... daily care routines and activities are often disrupted," Sue said.

Her Dad jumped in. "Have you thought about snow removal this winter? If you're going to hire it out, now would be a good time to start looking for someone."

Not knowing quite what to say, April borrowed from Alcoholics Anonymous. "I'm taking it one day at a time."

Sue fiddled with her toothpick drink spear. "Have you considered that maybe you moved too quickly to divorce?"

No one said anything and remained still in their seats.

Sue kept going. "I'm not saying that divorcing was a bad idea but maybe you jumped the gun."

"It wasn't a decision I made overnight. Justin was happy with the way things were going and I wasn't. I wanted more." April said.

Work was April's constant. When she told her co-workers about her impending divorce, they spared several minutes of sympathy. They extended compassionate guidance: "You'll get through this." Several suggested, "Make sure you get a good attorney."

Post-divorce, she contacted the Human Resources department to change her tax form and other documents.

When the HR representative asked who her new emergency contact was, April was stunned. She stammered out her parent's names. Another lifeline connected to Justin was cut away.

The house was emptier and lonelier without him. Extinguished was the comfortable routine of sharing, cooking together, and hearing him load the dishwasher or set-up the lawn sprinklers. April missed the everyday noises of living with another. In the quiet, there was plenty of time to think, and she wanted to avoid thinking. April was unhappy and home-sick. Small moments of vibrancy and color occurred, and she tried to hang onto them before they faded.

The rarity of social invitations had become April's norm. A divorced friend had once told her that divorce fractures a couple's social strata. Some of her and Justin's couple friends had sided with Justin and ignored her. A few maintained a relationship with both of them, and many had disappeared. April found her 'new' friendship roster bleak.

The lessening daylight and October temperatures triggered the trees' dormancy. Red, yellow, and rust colored leaves dropped and layered her home's front and back yards. April raked up six bags in resigned acceptance of her longer chore list. Halloween, the precursor to the upcoming holiday season, was near. This Thanksgiving would be April's first family holiday as a divorcee.

Justin was becoming memories and old photographs. She

still had her wedding pictures. Throwing them away seemed wrong, but she wasn't sure what to do with them. They stayed in plastic containers with her school yearbooks.

April had thought divorcing Justin would help solve her happiness problem. She had accomplished the logical and promoted benchmarks of graduating high school and then university followed by career and marriage. Hadn't she done what she was supposed to do? She reprimanded herself at the acknowledgment that her first-world life was good, and she should be appreciative and not discontent. Was this all there was to her life?

Colder, quiet November arrived. The neighborhood tucked itself into their homes. April's furnace noises rattled and echoed in the house if the television was not on.

It was the Friday night before Thanksgiving. April held the freezer door open and stared at her meal options. Instead of deciding between pasta or pizza, her thoughts ran: *I should have gone to the gym after work. I could bundle up and go for a walk. It's too cold. It could start snowing. I should be on a date. It's supper in front of the TV again.* She had been standing there long enough that the temperature gauge had triggered the blower to replenish the frozen environment.

She closed the freezer and moped to her living room television. Maybe comedy and dancing programs could stall her frustration, and now restlessness.

April had started dating again with the help of online apps. Last weekend's date had been a bust. The sushi was tasty, plus it had been refreshing to have supper that wasn't delivered or picked up in a drive thru. Her date was a nice guy whom she had much in common, but there had been no spark of interest for either person. When it came time to leave the restaurant, the awkward moment of deciding whether to shake hands, hug, or walk away with a goodbye tossed over the shoulder could stall the parting, but she appreciated this last guy. He hadn't wanted to hug and linger. The huggers exasperated her the most. There was no need to embrace a stranger when the meetup had been more interview than romance. Her experiences back in the dating pool were lackluster.

April tossed aside the couch blanket. It was 10:30. She could go to bed, but why bother? She had nothing scheduled and nowhere to go tomorrow. What had been the point of changing her life if she had nothing to look forward to?

The next morning, April lay on 'her side' of the bed, feeling sorry for herself. She was living less than before the divorce. There had to be more. She needed help.

Maybe this weekend she would buy a self- help book. It could give her some direction or inspire her to more happiness. Or was it joy? She couldn't recall which one she was supposed to pursue. It was probably both?

Two days before Thanksgiving, her Mother telephoned. "Hi Honey, just wanted to check what time you're coming on Thursday? We'll be eating around one."

"I'll be there by noon."

"Why don't you come earlier? You'll have more time to catch up with everyone."

April rubbed her forehead, "I'll have all afternoon to talk with them." She dreaded her family's questions about her new life minus Justin and the pitying looks that were bound to occur. There was no avoiding going.

As for Thanksgiving, her Mother didn't relent. April gave in and arrived early with her assigned pumpkin and apple pies. Her brother Kevin opened the front door of their parent's split-level house causing the attached autumn fabric wreath to bounce.

"Saw you come up the walkway," Kevin said.

"Thanks for opening the door."

"Yup, just to let you know Mom's told everyone not to mention Justin."

April sighed and slouched against the now closed door. "She didn't need to do that."

Kevin shrugged. "Aunt Kathy already started in about how much she likes Justin, and why couldn't you stay married to him. I'd advise taking an adult beverage with you before saying hello to her."

"Thanks for the advice."

Kevin grinned. "Helping where I can."

"Do you think my divorcing Justin was a mistake?"

"Do you?" Kevin asked.

"I'm second-guessing myself."

"People can change and want different things. Maybe it was a starter marriage for you."

"Thanks for not deriding my choice."

"I like Justin, but you're my sister. Loyalty first. It's straightforward to me."

April had thought the divorce would have been straightforward for her.

Sue wearing a leaf-appliqued apron approached them in the house's foyer. "April's here," their mother called out.

Kevin leaned in. "Remember my beverage suggestion," and moved out of the way as Sue side-hugged April.

"Why are the two of you whispering by the front door?" Sue asked. Before the children could respond Sue asked, "Could you two add another leaf to the table? We need more space."

April took Kevin's advice, then pitched in to help with the cooking and cleaning. The activities minimized personal one-on-one conversations. She went home at the earliest opportunity as her family relaxed in their sated post-meal reposes and played card games.

She pushed through Christmas Eve and Day in a similar

manner. Days before New Year's, April's loneliness reached a level unlike any she'd experienced before. She felt stuck in her life, her home, and the winter.

An extended acquaintance invited her to a New Year's Eve house party. Among strangers wearing sparkly paper hats, April laughed too loud and indulged in the early evening cocktails and later night champagne until she saw the room become blurry. At midnight the revelers blew foil horns and pulled poppers. The amplified cheer blasted into her drunken haze. In seconds, April felt disconnected from the celebration. She wanted to go home.

While she waited for her Uber driver, April stood in her party host's windowed front porch. The enclosed cold cooled her overheated body. Music and laughter seeped through the wall and invaded April's solitude. As each minute piled on top of the previous minutes, a self-created misery infused with her loneliness. April decided she had to do something different.

CHAPTER FOUR

April was disinterested in making a new year's resolution, but she knew she needed some type of change. Her present life was no different from the previous fall. She was stuck in an emotional muck. April needed something different to move herself in a happier direction. Seeing a therapist was an option under consideration. Before she pursued that choice, April decided to read self-help books hoping they would point her towards what she wanted.

In the second week of January, April went to the library seeking help. She felt awkward standing in the aisle browsing titles. People walking by would know she couldn't get her life together.

April skimmed the standing book spines and saw the repeated words: happiness, change, steps, new, and healing. Which ones would help her? Her shoulders started to tense. There were bound to be a few duds on the shelves. April detected a small headache beginning to form.

Selecting a book should not be causing her anxiety. She ordered herself to pick a small stack. She chose the books with the slimmer spines betting that she'd read the entirety of those books over the thicker titles.

Later in the evening, she folded laundry and revisited her awkwardness at the library. April paused in triple folding a bath towel to stare at the library books stacked on her coffee table. No one had been watching her or cared which books she had chosen. She might as well read one. Maybe something in the pages would help.

April picked up the unfolded clothes from the couch and dropped them on top of the folded laundry already in the basket.

After choosing the book on the top, she sank into her couch. April hoped for anything that would help and reduce her misery.

For the rest of January and into February, when she wasn't at work, April mined other people's ideas about happiness, meditation, cognitive reprogramming, color therapy, rearranging furniture, Eastern thinking, and nutrition looking for gold nuggets.

Some authors' claims inspired her in the first chapter but didn't carry her through to the last page. When she was done with a book, she grabbed the next one from one of the piles on her bedside, kitchen, and coffee tables. She revisited the library for the next rotation. The books, and then later podcasts, blogs, and ebooks, helped April accept that significant life changes required processing time, taking her future in steps, and getting a hobby. One of her biggest realizations had been the recognition that she burdened her marriage with the whole of her unhappiness.

A week before Valentine's Day, April needed groceries. She rushed into the store with a shortlist and avoided the holiday card section. She pretended to not see the red and pink hearts hanging from the ceiling. She looked past the heart-shaped candy boxes near the checkout lines. April didn't hate the holiday. She wanted the day of love to go by without her noticing and feeling bad about her uncoupled state. If she was totally honest, an undercurrent of envy hued her avoidance desire.

On Valentine's Day, co-workers displayed delivery bouquets on their desks. April ignored the blooms until a bountiful arrangement of stargazer lilies, pale pink roses, and coordinating bubble gum tulips sent by her parents arrived. Their sweet public gesture, and the strong lily scent, made April feel self conscious.

There was no way she was taking them home, nor did she want to see them on her desk but throwing away the innocent blooms felt peevish and wrong.

After work, April hauled the uncovered flowers to her car. The lilies' muscular scent filled the vehicle, making her sneeze. She opened the door window. The polar temperatures stopped her sneezing and made her nose drip.

She grimaced. *This is my life.*

After pulling into her garage, April pondered the unwanted Valentine's gift.

No way was she taking the bouquet into her house. What should she do with them? Leaving the blooms in the car wasn't an option.

April went with the easy choice. She placed the arrangement in a dim corner of the garage. When she was halfway across the room, April turned around and went back to her parent's gift. On second thought, she'd take the tulips inside the house, their bobbing flower heads more a sign of cheerfulness than romance.

At moments in the evening, April caught whiffs of lilies invoking self-pity. It was like the flower scent had squatted in her nostrils.

The next morning April sniffed the air. Thank goodness, no lilies.

Relieved, she readied for work. In the kitchen, April paused and wondered what she would eat for lunch. Her grocery store mad dash had lessened her Valentine's exposure but also meant she failed to buy enough food.

There must be something pre-made she could take? She would eat breakfast and figure out lunch.

April dropped two pieces of bread into the toaster. She rummaged through her pantry cabinet pondering her canned goods. The late-winter weather had propelled her to eat soup, and she had consumed all in the house. It appeared she would be going out for lunch. She chided herself for not being more organized. If April was better prepared, she could make salads in a jar like her co-worker Kari.

The microwave clock told April she was running behind. She skipped the butter to save time. She balanced the plate of toast and hooked her shoulder underneath her messenger bag. She stepped outside. Her skin tightened, and her muscles clenched at the below-zero temperature. April reversed and went looking for a coat.

A coffee spill from the day before meant her daily winter coat was unavailable. April pulled open the hallway's bifold closet doors. Crammed between all-seasons outerwear, a vacuum, and an assortment of forgotten household items was her knee-length black dress coat. She startled when she saw an old jacket of Justin's.

How had she missed seeing it all the months since Justin had moved out? She used the thought's annoyance to bump the door shut. This weekend she would clean out that closet. Maybe it was time for a spring cleaning?

April did the winter shuffle across hardened shiny, bumpy ice and snow to the detached garage. She didn't dislike the twenty-five-minute commute to work and regulated it to the 'required' adulting list. Arriving at the corporate parking lot, she opened her window, flashed her keycard at the scanner, and parked. Walking into the office was like entering a beige paint can—all sedate and professional. Even the plants behaved in an appropriate, upright manner.

April reminded herself she would need to finish the quarterlies before the workday was over. Her computer background had a Bahamian image showing cerulean water and a white sand beach. The seaside picture was the sunniest view she'd see today. She thought more about her day ahead. The project status staff meeting was on her calendar.

Coffee first, then meeting.

April would need to be quick to get coffee, and early for the meeting, to claim a seat nearest to the door.

Upon her late arrival, colleagues occupied the desired seats. What remained was a spot between Kari and Gary. April supported people participating, but Kari wanted to be involved and know everything that was going on. Gary was a true and false question asker. During meetings, April would think to herself, "Here we go again," as Gary used his favorite meeting conversation phrase of 'True or False.' True or false: If the company decides to renegotiate the Breem account, then we can adjust the timeline for completing the Robertson project? Gary preferred the world to be the choices of this one or that one. April mocked and partly envied Gary's simplistic approach to living.

The meeting was productive and prosaic. At 4:30, April turned off her computer and readied to leave. Avoiding eye contact, she tossed distracted goodbyes to her co-workers and left. She started the car and enjoyed the cloister of frost-fogged windows. The quiet engine idled while she reviewed her day. Today was the same as yesterday and the workday before.

April knew the mundaneness of her life was something many people craved. She had a well-paying job with benefits. April cared about the project development component of her career. But lately, she couldn't seem to ignore her co-workers' quirks, and her irritation was on the rise.

April wrote emails that were sarcastic and snarky, and sometimes even mean. She couldn't add the sender's email address until hours passed, and she had edited the body and tone of the message. The discovery of finding a co-worker had failed to cancel the remaining time of a previous microwave use could initiate an internal angry response unwarranted to the situation.

The cold of the seat fabric seeped into her coat and April shivered. Her thought train stopped. April turned on the defrost. She'd better get to class.

Following the 'get a hobby' directive, she had signed up for a community tennis class. The exercise helped to channel her angst in a different direction. April knew her recent emotional responses were extreme. Yet, she wanted to revel in the flash and feel of her animated anger. It felt warm and energizing, unlike the stagnant hibernation of her depression. This agitated state made falling asleep difficult. Enough common sense remained to keep her mad rushes in check. She didn't want to lose her job or cripple her relationships.

The safe place to release this vexation appeared at tennis. She swung her racket hard and moved quickly on the court, focusing on improving her game.

April doubted anyone noticed her walk onto the tennis courts a few minutes early for tonight's class.

Coach Deborah shouted brusque commands: "Don't just stand there. Get warmed up. Swing those arms high. Not like you're a mass of gelatin. Stay strong."

Then the coach yelled the first set of drill instructions. The class of twenty students ran to the court's baseline. A student was to run to the service line, and then the coach hit a ball over the net. Next, the student was supposed to return the ball to the opposite quadrant and then run back to the baseline to be replaced by another student. Faster and more irritated instructions were shouted at the players. The drill was a lost cause from the start.

April rushed the net at the same time her classmate Shannon exited the court in the wrong direction. April pivoted hard, jerking the full swing of her racket back and avoided hitting Shannon.

"Shannon," Coach Deborah yelled, "wrong direction, other way!"

As the class ran the drills, Coach continued to holler, "Shannon! Wrong way!" The students may not have known everyone's first names, but they all knew Shannon's.

Rushing to hit a ball, the sweat on April's hand loosened her grip. She swung the racket; it almost flew out of her hand. A last-second regrip kept the racket from colliding with the green court floor.

"April, control your racket," the tennis general commanded "Hustle. Hustle."

April raced to the starting line and her classmates. She waited and wheezed. If only the velocity of her breathing could have been transferred to her racket moments earlier.

When the drill was over, four more punishing drills, partnered with Coach Deborah's megaphone volume instructions, followed. The students' ability to line up fast enough diminished. Quiet grumbles and muttered swear words began to circulate and grow a mutiny. Coach blew her whistle shrill and long, ending the class. April limped to the courtside benches.

She heard a classmate say, "I don't think I can feel my legs."

Another responded, "Legs? I lost a lung back there."

"Does the coach remember that this is recreational tennis?"

April said, "I'd like to take the Coach's whistle and hide it."

"She'd probably move up to a blowhorn," Shannon replied.

April groaned. "You're probably right. Are you coming back next week?"

"Maybe. It depends on if I feel like being yelled at or my ability to walk and run ceases tonight."

April swallowed a laugh. "I hope you're okay. Have a good week."

A soreness smarted in her legs as she moved around the perimeter of the courts and proceeded to the exit. Stopping short of the gym's iced over, glass door entrance, April saw the outline of her hunched shoulders before she hobbled into the dark, icebox of an evening. The crunching sound of her running shoes that she hadn't bothered to change before leaving the gym was the only noise.

The stillness caught April's attention. Her exhalations puffed out in front of her face in petite winter clouds. April could almost feel peace touching her person, but she couldn't connect.

On her way home, thoughts about tomorrow made her weary. It was just another day.

She entered her neighborhood and looked at the houses. April admired the cordial glow of lamps and light showing through the curtains and windows. It made her wonder about the occupants.

Are they content? Satisfied? If so, how'd they do it?

CHAPTER FIVE

The warmer daytime temperatures of April continued to melt snow and expose last fall's dried yellow, flattened grass. Green tufts of vulnerable blades sprouted up. Shaded spots in April's yard held dirty, small piles of lingering snow. Purple crocus busted through the waking topsoil.

Eight months had passed since April's divorce. Other than tennis class, her daily pattern was a foot drag to work and home with occasional side trips for groceries, the gym, and infrequent social occasions.

April's tennis classes abated her anger and restlessness. It was after tennis when she could sleep the best. Last fall, she escaped her world and thoughts through slumber. In March, her ability to fall asleep easily and stay asleep through the night were infrequent.

Worrying about what to do with her future and thinking about the past had become an unwanted home hobby. The discomforting memories of slights and cuts she had inflicted on others piled on and infused her with additional regret and shame. Nights of interrupted sleep marked her face with dark half-moon bags under her eyes.

Her part-time insomnia was becoming a health issue. April returned to the self-help guides' suggestions. She tried sleeping with a fan on, taking Epsom salt baths, buying new pillows, and sipping chamomile tea before bed. One night as a Hail Mary, she drank warm milk and gagged at the first sip. Maybe other dairy would work.

She slow-chewed a hunk of cheese. An hour later in bed, April stared at the ceiling and passed gas. At least she was alone in this failure.

April laid there, shifting and searching for any position that would promote sleep and sanity. She was tired of feeling bad about her lack of direction and herself. She was lost. Aside from work and homeownership, she was stumbling through adulthood. Her taxes were due soon. April could no longer bury the paperwork under junk mail and clothing catalogs.

Justin had done her taxes when they had dated and when they claimed the label of joint-household. He hadn't griped. Justin completed the required forms and told her the outcome. She could always depend on him to help take care of things. She missed that.

At what had become her regular after-supper evening routine, she sat in her living room, a side lamp emanating a bright white light, and started and stopped television series. An image of a multi-deck cruise ship floating in-between icebergs as craggy and majestic mountains filled in the background grabbed her attention. The scenery was beautiful. April was surprised by her response. It had been months since a beautiful image had produced awe and appreciation within her. Starting a handful of months before the divorce, her life had been more in grayscale.

The footage was the introduction to a history show about the Klondike Gold Rush. The area was located in the northwest corner of North America and connected part of the United States' southeast Alaska and Canada's Yukon.

A black and white image showed a long line of men hauling bags and boxes on their backs as they hiked up a snow-covered mountainside. At the top, they crossed Chilkoot Pass and continued hiking and boating towards the bonanza goldfields. The wilderness route they traversed was called the Chilkoot Trail. The program showed the current-day landscape of massive mountain ranges that extended beyond the camera's viewing lens. Curiosity propelled April to open her laptop.

The furnace started another cycle of pushing heated air into the house. She typed the search words 'Chilkoot Trail.'

The 'Chilkoot Trail – Klondike Gold Rush National Park' was listed on the first page of results. Her finger clicked on the link--one tap. Not enough pressure to turn on a light switch, but it opened a webpage of historical adventure.

An estimated 100,000 miners, outlaws, lawmen, and every other career and kind that supported and thwarted gold rush dreams used the Chilkoot Trail during the 1896-1899 Klondike Gold Rush. Today, the trail was one of the world's longest, and hikeable, outdoor national park museums surrounded by mountains, forest, and history.

April was entranced by the idea of discharging one's life and livelihood to risk gold mining in a remote wilderness.

Scrolling down the webpage revealed an image of a wood-planked path snaking through a bog and filled with a forest of towering trees. The next picture showed skinny trees wrapped in paper-thin white bark and shiny green leaf canopy shadowing a dirt trail.

It was like an archway into a magical kingdom. She wondered what it would be like to walk through there.

Later that night, April dreamt that she was driving on a road similar to her house street. Snow piled up on the ground. A wind blew in and took away the snow. The cold evaporated. The trees bordering the road leafed out in multi-colored blue, lime green, vermillion, yellow, purple, and other colors she couldn't name. Spindly trees hung low and bowed with the weight of abundant foliage. April wanted to see the forest up close. She stopped the car and got out. April started on a gravel path. The further she walked down, her eyes adjusted, making the vegetation easier to view.

It's nice here.

She started to wake. No. Not yet. She didn't open her eyes. April tried to go back to sleep and recapture the dream. She pretended minutes hadn't passed. April wanted the dream back too badly to feel ridiculous.

The tiniest gap between her eyelids and lower lids allowed the dawn light through.

Lauren's words sounded within her: get up, and take a shower.

April did. The strange beauty of the dream intruded. She couldn't remember if she used shampoo. Instead of drying off, she left the bathroom dripping water onto the bedroom carpet.

She wondered where she had been driving to in the dream.

April paid no attention to the clothing she dressed in. The essential pieces were pulled on, buttoned, and zipped. They might have matched or not matched.

April ate a handful of tortilla chips for breakfast. She crunched and mused on the vibrant trees in her dream. April had enjoyed walking that fantastical path.

It was time to leave for work. Her hair was still wet. She put on a winter stocking hat. The commuter traffic flowed and passed around April as she drove to work. It was as if her vehicle was an obstacle to maneuver around and leave behind.

A few steps into the building April studied the sedate, professional abstract wall hangings, the identical brown leather chairs with their brushed nickel armrests, and the pods of cubicles with their fabric-covered walls and laminate worksurfaces.

Everything looks the same. Very dependable.

It was early. Few employees were in their cubicles. She sat at her desk and turned on her computer. The space between waiting and work gave her a minute to think.

April's heart strained for something different, something new. She had started the year in a muddled place. The likelihood of her future continuing in that direction was strong.

An image of her standing on a flat rock ledge popped in her mind. She could walk back the direction she came or take a turn and walk the other path.

It was time to make another choice.

CHAPTER SIX

Two days later, April's first wedding invitation since her divorce arrived. She had no boyfriend or date. Should she go or skip?

April telephoned Lauren. "Hi. Can we meet for coffee?"

"You sound upset," Lauren said.

"I am. I received my first post-divorce wedding invitation."

"Ohhh. Let's meet at Como Park tomorrow night at seven. We can talk while we walk around the lake."

The next evening, April arrived early. From her parked vantage, she could see sunglass-wearing runners, walkers, and bicyclists on the multiuse circuit. Yellow-cupped daffodils and vase-shaped white tulips growing in front of a thicket of protective squat trees swayed in a promising-summer breeze.

April heard her name called and saw Lauren in the sedan's side mirror wearing yoga pants and a short-sleeved shirt bearing the logo of her children's elementary school.

Lauren waved. "Hi! Am I late? It's nice out."

"You're on time. Summer is almost here."

Lauren pointed at the lake. "Do you want to walk around or go through the park?"

"Let's go around the lake."

The women started on the pathway around the water.

"Aside from the wedding invitation, do you have any plans for the summer?" Lauren asked.

April shrugged. "Nothing yet."

"Are you going to the wedding?"

"I don't know."

"You don't have to go," Lauren said.

"I know. But, I don't want to avoid it because I don't have a date."

"Do you want or need a date?"

"No. Maybe. Weddings are more for couples and families. If I went by myself, I'd stick out."

If April took a date, or a friend, to the wedding, it was because she wanted to bring that person and not use her plus one as an unpaid hired helper. Going everyday places alone wasn't difficult--though sometimes lonely.

"Could you think of the wedding as more of a party than a couple's event?" Lauren asked.

"I suppose." April had gone to the New Year's Eve party by herself. Beyond the presence of couples, the wedding was another example of other people moving forward in their lives while April tried to figure out her next step.

Lauren asked, "Are you still going to tennis?"

"Yes. The class lasts a couple more weeks. I'm nervous about how I'll fill my time when it's over. I'm not sure what I'll do."

April's thoughts about her life's direction had begun to lose the fogginess that settled in the previous fall. She was still unsure. Within her marriage, there had been reliable well-defined status and expectations. A developing clarity and determination she hadn't known in a long while were slow-building inside her. There was also a fait undercurrent of excited curiosity. Last week, April had felt a similar reaction when she learned about the Chilkoot Trail.

Those miners went looking for gold. Why couldn't she look for her own gold? She wasn't tossing aside her life to go prospecting, but perhaps she could take a vacation somewhere new by herself? Nervousness at the possibility made her neck and chest flush red.

April had vacationed with Justin, her family, and friends and had traveled for work. The idea of a solo personal trip thumped in her heart. She had friends who went on their adventures without the requirement or desire for another person. This way of travel was foreign to April, yet it was not unimaginable.

Vacationing by herself wasn't something April did. Was that true? Could she be brave enough to do it alone?

One self-help book advised, regardless of the destination, you always take yourself with you. Was this trip idea best to explore or ignore? If she didn't try, what would happen? Nothing would. April's life continued as it had since her divorce.

Her decision to divorce had transformed her more than she expected. Taking a trip would be an exploration and adventure to a new place in the world and within her. What if it shifted more chunks of past decisions, thoughts, and feelings and revealed a new path? Would she like what she excavated? Was it best kept buried? April didn't want to shovel and shift more bitter scoopfuls. Or, what if it was nothing special? Just ordinary rocky soil that lacked the shine of quartz or fecund vegetation.

She wanted to be done waiting for the answers to rise to the surface. It was time to move beyond the self-help guidance and try new tools to dig and discover what satisfied her. She made big choices for herself before. She'd make another one. Where did she want to go? Asking the question emboldened April.

Questions flowed, rose, and dropped in her brain. What

would people say? Would she be safe? Would she know what to do? How would she do this? Was April too old to backpack Europe? Was she the type to go to an exotic country? She didn't know until she tried.

Excitement was building inside her. It started as a quiver, then a flutter, and now was a frequent feel.

Maybe it was best to pick a popular place? Somewhere nearby, or far away? Beachy, mountainous, or a big city full of people where she could blend in? Did April want to be hidden or seen? Or some of both? She'd had enough hiding during her divorce depression.

Traveling to Mexico and Florida sounded more like a retreat with the likelihood of a spa massage. Port hopping from a ship would be relaxing and yet seemed to be missing the self-discovery component.

April knew she wanted somewhere beautiful and a geographical distance that took her out of her comfort zone. Activities such as bungee jumping and hang-gliding induced survival scare more than joyful living.

Maybe she should go to a national or a state park? A trip to southern Utah, Western Montana, or the Oregon Coast could be possibilities. Was she thinking too big?

April sensed she was coming closer to her destination.

While locations arrived and departed off her mental list, her life continued no differently than the new normal it had become.

On Saturday morning, April wanted a liveliness she didn't have at home. She went to the Bean Perking coffee shop. April waited in line to place her order and studied the 'for sale' artwork hanging on the walls of the hipster café.

Even the artwork gets to go somewhere else.

Lounging customers waited for their drinks. Near the group was a gentleman who April guessed, was in his sixties. He wore grey hiking pants and running shoes, an uncommon look found in this urban cafe. Hanging from his shoulder was a limp and worn backpack with patches sewn on it. Each faded patch was a different shape, color, and design.

One patch drew April's focus. It was a 2x2 square with a background of white and blue mountains, and a foreground with a gold pan next to the words 'Chilkoot Trail.' April gaped as the man reached for his paper coffee cup and then moved to a bistro table next to the street-facing windows. He opened his pack and withdrew an electronic tablet and started to read.

She approached the order counter as another customer stepped away. April wondered what it would be like to be on the Chilkoot Trail.

After collecting her order, April walked over to the travel man's table.

Before she could curb herself, she interrupted, "Excuse me."

The gentleman raised his head and said, "Yes?"

"I was wondering if you hiked the Chilkoot Trail?"

The man tilted his head. "I have. How'd you know?"

"I saw the patch on your backpack. I'm curious about your experience."

Chuckling, the man said, "Forgot about that. The Chilkoot is a fun hike. Incredible scenery. A comradery with the other hikers occurs. Are you thinking of hiking it?"

Excitement made her muscles tingle. She pressed her free hand into her thigh, "I don't know."

"My name is Dan. Do you want to sit down and talk?"

Minus hesitation, April pulled out the opposite chair and sat down. "Thank you. I'm April. Nice to meet you. Was the Chilkoot hard to hike? How did you get there?"

"It's a plane ride or a drive. I flew into Whitehorse, Yukon. Then I made the short drive to Skagway, Alaska. The hotel I stayed at has drop-off service to the Chilkoot trailhead. If you wanted to make your trip longer and more adventurous, you could fly into Fairbanks or Anchorage, Alaska and road trip to Skagway."

"How long did the hike take you?"

Dan's smile contained pride, "I hiked the trail in six days. A person could do it in two or three. I wanted to make the most of my time on the trail. The mountain scenery is incredible."

Dan's face softened and took on the look of someone gliding into a memory.

"The trail starts at the abandoned town of Dyea, Alaska. The first section is in the rain shadow of the coastal forest. You hike through cottonwoods and ferns and across beaver bogs and rivers climbing further into the mountains. The higher elevation takes you into conifer forest."

Dan took a sip of his coffee.

April impatiently shifted in her chair while she waited for him to continue speaking. She was eager for more.

"The hardest day is to and over the Chilkoot Pass. You hike through valleys to reach the Scales, climb up the Stairs, and over the Pass into Canada. Then down the other side through more beautiful valleys and past more waterfalls until you reach Bennett, British Columbia. At Bennett, you can catch the train back to Skagway."

Dan's focus reoriented on April. "The amount of snow in the trail's middle varies each season. Some individuals have hiked or run the trail's thirty-three miles in a day. The time you spend on the trail depends on your physical level and the time you have available."

"Was the hike difficult?" April asked.

"Sometimes. My older knees go slower than most. The climb up the Stairs is the most difficult part. The park rangers have a ready path marked for hikers." Dan's finger made an invisible wiggling line on the tabletop. "The longer daylight allows more hours to hike. How did you learn about the Chilkoot?"

April blushed. "I watched a television program about the Klondike Gold Rush earlier this month. Your backpack patch surprised and intrigued me. I was curious."

Dan leaned forward. "The Chilkoot is a special adventure. If you can do it, do it."

April said, "I don't know if I have the time, or bravery, to go that far away. Thank you for telling me about your Chilkoot hike."

Dan smiled. "Sure thing."

"I had better get going. Thanks again," April said and left the café.

The outdoor sunshine made April squint. She slipped her sunglasses on. The conversation with Dan started to replay in her mind. April considered the serendipitous encounter.

She and Dan were thousands of miles away from Alaska, and yet they had met. April stopped for the red hand of the walking signal. Other than him, she knew no one who had hiked the Chilkoot. This could be a singular trip that was all her own without the coloring and recommendation of someone she knew. April could hear her heart beating in her ears. The idea of the Chilkoot Trail nudged her brain, and maybe even her soul.

April's month of April had a few days left. The Chilkoot floated on the periphery of her mind. Hitting tennis balls, watching television, or reading books could not silence the desire she was half-trying to ignore. The Chilkoot wouldn't go away.

If April went, then she would answer several of her questions. Did she have it in her to do something bold and new? Would such a trip make her happier? Braver? Stronger? Could she create a future different from last week and the year before?

On Tuesday morning, the commuter traffic had stopped on

the interstate. April looked around at the drivers and passengers surrounding her. Some people were on their cell phones. Others sipped from travel mugs. Everyone waited. She felt itchy in this lack of motion.

April decided. She was going to hike the Chilkoot.

CHAPTER SEVEN

April needed to learn more about the Chilkoot Trail. When was the best time to go? How much would a trip like this cost? How did she physically need to prepare? What did she need to know that she didn't realize she needed to know? That evening at home, she sat on the couch with her laptop, feet propped up on the coffee table, and began researching. Driving from St. Paul to Skagway would necessitate crossing multiple states and half of Canada. The quickest, efficient way was to fly.

Where would she fly to? Dan, the travel man, said she could land in Whitehorse, Canada, or somewhere in Alaska.

According to the National Park Service website, April was required to apply for a Chilkoot Trail hiking permit reservation. Would reservations still be available this year? What if there were no open reservations for the dates she wanted? What if a reservation was during bad weather? She didn't know how to hike.

Panic made April drop her feet to the floor, where she kicked a stack of self-help books. She told herself to calm down. A late August reservation would allow her all summer to learn to hike and camp.

Her camping experience included several summer trips with her parents as they camped in a rented recreational vehicle. They drove their lodging and food to a spot and locked the door at night. The Chilkoot hike would involve multi-day backpacking with gear, food, clothes, and tent camping.

What if there were no camp spots for April to set up in the campgrounds? It's the wilderness. There's plenty of space to set up tents. More weird and valid worries crowded into her planning.

Maybe this trip wasn't a good idea. Anxiety had her up and pacing the living room.

Maybe an organized tour with amenities included somewhere else? No, April would learn how to hike and camp. She reminded herself she didn't know how to cook 'camping food.' Maybe she could eat energy bars for each meal?

April crossed over to the living room windows that looked onto the front yard. The soft early evening light gave the neighborhood a cozy feeling. From where she stood, April discerned the tight almond-shaped buds on the trees. In days, the neighborhood crab apple trees would flower ivory and pale pink blossoms.

At the end of the trail, how did April get back to Skagway? Dan mentioned something about a return train. How was she to plan all this thousands of miles away?

April opened a window and smelled the invigorated moisture of building spring showers. The smell soothed her. She'd take it all one step at a time.

On Thursday, April submitted a leave request for late August. The request was denied.

Maybe this meant she wasn't supposed to go. April's momentary relief flipped to anger. She was ticked off.

Would April defy her boss and jeopardize her job for this trip?

She reminded herself to stop acting crazy. April would not make rash decisions because she wanted to go on this trip. Though she wasn't so sure.

Why had the request been denied? She'd ask again.

Her annoyance lessened by a small fraction when she reached her boss Judith's office door. April knocked.

Judith's head came up, and she smiled. "Come in. What's up?"

"I saw you denied my leave request. I was wondering why."

Judith raised her hand and indicated that April should sit in either of the chairs in front of the desk. "August is not good timing. The Macstall contract is renewing. We're going to restructure processes with the renewal. I was going to tell everyone at next week's department meeting. You can request time before or after August."

It was almost May. April needed time to learn to hike and camp. Be easy, she told herself. She needed Judith on her side.

Judith continued, "I'm sorry you're disappointed. We need August to help with the review and rework."

"I disagree. The data can be compiled starting in May. The recommendations made in June. Then the project review starting July 1. All initial hiccups or forecasted bottlenecks will already be attended to by August."

Judith shook her head. "I think we need to build in more time. Again, consider a vacation before or after August or during the winter holidays," Judith said.

"I understand."

"Thank you. Was there anything else you wanted to discuss?"

"No, that's it. Thanks," April replied as she plodded from Judith's office.

How was she supposed to figure this trip out if it didn't get off the ground? Was this providence saying "lousy idea" and "no"? What had April been thinking? This half-baked journey was a foolish attempt at some fanciful fantasy of discovering herself elsewhere. She should get it together right here, right now.

After a sandwich supper, April stood at her kitchen patio door and stared at the dusky blue backyard. She thought about work. April was keen on the upcoming Macstall project, but she wouldn't deny the disappointment of the schedule conflict.

Put the vacation aside. At least for a while until work slows down. Work is important. This trip can come later.

April's thoughts were mature. But, she couldn't deny that she felt disappointed and stuck. As if she twisted herself deeper into the same ground. April felt as if her kitchen walls were moving closer, boxing her in.

She needed air.

Opening the patio door, April went into the backyard in her bare feet. She stood on the stone pavers that she and Justin had laid two summers ago. The bottoms of her feet pressed into the cold burn of the smooth stone.

She told herself to choose another destination and time.

April considered easier trips. Locales not across a continent or on a historic trail, but the desire for the Chilkoot Trail was persistent. April was unable to let it go.

She was going.

The ground didn't quake or entangle her.

On Friday, April submitted a second leave request for the end of July. After the email was sent, she exhaled. She hadn't been aware that she was holding her breath.

This is silly. She was an adult making vacation plans. She'd have to wait and see what happened.

Reports and meetings took precedence. It was late in the

afternoon when April saw an email from Judith. A yes crowned this request. April lofted a triumphant fist into the air. Then she remembered her co-workers could see her. She lowered her arm, then half-stood and half-crouched to look at her department. No one had noticed her.

April was antsy to get home and continue planning. Upon entering her house, she dropped her coat and messenger bag on the kitchen table and fast-walked to her laptop in the living room.

A blog recommended checking simultaneously that Chilkoot Trail hiking reservations were available as well as open seats on the train back to Skagway. If a day's trail reservations were closed or there were no seats left on the train, then scheduling adjustments were required. She would hike the Chilkoot over six days and five nights of camping. On her first day, she'd hike seven and a half miles to the Canyon City campsite. The next day she'd hike another six miles to Sheep Camp. The third day would be her longest and hardest making the seven and a half miles to Happy Camp. April found the name optimistic.

This was the day of the Golden Stairs. The Stairs sounded beautiful and charming. A treat in the middle of the trail. In reality, it was a boulder field up the mountainside and over the Chilkoot Pass into Canada. If a hiker didn't climb the Golden Stairs, the alternative was to walk back to the beginning.

If Dan could successfully climb the Stairs, so could April, she told herself in a voice that sounded similar to her mother's.

The fourth day would be five and a half miles to Lindeman Lake campground. April decided to build in an extra day on the backend in case weather and/or terrain caused a delay. Her last night on the Chilkoot Trail would be at Bare Loon Lake. The last day would be a four-mile hike to Bennett. There she'd catch the late afternoon White Pass & Yukon Route Chilkoot Hiker Service train back to Skagway.

April successfully made her Chilkoot Trail hiking reservation and bought her return train fare back to Skagway. The next day, April purchased her plane ticket to Whitehorse. Her flights' arrival and departure times conflicted with the bus and train schedules from Whitehorse to Skagway and back, necessitating renting a car. The perk of her company's corporate discount eased the sticker shock of the rental price. Another new side adventure was added to April's itinerary.

The next task was to find a place to stay overnight in Skagway the night before her hike began and the night she returned to town.

She wondered what condition she'd be in upon her return to Skagway? Exuberant? Please, let it be that. Limping and defeated? Please, not that.

April booked reservations at a historic inn that had previous iterations during the Klondike Gold Rush. It provided a drop-off service to the Chilkoot Trailhead in Dyea.

The last tasks were to learn how to hike and camp. For experienced hikers and campers, this hiking trip was probably easier going, but for April, this required her almost nonexistent skillset to leap forward.

How was she going to learn to be "outdoorsy"? Why did she think time off was such a big deal compared to learning about walking in nature? Had she bit off more than she could chew? April was exasperated by her second-guessing and lack of outdoor skills.

At home, with a quick chicken salad sandwich in one hand, she opened her computer with the other. She typed in 'how to hike.' The digital search delivered pages of webpage links. She searched a familiar outdoor retailer's website. The site included information and offered classes regarding hiking, layering clothing, and gear. April clicked on the words 'Camping Information.' Another page opened and listed out tent setup, water needs, GPS, hygiene, survival, and more. The word 'survival' ignited bright and hot lightning bolts of concern into April's body.

She decided to read that section another day.

Her eagerness accelerated with the volume of her research. The most fun was delving into people's Chilkoot Trail blogs that often included a packing checklist. Most of the websites posted recent trail pictures as well as black and white historical images. There were aerial panoramas of mountains and photographs of the trail itself.

The blogs ranged from the experts of "it was a moderate hike" to the "it was hard, but it was on my bucket list" and "I'm glad I did it." The bloggers' stories excited April. They all spoke about the beauty of the trail and the pleasure of the experience.

Sometimes the pleasure was dampened by rain, snow, and cold. A few stories reported of snow-packed trails and others of it raining every day. These unnerved April. The Chilkoot Trail had multiple river crossings. She hoped the bridges wouldn't be washed out.

On her to-do list was telling her parents and Lauren she was going.

April met Lauren for brunch. A week had passed since April had made her Chilkoot Trail reservation. As Lauren took her first bite of her runny eggs benedict, April said, "At the end of July, I'm going on a hiking trip."

Lauren stared at April. "This is out of the blue. Who invited you?"

"No one invited me. I decided to go."

Lauren set down her fork, put her forearms on the table, and leaned forward. "Are you going by yourself?"

April stumbled, "Yyess."

"When did you decide this?"

"I've been thinking about a trip for a while."

"A hiking trip? Where are you going?"

April hesitated. Lauren waited. "I'm going to hike the Chilkoot Trail. It's a thirty-three-mile trail that starts near Skagway, Alaska, and goes into the province of British Columbia."

Lauren's eyes widened. "As in the other side of the continent and at the top of the earth?"

"It's not at the top of the earth," April said.

"Close enough. Why there?"

"An adventure. A vacation. The Chilkoot Trail is part of the route the Klondike Gold Rush miners used in the late 1890s. The scenery online looks beautiful."

"Couldn't you have chosen a trip or trail closer to home?" Lauren's question pressed April.

"Probably."

Lauren replied, "okay," as if the word had double the sounds of its four letters. "You still haven't explained why you want to hike this particular trail?"

April was uncomfortable. She scraped her fork tines across her deflating pancakes making lines on their tan surface. "There's something special about the Chilkoot Trail that draws me."

"I see. April, do you know how to hike and camp?"

"I'm starting to learn."

"I think this trip is kind of peculiar, but if this is what you want, then I'll support you," Lauren said.

"You're not going to tell me to stay home?"

"No. Know what you're getting into. Don't do anything dangerous. Call or text to let me know you're safe."

"I can do that." April paused, "thank you."

"You're welcome. I'll go walking with you, but do not expect me to take up hiking."

"Are you sure? You may like it." April laughed. "There's some shopping involved to get ready."

Lauren lifted her fork and pointed it at April. "Now *that* has my full participation."

CHAPTER EIGHT

After brunch, the women went to an outdoor recreation retailer to outfit April for her Chilkoot hike. The warehouse-sized store they stepped into had kayaks suspended from its ceiling; a table of t-shirts printed with the words adventure, epic, and nature; and colorful bikes lined up along the nearest wall.

A salesclerk with a tidy man-bun and wrinkle-free khakis approached. "Can I help you, ladies?"

"I need hiking and camping gear," April said.

The salesclerk focused on April. "What exactly do you need?"

"Everything," April referenced the packing list she had created by merging various Chilkoot hiker packing lists. "Let's start with a tent."

"Follow me. How many people will be sleeping inside the tent?"

"Just me," April said.

Thirty minutes later, April chose a two-pound green polyester tent with a see-through black mesh top. Its lightness and easy set-up merited the several-hundred dollars investment.

The clerk held up the tent's gray and white rainfly and pointed, "I've heard that this rainfly can withstand some hail."

Hail! Another thing for April to worry about.

"There was no mention of hail in my research," April said.

"Hope not. You'll be ready if it does."

Next followed a selection of sleeping bags.

"How cold will it get at night?" the clerk asked.

"Chilly. I'll be in the Alaskan and Canadian mountains in July."

"A thirty-below bag will be more than sufficient," the salesclerk said.

April cringed. It couldn't get that cold in summer, could it? What if it does? She made a mental note to check actual evening temperatures on the Chilkoot. Her essentials gear list continued onto a sleeping pad, camp stove, footwear, and more.

"According to my research, I need a water filter. There's water along the trail. I only have to carry the water I need each day," April said.

"Why do you need to filter water?" Lauren asked.

"To prevent giardia."

"What's that?"

"A water parasite that causes vomiting and diarrhea."

Lauren crinkled her nose. "Yuck."

April selected, per the salesclerk's direction, a water filtration system that resembled an IV bag called a reservoir, emergency iodine tablets as a backup, and a filtering straw that screwed onto a water bottle and allowed immediate drinking from a water source. April and Lauren were learning camping and hiking jargon as the camping gear was added to the black plastic shopping baskets they carried.

The last big-ticket item for the day was the backpack. Another clerk called their guide away. April and Lauren stood in front of the wall of nylon/polyester packs with their multiple zippers, buckles, and straps.

"There's a lot of them. Where do you start?" Lauren asked.

"I need a multi-day backpack. They're the bigger ones," April said.

"Makes sense. You have been learning a lot about all this."

April turned from inspecting a group of women's slimmer bright-colored packs and replied, "I've been researching. I want to be prepared."

A different sales clerk with short-shorn curly hair thudded towards them wearing hiking boots. April took her footwear as a good sign.

"Hi ladies, I'm Courtney. Can I help you find packs?"

Lauren spoke first. "I'm the friend. April needs a multi-day backpack. She's hiking the Chilkoot Trail in Alaska and Canada for a week in July."

April was surprised and warmed at Lauren's announcement. Lauren appeared proud of her. She believed April could do this adventure. April hoped Lauren was right.

Lauren tapped April's arm.

"Sorry, I was thinking. What did you say?" April asked.

Courtney pointed to the wall of backpacks. "Are you interested in any particular pack?"

"I like the blue one."

Oh, jeez. April chose a color and not a requirement.

Courtney cocked her head. "Okay. Which blue one?"

April held up her hands. "This is all new to me. What do you suggest?"

Courtney swung an arm wide. "Let me show you this group of packs. We'll figure out what fits your needs and body frame the best."

For the next hour, April tried on backpacks loaded with weighted bean bags and then shuffled about the store. Her newly expanded body felt strange and cumbersome as she skirted customers with caution. Courtney ascertained a good fit while Lauren watched.

Wearing an indigo-colored backpack, April took a corner too sharp and bumped into a metal water bottle display, making the colorful assortment swing and clink. She scurried over to Lauren and Courtney.

"How does it feel?" Courtney asked.

That April was a poser, and everyone knew. Courtney probably pitied her and doubted she'd come back alive.

"The pack feels fine," April said.

"The pack fits your body and will hold all your gear. Are you comfortable? Do you like it?"

April was worn out and wanted to leave. "I'll take it."

Before she and Lauren could leave the backpacks, Courtney convinced April to purchase a red day-hiking backpack with a pocket to insert a plastic water reservoir connected to a hose and mouth nozzle attachment for convenient water drinking while hiking.

After April paid the eye-popping bill, Lauren suggested, "Let's get something to eat."

As they walked across the parking lot, Lauren asked, "Now that you have your gear, where will you practice?"

"I start car camping next weekend. In June, I'll move onto backcountry camping."

"Is that enough time to learn?"

"I hope so."

"Are you joining a camping group or going by yourself?" Lauren asked with her eyebrows raised.

"By myself. Unless you want to go too? Your whole family could come. We could practice together."

Lauren snorted. "I did some camping when I was a kid. I didn't enjoy it."

"Come on. It will be fun," April semi-pleaded.

"Fine, we'll go camping with you for two weekends, but that's it. I like my bed and indoor plumbing."

"Your husband and kids will love it."

"Maybe. Let me check the kids' summer schedules. I'll get back to you with dates."

April opened her car's trunk. "Do you think I'm crazy?"

"Yes, you just spent a boatload of money on hiking and camping gear."

"You know what I'm asking."

Lauren placed a shopping bag in the trunk. "Part of this hiking idea is crazy, and the other part isn't. If this is important to you, then do it. Face it: there are more dangerous adventures you could be considering."

"Aside from flying thousands of miles so I can solo backpack in a wilderness full of bears and other wildlife?"

"You haven't started cliff-diving, developed an addiction, or joined a cult. I'd say this adventure is fairly healthy in comparison."

"Thanks," April said.

"Your welcome. Let's finish loading the car and get something to drink."

"Coffee?" April asked.

"Oh, puh-lease. Margaritas."

That evening, April laid her day's purchases on her living room floor. She didn't want to remove the price tags. She needed to commit or return the gear.

It was as if there was another invisible gap to cross. April leaped across the first space when she had decided to hike the Chilkoot. Then she jumped again planning her itinerary and trail and flight reservations.

To quiet her trip fears and buyer's remorse, April decided to pitch her new tent in the living room. When she had it all set up, she stood back with pride admiring its construction. She liked seeing it. A wild idea flew into her brain. Should she sleep in there tonight? Try it out? April could move the shelter to the backyard and sleep outside. The idea that the neighbors may see and then wonder about April's sanity stalled her enthusiasm.

The second weekend of May was April's first solo car camping practice. She decided to go to a nearby state park that had restrooms with showers in the campground. The facilities made it feel a bit like cheating, but it also felt more familiar.

When her recently purchased state park vehicle pass arrived in the mail that week, she felt buoyed looking at it. Being an owner of that plastic decal granted a status of legitimacy to her training. A secret desire to show off her new vehicle adornment surprised her.

When the inaugural weekend was a day away, April tried to convince Lauren and her family to come.

"It's still chilly out. We're not camping out with you," Lauren said.

"Come on, please."

"Nope. We'll camp with you in June."

April wanted to say, 'I'd feel better if you'd come this weekend. I'm intimidated to go on my own and sleep outside,' but she kept those thoughts unspoken.

During her Friday workday, the department celebrated a co-worker's birthday. Colleagues chatted while eating white frosted white cake from the grocery store.

Kari asked, "April, what are you doing this weekend?"

"I'm going camping," slipped out of April's mouth before she realized she'd spilled the beans about her outdoor training. Several side conversations quieted.

Gary leaned over as if he misheard. "Did you say camping?"

"Yes, camping."

"New guy?" Kari asked.

"No. I want to get outdoors more."

Another co-worker asked, "Isn't it too cold at night to camp?"

"Spring is here, and nighttime temperatures are warming up. I'll be fine," April hoped.

Before leaving the building, she changed from business casual to a pair of yoga pants and a fleece top over a t-shirt.

Would she be warm enough? Maybe long underwear was a better idea?

April surmised that her expensive tent, inflatable sleeping pad, and her puffy, mummy-shaped sleeping bag would keep her warm.

Maybe she should have camped in the backyard first? Or began with a single overnight and not a weekend?

Under a blue-white sky, April drove beyond the sight of the skyline, rectangular strip malls, and suburban housing. The metro area flowed into black-brown fields of overturned topsoil clods and barbed-wire fencing enclosing short-grass pastures. The sun began to set and colored the sky lilac, and the clouds resembled pink cotton candy.

A broad sign attached to a shortened telephone pole announced 'Winding River State Park.' A squeak of excited nervousness popped out of April. She turned into the park's entrance. The dimming evening light and the tall, thick-trunked with few leaves paralleled and shadowed the straightway blacktop road into a series of turns and camp-grounds.

Her campground was encircled by trees. April noted a handful of RV campers with light leaking from their curtained windows. No one parked near her campsite. This gave her a measure of relief as she wanted her first camping movements unobserved.

The evening daylight was almost gone when April began

unloading the trunk. It was then she realized she had forgotten to pack a flashlight or headlamp.

How could she have forgotten? Should she ask another camper to lend her a flashlight?

That thought made April cringe. She wanted to be one of them. Who was 'them?' The outdoorsy people who are competent, confident, and not foolish.

April required a plan. Here was the plan: she'd drive home. Try again next weekend.

She began tossing camping gear into the backseat. *I tried.* April told herself. *I wasn't ready.*

April backed out of the small paved parking square and reentered the campground loop road. When she saw the park gate up ahead, she asked, did I try?

That question had April easing off the accelerator. Had she given this a real chance?

April turned the steering wheel to the left and began the loop again. This time her eyes found the spot first, and her headlights followed. She sat in her idling car. *This is nuts.* Should she go home or stay?

Not knowing what to do, April remained still. She stared at the darkening campsite. The headlights lighted up the flat area for her tent, a picnic table, and a fire pit. That was it. April could leave the car lights on while she set up camp. She was staying.

April turned off the engine and left the car's headlights on. After retrieving her gear from the backseat, she used the illumination to pitch her tent.

Another thing conquered. Supper next.

April opened the cooler. She stared at the hotdogs that had seemed appropriate, and traditional, to dine on in her first night. Her anxiousness and fear had tired her out. Setting up the new camp stove was better left for tomorrow. She sat at the picnic table, eating handfuls of trail mix chased down with water. Between the work week and the emotional swings of settling in at the campground, April was tired. It was time for bed.

Brushing her teeth seemed too much exertion. April loaded the cooler into the car's front passenger seat and shut off the headlights. Crawling into the tent's vestibule, she then removed her running shoes, to not track dirt onto the floor, and set her phone and keys inside them. Still wearing her day clothes, she slid into her sleeping bag.

Tomorrow will go better.

Laying there, April discovered she had to rest her arms by her sides to keep them on the sleeping pad. The campground was still and too quiet. There was no street noise, no wind, and no ambient lighting. April wished again she had brought a head-lamp. She had seen online pictures where savvy campers had hung a headlamp from the top of their tents, creating overhead lighting.

April felt out of her natural habitat and nervous. If she were at home sleeping in her bed, there would be real walls between her and the outside.

What if there's someone out there walking and going into people's campsites? She reminded herself there wasn't. What if a wild animal investigated her tent? It was only fabric walls separating her from the animals. She was thinking crazy. A squirrel was not going to get her. But a big, wild animal could. Maybe she wasn't ready for this. Tomorrow, she could pack up and go home.

Then she thought she heard a snap. No, it was more of a crunch. Fear heated her.

There is nothing out there. April told herself. She needed to relax and close her eyes. But she wanted to see her attacker before it happens. It was probably a small rodent. Or a wolf?

Then she heard something scrape the tent fabric, and before

she could consider other choices, she peeled back her sleeping bag and tent zippers and grabbed her shoes. In stocking feet, April moved like a slack-loose marionette and fell into the car's front seat and locked herself in. When her shaking transformed from fear to chilled, she knew she needed to decide her next move.

She could start the car to warm up. The other campers would hear. Who cares? April should go home. She would have to take down the tent, in the dark, or leave it behind. All that gear was hundreds of dollars. What was she going to do?

April scrutinized the murk for danger. Seeing nothing, she opened the door. Wearing her shoes this time, April ran to her tent. With shaking hands, she pulled her sleeping bag out and dashed back to the car's backseat. Using the key fob, she relocked the doors.

She shimmied into her sleeping bag. Before dozing off, April thought, "being terrified is tiring."

CHAPTER NINE

April awoke cold. She wondered if her furnace had gone out. Then the memory of fleeing to her car pushed open her eyes. She saw the backseat's gray fabric. Uncurling her body, she heard the shish, shish of her sleeping bag's nylon as April stretched her legs half laying and half hanging across the seat. A crink hindered her turning neck. The side window was frosted opaque.

This was not how she imagined she'd wake up.

Picking up her running shoe, April checked her phone. The screen showed 7 a.m.

Using her fleece sleeve, April rubbed at the window's thin icy covering. Through streaks, she saw a pearl-gray sky and moss brown tall oaks. The overcast daylight made her want to remain in the sleeping bag. Her bladder didn't feel the same.

Shoving her feet into her shoes, April returned to her tent. She dug into her backpack with jerky movements pulling out a light-weight coat too thin for the early season and a black stocking cap she had thrown in at the last minute. It was better than nothing.

She shivered as she walked back from the new-season clean restrooms stocked with toilet paper and absent of people. The woods surrounding the campground smelled of a crisp, dewy earthiness.

Back at the campsite, April stood next to the firepit. A campfire would be warming and welcome. She hadn't thought to bring matches and wood. April was kidding herself. She didn't know how to light a campfire.

April brushed her foot back and forth across the dirt, making lines while she considered what to do. She wanted to warm up. Should she turn on the car? The RV campers have heat. April was supposed to be learning how to be a proper camper. When does that happen exactly? Eating breakfast may make her optimistic and warmer.

Sitting at the picnic table with her new stove, April followed its instructions. She twisted the fuel cylinder onto the burner mechanism. Next, she filled the stove's large metal cup with water and turned the valve; the gas hissed in release, then she pushed the ignitor button. A whoosh proceeded a flame.

She did it!

In less than a minute, water boiled and climbed the cup's sides. Not sure what to do, April pulled her sleeves over her hands and lifted the cup and set it onto the picnic table. The cup's heat flooded her cold-stiff hands. She poured hot water over a mug of instant coffee and a bowl of oatmeal. The smells of cinnamon and apples lofted above her chattering teeth as she stirred the rehydrating oats.

April was cold. Who cared what the other campers thought she was starting the car.

As heat blasted through the car vents, April sipped hot coffee and spooned cereal. Her teeth quieted, and a cozy sleepiness overcame her. She rested her forehead on the steering wheel and into the direct pathway of blowing heat. April contemplated last night and the day ahead.

Maybe one night in the campground was enough accomplishment this weekend.

The thought simultaneously elated and dejected her. She knew last night was not a success. Sitting in the car, warming up was not 'campy.'

How would she be ready in time for the Chilkoot?

April knew fumbling and mistakes closer to home was safer than two thousand miles away. When she planned this inaugural weekend, she had chosen several manageable hiking trails. Keeping to that part of the itinerary seemed a good idea. She'd start hiking at nine.

What would April do until then? Who knew camping was kind of boring? Next time, April would bring a book.

Her breath caught. She was planning for next time.

April was still in the game.

She decided to read the news on her smartphone. During this time filler, it occurred to April that last night she could have used the flashlight on her phone. Instead of berating herself for not remembering, she chose to chalk it up to stress-forgetting, and relegated it as a new camping tool. Next, she rejected changing clothes as that would require exposing skin. Yesterday's underwear would suffice.

At 8:55, April left her car. She checked for gear and trash scattered about her campsite and zipped the tent. April opened her prepacked new red day-hiking backpack verifying the contents of water, map printouts, trail bars, a pre-made lunch from home and tossed in her phone. A glance at the other campsites confirmed no one was paying attention to her.

April began walking the campground loop, searching for the trailhead. The warmth of her exhales turned the air in front of her face into smoky puffs. It felt strange to have the pack on her back, and the waist and torso straps buckled snug. The pouch reservoir filled with water sloshed with her steps.

On the opposite side of the campground, she saw the words 'Trout Hook Trail' etched on an arrow-shaped brown sign nailed to a post. The trail was hard-packed dirt with shouldering tall oaks with young leaves. Between the rough, scratchy bark trunks, the ground rippled in uneven mounds covered in buff and brown leaves and fallen branches. No breeze or bird calls disturbed the air. Was it too cold for the birds?

Hiking generated body heat, and April's discomfort lessened.

What was she supposed to think about while hiking? Maybe dissect life in some profound, nature wanderer way like Thoreau or that other guy? Wasn't she supposed to be in some nature induced peaceful state?

Textbook and media images of explorers and adventurers with chests out and chins up claiming destiny and wealth as they moved across the wilderness flashed in April's mind. She wasn't doing either. Today's task was to learn to hike. Pay attention to the trail. Watch out for animals and danger.

Firm-footing helped her pick up speed as she stepped on loose gravel, and molding leaf debris. More berating thoughts bullied into April's headspace. Did she belong here? Why did she think she could do this? April was becoming frustrated. She hadn't slept in her new tent. Being in nature wasn't creating bliss-filled moments and life-changing deep thoughts.

She didn't dawdle to admire the tightly wrapped pencil eraser-sized bright green buds growing and poking out of branches. At an inclining rockpile of stones and smaller rocks, April had to stop the mental attack and traverse a zig-zag pattern to climb up and over.

On the other side of the obstacle, April looked back. She was surprised at the distance she had traveled.

How long had she hiked?

A phone check relayed an hour and half had passed. She was surprised. April couldn't recall much of the landscape she had passed.

I need to pay less attention to me and look at what's around me. April turned in a slow circle, studying the upper tree limbs that arched over the path. The limited leafing out allowed sunrays to dapple light on the trail. She sniffed the air. It smelled like a new bag of potting soil.

She decided to walk slower and look around.

For the next hour and a half, April focused on the woodland. The trail had a pattern of oaks clumped together, followed by open meadow where a trick of sunrays made old and new native grasses look golden. A pair of hawks with brown wings glided overhead on invisible jet streams. At the fifth or sixth meadow, April opened her water valve and sucked at the nozzle. A flavor combination of frigid cold water and new plastic rushed into her mouth. This section's lack of tree cover warmed and brightened April and her surroundings.

It's nice here.

Then she took out a compressed food bar of ground oats, nuts, and chia seeds drizzled in chocolate. The taste straddled salty and bland.

April had been on the trail for a few hours, and nothing bad had occurred. Tonight, will be different. Next time will be different. At least she didn't leave. April came close, but she redirected and gave it another shot.

The last thought made April feel more spunky. She continued on the trail. Faint burbling fountain sounds became running water as April entered another acre of trees.

There must be a stream ahead.

The trail moved closer to the water. Soon she walked along a slow-flowing river. April stopped at a weather-bleached log lying near a tree-filled riverbank. It was earlier than usual to eat. The combination of exercise and the cooler temperatures had her stomach emitting growls and rumbles.

She surmised the log might be a homestead for forest creatures. Not taking any chances, April banged a stick against the wood attempting to evict any dwellers. Nothing exited. April unbuckled her daypack and set it and herself down.

While eating a ham and Swiss sandwich, a snack bag of chips, an apple, and a pouch of nuts, she watched orange and black pocket-sized songbirds fly and hop from high branches. Their whistles and warnings traveled the acreage. When lunch was over, April realized she was cold.

Time to get back to hiking.

In the next trail section, the river widened to a smaller lake size. The currents moved quicker. April saw boats with fishing poles arcing over the water. Maybe she would learn how to fish. April would have to buy more equipment. It was best to learn to camp first. She hoped the trail's junction was near.

A sign with two arrows marked the intersection. One line of the trail continued along the river, and the other circled back to the campground. April was happy to begin the three miles back.

She knew hiking six miles today pushed her, but she wanted to maximize her time on the easier flat trail. Tomorrow's hike would be a shorter four-and-a-half-miles with elevation gain. April would be home in less than twenty-four hours.

She arrived back in the campground close to 4 p.m. April was happy tired. Taking a nap before supper made an excellent addition to her weekend.

Inside the tent, the walls diffused the late afternoon brightness giving the light a greenish tint. Removing her left sock, April rubbed at a quarter-sized raised patch of heel skin, relieved, it wasn't a blister. She'd need to start practice walks around her neighborhood during the week to build up her feet and stamina.

April thought about her new trail running shoes sitting on her living room carpet. When she lifted the shoes to pack for this first weekend, they had felt too new and special, as if they belonged to someone else. Practicality demanded April start using those shoes and ready them for the Chilkoot.

She rezipped the tent and laid atop her sleeping bag.

April had hiked. She didn't get hurt or lost. If her parents and Lauren could see her, they'd be shocked. Justin would be surprised. She wondered what he was up to?

April closed her eyes. She didn't want to go further into that last line of thinking.

When April woke, she didn't know if it was afternoon or evening. She listened for birdsong and heard a soft breeze rustle her tent. She checked the time. It was 6:30. She hadn't intended to nap so long.

She sat up. Her muscles elicited a new tenderness. When April laced up her shoes, her feet felt jammed and suffocated. She'd need to get a pair of slip-on camp shoes. April had hoped she was done buying gear.

Supper was two boiled hotdogs slathered with ketchup from restaurant sachets and potato chips. April desired something sweet. She hadn't packed any dessert or candy. She added another item to her future packing list.

The sun dropped behind the trees making the light in the campground a dense teal. Objects became dark shadows. Generators hummed as campers used electricity. Several stationary, wavy campfires sent sparks and smoke upwards.

April caught a movement from the corner of her eye. Thirty yards into the treeline, a doe took cautious steps into the clearing. The animal stopped and assessed her. April slowed her breath and held still. Each waited to see what the other would do. An RV door opened and thwapped closed, startling the deer into fleeing.

She imagined the animal could hear her silent words: I know how you feel.

The evening moved, and a thick quiet followed.

April's phone flashlight lit up the inside of her tent. She changed into a clean shirt, underwear, and yesterday and today's yoga pants before crawling into her sleeping bag and pulling the zipper up, exposing her face.

Thoughts budged in front of sleep. Is being encased like a sausage a safe choice? I don't want to be scared and have to sleep in the car again. What will tomorrow's trail be like? Will it be easy to find and follow? What if there are sections I'll need to bushwhack through? What if I encounter a wild animal? What if I trip and fall? How will I get help or back?

What if it goes well like today?

April woke the next day to an outdoor dampness coating her tent. She checked her phone and saw it was 8:10. It was late.

April was more tired from yesterday than she realized. She moved a bit, checking her muscles. There was a trivial soreness in her legs. A similar feeling in her shoulders and back where the backpack had hung.

The tent zipper's brisk downward whisk gave a brash, elongated 'z' sound. April's fingers were clumsy with cold as she dumped out fine gravel and dirt from her well-used gym shoes. She added gloves to her packing list.

While eating oatmeal, April eyed her tent's discoloration of dew-covered flaps and sides.

Should she take the tent down now or before leaving? She'd leave it for later.

April added the same food inventory as yesterday to her backpack then put the rest of her gear into the car's trunk. Time to hit the trail.

Today's route was a shorter and more challenging out and back that started from the campground. It ventured into a different part of the park. Trees gave way to a long, empty field of bent last-season straw-yellow grass. The pressure of April's footfalls disturbed the groundcover releasing a smell of spring mold similar to overaged mushrooms. She decided to give her attention to what she saw and leave the worries and mishaps at the campground.

April saw woods in the distance. An atmosphere of companionable solitude accompanied her physical fatigue. This helped subduc her internal 'what ifs' and worries. Her body loosened and warmed, decreasing muscle soreness. She began a gradual hill climb up the river bluffs. The higher vantages looked down on the river. April's focus went from expansive to narrow as she stepped over downed trees, around buried rocks, and adjusted her stride as the pathway's grade steepened. When she reached an open outcrop of rock slabs stacked like books, April paused and drank water.

It was another hour before she reached the trail's summit and end. A three-hundred-and-sixty-degree view included the park's trees and meadows, the bluffs, and a winding river. Two boats floated down below.

On a flat, gray-white rock the size of her vehicle, April rested and ate lunch. A breeze made the spot cold, and she kept her coat zipped and whichever hand was free in her pocket. She backtracked to the campground, finishing faster than it had taken to do the first half. April disassembled her tent and left the campsite as she had first encountered it.

Her first practice trip was over. Inside the car, traffic prevented April from a concentrated assessment of her first hiking and camping adventure. The weekend's excitement, nerves, fear, and adrenaline that had bloomed and ridden roughshod was weaker.

At home, she unpacked, scattering her gear about the living room.

Staring at the camping contents, she wondered, am I ready to do this again next weekend?

She wasn't sure of the answer.

CHAPTER TEN

The next morning, April stood in the work staff breakroom filling her water bottle.

Kari sidled up. "Hi, April. How was your weekend?"

"Morning, Kari. My weekend was fine."

"Did you go camping and hiking?"

Kari is so nosey, April thought, but still said, "I did."

"Wow. I'd be so nervous going by myself."

April should have known a co-worker would ask. Why didn't she prepare something to say on her way to work?

"Everything went fine. No problems," April lied.

"Did you see any wildlife? Was it cold?"

"A few birds and a deer. The mornings were chilly. I'd better get back to work." Before Kari could ask another question, April escaped to her desk. That conversation had been different from her talk with Lauren on Sunday night. Before April had left the campground, she saw a text from Lauren asking how the weekend went.

April waited to call later Sunday evening when she knew Lauren's kids were in bed.

"Hi! How'd it go?" Lauren asked.

"The hiking went well. The camping not so much."

"What happened?"

April sighed. "I forgot my headlamp. I had to use my car headlights to set up my tent and smartphone's flashlight at night. I spotlighted my ineptitude."

"You problem-solved. That was smart. What else happened?"

"The first night, I was frightened by a squirrel or some other critter. I couldn't scramble out of my tent fast enough. If you had seen me sprint to my car, you would have laughed. I slept in the car that night."

"That's okay. You stuck out your first night."

"I'm probably the only person who had a perfectly usable tent steps from their vehicle they slept in." April said.

"I bet when it rains, tent people get into their vehicles. Did anything else happen?"

"I almost left within the first hour of arriving at the park. I turned around at the park entrance."

"What made you go back?" Lauren asked.

"I wanted to give the experience a fair shot. I didn't want to quit."

Lauren cheered. "Good job. How far did you hike?"

"I hiked six miles on Saturday through forest and meadows. On Sunday, I hiked four and half more up a bluff that looked over the river before packing up and driving home."

"Did you enjoy it?"

April paused before answering. Had she? She enjoyed the hiking. Seeing the deer was amazing.

"Most of it. A deer ran through the campground. The sunshine made a lovely pattern on the trail. I liked the river view from the bluffs. It felt good to move and be outdoors."

"Good. Are you going again?"

"I think so," April said.

"You don't have to do any of this. You can change your mind."

April could make a new choice. Her Chilkoot adventure could be rescheduled for next summer or canceled, but she wasn't ready to stop.

Monday evening, after work, April walked three miles around her neighborhood. And, again, the next night. On Wednesday, April added another mile. On Thursday afternoon, she wore her new trail shoes.

After Thursday evening's exercise, she sat cross-legged on her couch, staring at her compressed sleeping bag where she had dropped it after camping. Each weekday, April picked her way about her living room, not touching the gear as if each item was a campfire.

Her next reservation was at Blue Pond State Park. The park's multi-use trail system wound and encircled various sized lakes and ponds.

Was she going on her second practice weekend? Last weekend started with a couple of mishaps. It wasn't a disaster. April slept the first night in the car. This weekend could be worse than last time. Or it could be better. If she went and didn't want to stay, then she'd return home. No one would know except for her, and maybe Lauren.

April stood up and bumped the bag with her foot. She reminded herself to pack her headlamp. She was trying again.

As the Friday work afternoon closed out, Gary swung by April's desk. "Hey April, are you camping this weekend?"

"Yup."

"If you're lonely at home and need to pass the weekend, it's good to get out."

April's initial annoyance at Gary's unsolicited advice streaked to aggravation. "I'm going because I like it." Not exactly true. There had been few highlights last time. April would not admit to Gary that she wavered in her recreation.

Kari bounded up to their conversation. "Hi, everyone! What are you doing this weekend?"

Gary answered for both April and himself. "I'm watching the game on Sunday. April's going camping again, so she doesn't have to stay home alone."

"I'm going because I want to. It's good exercise," April verbally swatted back.

Kari cocked her head. "You're going again? Alone?"

"Yes. I need to finish these reports before I leave for the day. Enjoy your weekends." April turned away and hunched towards her computer screen. She pretended to go back and forth between the papers on her desk and the monitor.

Last night April readied for her out-of-town weekend. She had no intention of repeating her lack-of-light circumstance and packed both a headlamp and flashlight. April checked several times, verifying the batteries worked in both.

She decided to simplify her outdoor cooking. April chose items that required nothing more than adding hot water. Instant oatmeal and coffee for breakfast and noodle boxes for two suppers. Lunches would be peanut butter and jelly sandwiches and apples, then pre-made trail mixes and energy bars for snacks. She reread her packing list a third time, looking through the piled gear. Staring at the items, April asked, what was missing?

Unable to come up with anything extra, she packed her duffel and day hiking backpack. As she loaded the bags, tent, and water jugs into her trunk, it occurred to her to bring a lawn chair. A lawn chair would be more comfortable than the picnic table.

She locked the car and walked back into her house. The memory of her morning wait in the car flashed in her brain.

April needed to bring a book. Maybe she was getting better at this?

After work and to avoid co-workers, April went to a different floor to change into her camping clothes. Instead of yoga pants, she dressed in the multi-pocketed hiking pants with zippers below the knee that could transform the pant legs into shorts. The outdoor store sales clerk had recommended them.

She exited a door on the other side of the building. April maneuvered in and around rush hour traffic heading northwest to the next park and adventure. She checked in with her feelings and acknowledged her skittishness. April wondered again if she was foolhardy, foolish, or a fool.

With the aid of May's extended minutes of daylight and an earlier park arrival, she found her camping spot and pitched her tent with ease.

After her temporary home was set up, April assessed the other campers. A few sat at picnic tables, and others relaxed in foldup camp chairs around firepits. Other campers were still arriving. It was too early to eat. April wasn't sure what to do.

Maybe she should find tomorrow's trailhead?

Since her split with Justin, April noticed an uptick in conversing with herself. She considered asking her single friends if it was normal. Do you talk to yourself a lot? Do you answer back? Sometimes the voice is helpful and other times not. If April asked her friends, would they think she was a bit mental?

Stymieing those thoughts, April walked twice around the campground and located a path that cut through to an adjacent campground. On the far side, she found tomorrow's trailhead. An elevated, wood-framed sign displayed the park map. Within the black line of the park's boundaries were green and brown wiggling, looping, intersecting, and straight lines of trails, plus tiny images of buildings and points of interest. The longer evening prompted her to investigate the first section of the trail. Beige pulverized jagged rock atop dirt led April into a red pine forest.

Thirty minutes later, she realized that she needed to walk back to the start as the light was diminishing and her hunger growing.

Going back, she picked up her pace and reached the trail marker as the sun began to set behind the trees. At her campsite, she added boiled water to a paper box of Thai noodles. Sitting in her lawn chair, April thought about what she wanted from this weekend. The goal was to become a better hiker and camper. If she could enjoy this experience, that would help keep her plugging away at this crazy idea of flying to the Yukon, driving to Alaska, and hiking the Chilkoot.

When more people learned about her weekends and upcoming vacation, they'd have questions. April dreaded answering. She wanted to become outdoor proficient and confident. If the Chilkoot went well, she'd talk about it. If it were a failure, she wanted fewer people to know.

April cleaned up her supper dishes. She decided to turn in early. A stop at the campground restroom was required before crawling into her tent. At the camping store, the man-bun sales clerk had mentioned buying a fluorescent orange hand shovel.

In a knowing tone, the clerk said, "You'll need one of these to dig a hole before pooping."

Surprised by the advice and her new camping rule, April nodded and put the small shovel in her shopping basket. These campgrounds had bathrooms and porta-potties, and she had left that camping accessory at home. She hoped human waste was all she had buried when the summer was over.

In the tent, she put on her headlamp and read the book she had learned last weekend to bring. The larger number of campers meant more background noises, which comforted

April. She fell asleep listening to a family talking while throwing a frisbee.

April awoke early the next morning with a cold nose. The noises of last night's community were absent. She half-unzipped her sleeping bag to change her underwear and continued wearing yesterday's clothes. She added a light-weight coat, stocking hat, and gloves and zipped back up into her sleeping bag. Her early hour drowsiness hadn't dissipated, and she rested.

She was awake an hour later and ready to start hiking. She laced up her cold-stiffened new trail shoes. Other early risers breakfasted at picnic tables. She heard generators rumble, the clap of closing doors, and mumbled conversations. A breeze brought her campfire smoke.

April cupped her fresh mug of instant coffee and watched what the other campers did. Post-cleanup, it was time for her to return to the trailhead in the pine trees. The sky was cloud white. After repeating the previous night's segment, the trail began a slight incline becoming hilly. The lowest dips on the trail had stinky standing muddy water. She was able to walk around, except on one occasion. April light-stepped on the trail's squishy mud edge and stepped up onto a downed pine that became her impromptu bridge to the other side.

An hour later, she came to an oversized pond. A small flock of black curved-necked floating geese hugged the shoreline opposite her. Their paddling webbed feet caused the water to ripple. A month or so earlier, the ponds and lakes would have been covered in cracking ice.

April encountered no one on the trail for the first two hours. She startled when a group of young runners called ahead to her. April looked back at the horde running her direction. She stepped off the trail to let the group pass. Using their similar shirts as a clue, she guessed they were a high school track team.

When the kicking and cycling legs were out of sight, the ever-green quiet resumed its place.

April stopped in the middle of a weathered, wooden foot-bridge and leaned her belly into a plank and rested her elbows on a splintered and gouged railing to eat her lunch. Overhead the clouds were fixed into place like propped-up bed pillows.

This well-defined and cleared trail, plus her new exercise routine, eased her effort and allowed plenty of time to think. She was thinking about her life, her career, and her lack of happiness. April had had an inkling that Justin hadn't been her biggest problem, but she had proceeded with the divorce. She wondered if she had worked on herself sooner, would she and Justin have stayed together.

No. It would have delayed, but not prevented, the breakup.

They had matured in different directions. At some future point, either or both would have wanted a more emotionally satisfying relationship with someone else.

April noted the new spaces she created in her life. She sifted through the options and tried to figure out how she would fill those openings. She knew she was lucky for this opportunity and didn't want to squander it or crucify herself while exploring.

What did she want out of her life? What made her happy? Once she knew, what could she do about it?

She was challenged to answer. Not being able to readily answer questions was tiring and frustrating. April let them linger in the background while she refocused on the scenery.

That afternoon she took an incorrect right onto a spur trail sheltered by cottonwoods. The new leaves rustled louder than the morning's pine needles. The side-trip halted at the edge of a lake wider and longer than many sports stadiums. Near an island towards the lake's center, April could see white floating

balls. The distance hampered her vision. She guessed the balls
were swans.

Back at the tent, April fixed her boiled noodle supper. A
few of the campers had a crackling fire that complemented the
calm evening.

It would be nice to have a campfire. Maybe next time, April
would bring wood and figure out how to make one.

Since she didn't have anything more to do, April went into
her tent and affixed her headlamp. She read until her eyes and
brain were fuzzy.

April woke up early on Sunday morning to complete her
mileage before campground check-out. The temperature didn't
feel as cold. Sitting atop her sleeping bag, she changed her
clothes. Today's trail started outside the campground at the
Licking Rock Lake. A valley shaped like a shallow dish with
limestone edging cradled a jelly bean-shaped lake. The trail
followed the shoreline in a complete loop. The smell of dew-
damp rock reminded her of concrete after a rainstorm.

The easy-going terrain allowed April to slip into thoughts
about what events had brought her here. She worked her
personal timeline backwards. Learning to hike had become a
priority because she wanted to explore the Chilkoot Trail,
which had been served up in her living room, and validated by
her brief encounter with Dan that she could manage the trip,
during last winter's situational depression post her divorce.
What had prompted her to tell Justin on 'that' particular day? It
was an ordinary day in her ordinary life.

Somewhere within her, the time to tell him had felt right. In
the months before the 'talk,' April had known she wasn't in love
with Justin. She liked and loved him but more as someone with
whom she had grown into adulthood and shared a past.

April's memory went to many of their happy times: When
he tried to teach her how to snowboard, helping her up each

time she landed on her bottom. Celebrating over pizza and beer when either had been hired or promoted at a job. They each wanted better opportunities for the other. Laughter at a situation that wouldn't have been funny to anyone else but them. The review of their relationship before, in, and after marriage continued around the lake and back to the main trail.

Mixed with April's tiredness was the sticky residue of her introspection. She wanted to let it all rest. Seeking the sanctuary of her tent, April slid into her sleeping bag. She put on her headphones and shuffled a playlist. It took a while, but the music was louder than her brain, and eventually she napped.

She didn't know what time it was when she woke, but April knew it was time to go home.

The campground was quiet as most of the campsites were empty. April was alone, but her loneliness was fainter.

CHAPTER ELEVEN

April's work week was brisk, as her department's leading project entered its next planning stage. The increased activity had her team busy and conversations business-focused. This was a boon for April. No one asked about her latest camping weekend.

On Friday evening, April glared at the gold foil and ivory Saturday wedding invitation affixed to her fridge. The weight of the cardstock required multiple magnets to prevent it from sliding. Her next trekking would have to wait until the following weekend. On a positive note, any consternation about her outdoor skills training had shifted to 'no wedding date' gloom.

Why didn't April RSVP she was unable to attend? She could let the bride know tonight that she wouldn't be attending. She'd blame it on a work conflict. Then April could dash off to a state park for a getaway. Or, hide at home and binge-watch movies.

The last idea felt effortless and familiar.

April scolded herself to be an adult and go to the wedding. She had bought the gift. But she didn't want to sit through someone else's happy life and bright future while hers was unknown. Practicing for the Chilkoot was fragile ground for her.

She traced the borders of the rectangle invitation. Did April think of herself as weak? Was it a story she had made up?

April was trying something new. Her life wasn't different. That wasn't accurate. April had two hiking and camping weekends attached to her.

She turned away from the fridge. The wedding invite was tabled.

On Saturday morning, April again stood in front of the invitation requesting her presence.

Be an adult, she told herself. Go to the wedding and stay through the dinner. As soon as the dancing started, she'd leave. Her Saturday chore list had a vibe similar to cleaning the bathroom. Each task had to be dealt with and done.

In the early afternoon, April dug into her closet and pulled out a rosy peach summer dress and nude heels. She couldn't remember the last time she'd worn the dress.

When April was a few blocks over from the church, she hunted the neighborhood streets for parking. She saw couples, families, and groups of friends dressed up in their Sunday best with heels and ties, and a few wide-brimmed summer hats, stroll to the event. The sunshine and smiles made the guests extra shiny. April felt awkward and out-of-place. She knew her feelings would amplify sitting in a church pew with strangers. In a split second, April changed her mind. She was not attending.

April drove home without once looking back via the rearview mirror. She parked her car in her garage and turned off the ignition. The garage door retracted into the closed position. She stayed seated. There was a sense of safety in the dim lighting of the closed-up building. A hush saturated the space. April knew she should go into her house. She wanted to hole up in this place and detach from her life.

If she stayed here too long, her neighbors might think she was suicidal. She wasn't suicidal. Just feeling profoundly alone and unconnected, especially to herself and elusive contentment. Everyone has someone, and something, in their life. Well, not everyone, but lots of people. Her mom had her dad, her brother had her sister-in-law, and Lauren had her husband and kids. Even annoying Kari had someone.

Her thoughts tumbled fast. April tipped her head back against the headrest and she closed her eyes.

Who did she have? April had herself. She wanted more things to do other than her boring life. Why couldn't she feel fulfillment in what she already had? Why couldn't it be enough? Why did she have to crave more? April felt lost this year and last. There was no trail map to reach her goal or to go back. Back? There was no going back.

Unlike the hiking trails, April's life was a mix of defined direction, side paths, and unexplored territory. She was tired of thinking about all of it. Would she sit in her garage all night? No one would know. April had her phone, a snack bar in the car console, and a water bottle lying on the front passenger seat floor. No bathroom, though.

Thinking about hiding in her garage achieved a new low. She telephoned Lauren for help.

"Hi! How's your weekend going?" Lauren asked.

"Fine. You?"

"Kids activities and chores. Plus, we're supposed to meet my parents for brunch tomorrow. We're going to try that new breakfast place on University. Aren't you supposed to be at a wedding?"

"Yes."

"Why aren't you there? Where are you?"

"I'm sitting in my car in the garage, thinking about spending the night."

"What? Why are you thinking about spending the night in your garage? April, you're not going to do anything dangerous?"

"No. I'm just...stuck."

"I'm on my way," Lauren said.

"Honk when you arrive. I'll open the garage door. Lauren...thanks."

"Any time."

In half an hour, April heard Lauren's SUV honk. April pushed the garage door button. The raucous noise of gears and pulleys filled the room. She saw Lauren's teal shorts and ivory top through the passenger window. As Lauren slid into the car, April pressed the garage button, and the overhead door began closing.

April turned her head to Lauren and, in a forlorn tone, said, "Hey."

"Tell me what's going on?"

"I couldn't go to my friend's wedding. I made this big plan to go on a hiking trip in Alaska, in Alaska, for goodness sake. What if I get there and can't do it?" She tilted her head back and stared at the car's roof.

"Oh, April."

April gripped the steering wheel." I don't know what I'm doing with my life. I'm stuck in my garage feeling lonely, bad, and almost as unhappy as last summer."

"I know you're struggling. You want to be happy. I want you to be happy. Maybe instead of pursuing the big ideas of happiness and contentment, look for it in smaller ways." Lauren held her hands up like a balancing scale. "More of a cumulative effort than a grand event. I'm not saying don't do big things. Hiking the Chilkoot is a big thing. Go for it. But maybe focusing on smaller wins will help. At least think about that?"

"Okay. What if I do all the outdoor preparation and reach the Chilkoot trailhead and bail?"

"What if you do? I'm not saying you will. But what if, you get to the trail and change your mind?"

April rubbed her forehead. "I don't know. Come home."

"No one is forcing you to hike the Chilkoot this summer. Maybe wait until next year and ask a friend to go with. Other than me; you know I'm not interested in sleeping in a tent."

April could wait. She didn't have to push this trip. But she wanted to go.

Lauren continued to speak. "You're in a rough patch. It will pass. It sounds like you're stuck in the gap."

"What's the gap?"

"The place between the old and the new life. It can take time to bridge the two."

April blew out air as if she was filling a balloon. "I want to be on the other side of this."

"I'm sorry this hurts. You said that part of your dissatisfaction with Justin was that you felt stuck in a rut. You climbed out. You're figuring your new direction."

April let go of the steering wheel. "I'm having a difficult time knowing what that is."

"It's okay not to know. Figuring out what makes you happy takes time. It's an easy question to ask and challenging one to answer."

"I was in such a hurry to reinvent my life that I didn't think enough about what I wanted or how to get there. I just wanted different."

"How about no big decisions for a while?" Lauren suggested.

April snorted, "I'm in my garage. Big decisions are the least of my problems."

"How about getting through this weekend and then seeing where you're at on Monday morning?"

"I can do that. I feel like I let myself down."

"How?"

April rubbed at her eyes. "I was supposed to have figured this all out by now."

"By who's timeline?" Lauren asked.

"I don't know. Mine? Society's?"

"Cut yourself a break."

"Do you know how much time I have to think while I'm on the trail?" April said.

"Is that a bad thing?"

"Sometimes. There's no getting away from yourself when it's just you walking the trail. At least when I was depressed and sad, I could hide out at home and numb myself with television and sleep."

"Too much introspection and unearthing?" Lauren asked.

"Way too much."

"Why don't you join a hiking group? You'd meet new people."

"I guess I could." April refrained from telling Lauren about avoiding other campers on her practice weekends.

"We have our June campout. Do you still want to do it?" Lauren asked.

"Yes. I'd like that. Thank you."

"You're welcome. I have to get going. Am I leaving you in the garage or saying goodbye to you at your backdoor?"

"The door."

When April was inside her house, she switched on her phone's do not disturb feature, lowered her window blinds, and binged watched television. Later that night, she laid in bed and thought about how she had barricaded herself at home.

Was she trying to pause the world or speed it forward?

A part of her was remorseful at missing her friend's wedding. Another part of her was relieved the event was over.

When April turned on her phone to full function, she saw no missed calls or texts had been waiting.

Other people's lives went on without her participation. No one cared what she did today. Her self-pity was like ivy that climbed and covered until April was captured, and her vision obscured.

The next morning April stood at her living room window sipping coffee. Her self- pity remained. She was annoyed by her misery. She wanted to feel better and decided to walk around the neighborhood. It wasn't a hiking trail, but the exercise may help.

April changed into shorts, a t-shirt, and her new trail shoes. A couple hours later, April was cheerful and tired. The six miles of sidewalks and streets continued to build her distance.

Back in her neighborhood, she observed the households and yard activity of her neighbors. The neighbors were industrious in their actions to beautify their yards. Her yard needed to be cleaned and tidied. Her dad had mowed the beginning season's growth. It was now April's to take care of.

She'd do the work today. There was no park and campsite reservation. April had a Sunday to fill.

This was the first spring that she would be tackling the yard on her own. Justin's chore was now her's. It was another first in an expanding list of firsts. Changing into a wicking shirt, she went into the garage to retrieve the lawnmower.

April read the directions on the handle. On the fourth tug of the starter rope, the small engine emitted a rattling roar. She moved the bag-free machine back and forth across the turf until the shorter grass had a layer of cut grass on top of it. The aroma of warm, cut grass overwhelmed the dulled smells of gasoline and oil.

April mowed the front and back yards, developing sweat stains under her sleeves and a sore back.

I'd rather be hiking. April shook her head at the irony.

Another hour was spent pulling weeds out of the flower beds she hadn't bothered planting this year. She inspected a stinging blister on her hand.

April rolled the mower into the garage. She was hungry. Not the almost frantic eagerness for food she experienced on the hiking trails. This was a robust want to tuck into delicious food that was not supper cereal.

She didn't bother dusting the grass and dirt off herself before driving to the grocery store.

What did she want? Italian? Vietnamese? A hamburger?

April pushed her shopping cart around apple displays, past plastic mesh bags of onions, along cellophane-wrapped pasta shapes, next to cooler cases of fresh cut meats and well-traveled lake and seafood, and glanced at petite tubs of dairy products. She didn't pause at the slim cereal boxes. She ambled a second circuit about the store, thinking about what she wanted.

April wanted a BLT.

With the fixed idea, April went to the bakery section and chose a loaf of stout French bread that she could press a fingertip dent in. Next, she picked up ruddy, thick bacon. She bagged several multi-colored plump heirloom tomatoes and bib lettuce.

April had almost to unhinge her mouth to bite into the generous sandwich. She chewed thick-cut bread slathered with mayonnaise and layered with salt-savory crisp bacon, firm lettuce, and juicy, yellow-seed tomato slices, trying to extract all the taste before swallowing. It may have been an unimpressive supper at home, but for April, this sensory eating experience answered her current life question of what she wanted.

CHAPTER TWELVE

On Monday morning, April readied for her day. Something was different about the morning and her. She didn't have time to delve. Today was a busy workday. She turned on her work computer and immersed herself in project tasks, deadlines, and meetings.

During her drive home, April thought about the last twelve hours. There had been no existential angst or despair. She felt okay. Better than okay. She was satisfied with her work project's progress. Her upper arms were a bit sore, but she felt strong and sturdy. Lauren had come when April asked for help, and she knew there were many people, and things, that made her life so much better.

Today was a win. She felt good. It was nice.

Two days later, April went in for an annual vision test. It was supposed to be a check-up and nothing more.

"Your vision has changed enough that you require glasses for close up objects and activities such as reading," the optometrist said.

April's eyebrows lifted high. "I don't need glasses."

"You do."

"Can I buy a pair of eyeglasses from a pharmacy?"

"Yes, but because of your vision restriction, I would prefer you get prescription glasses."

"Fine," April sighed.

Ten minutes later, she was trying on various oval, square, rimless black, white, and red frames. After thirty minutes and numerous pairs, April wanted another opinion. She texted Lauren. When no immediate reply came, April telephoned her mom, Sue.

"Hi, Mom. Do you have time to talk?"

"I'm kind of busy at the moment. What do you need?"

"I'm trying to pick out eyeglasses. I need a second opinion. Could I Facetime with you? You could tell me which pairs you like."

"Hold on a second." April could hear her mother shift the phone and mumble something before saying, "Okay, I'm ready."

April switched to Facetime. Her mother's forehead and eyes filled the telephone screen. "Mom, pull the phone back."

"Got it. Let's see the options." Sue said.

April put on a pair of navy square modern frames and repositioned her phone, so her mother could see the result. "What do you think of these?"

"Distinguished." Sue then asked, "Girls, what do you think?"

April then saw her mother's church fellowship group peering at her. She heard, "too dark," "how about something a little bigger," and "she doesn't look bad, just not great."

"Mom, where are you?"

"It's the church ladies' afternoon tea."

Oh geez.

"April, put on the next pair. Loretta is asking if there's a cat-eye shaped pair," Sue said.

It took half an hour and modeling multiple pairs and some back and forth with four particular eye frames for April to choose and the church ladies to agree.

Sue said, "Now I like those. That's the one. Girls, doesn't April look nice? Smart and classy."

April was pleased with her choice and smiled at the ladies' unexpected help. She needed to tell her parents soon she was hiking the Chilkoot.

There was one more weekend before the Lauren and Family Camping Weekend. April decided she would try finding a day hiking group for the upcoming weekend.

At home, she searched the internet for local hiking groups. She found two viable options. April signed up for the planned Saturday half-day hike to a county park she had not visited. The web invitation told group members to meet group leader Gayle at the specified trailhead.

On Friday night, April filled her daypack with snacks and a full water reservoir. The volume was unnecessary, but she had to get used to carrying a heavier pack. The backpack didn't feel weighty enough. She added two small bags of rice. If the other hikers saw the inside of her backpack, they would think she was strange.

Worries about the afternoon clamored in April's brain as she laid out her hiking clothes, including a baseball cap. What if they were all more experienced then she was? Of course, they would be. April was learning. What if they thought she was a hiking fraud? Is there such a thing? What if April couldn't keep up? What if she embarrassed herself? April closed her eyes and started deep breathing. Adding the rice was unnecessary because all her mental crap did the job.

April's shoulders slumped. *When would this get easier?*

On Saturday morning, April drove to a regional park and searched for Gayle and the other hikers. She saw a group of women and men of various body shapes and dressed in outdoor fabric hiking shorts and short-sleeved wicking shirts milling near a trailhead. Some wore sunglasses and other broad-brimmed, floppy safari hats. They appeared 'hiker official' with their serious, boxy boots and high-end daypacks.

April was nervous. It was similar to the first day of school.

She walked over to the group in what she hoped was a calm and easy-going manner.

I'm an adult, for goodness sakes. If I don't like them, or the hike, I'll go home. Exactly how am I supposed to leave if I'm somewhere on the trail? The way I have before, I walk back to the car.

She stopped at the outside of the hiker circle and smiled with her mouth corners pushed up, and said, "Hi."

A woman, in what April guessed was her mid-fifties, extended a handshake to April, "Hi, I'm Gayle. You are?"

"I'm April. Nice to meet you."

"Welcome! It's great that you could join today's hike."

"Thanks. I've not hiked here before." April had not hiked most places before.

"We, I mean the group, have done this hike several times. It's great. You'll have fun. We're waiting for a few more people to arrive. Let me introduce you to the others. Everyone, meet April."

After introductions, the group slipped into the easy banter of people who spent time together. April listened and tried to remember whose name went with whom.

The last of the hikers arrived, and Gayle announced, "Okay, gang, today's hike is six miles. We'll take five to six hours, depending on our pace, breaks, and a quick lunch. We'll mostly be under tree canopy. Be sure to check for ticks throughout the day. Any questions?"

No one spoke.

"Let's go."

The group formed a line and began walking the trail. Three white-haired men commented on the recent warmer temperatures. A couple passed a pair of binoculars back and forth. Several others were speaking about a previous hike. April listened while cheering herself on: *I made it here. I'm hiking with others. Good job to me.*

Gayle set a moderate pace. The trail meandered through woods. Taller grass bent with its weight.

April mentally thanked Gayle for not speed-hiking. She assessed the hikers around her. The binocular couple was ahead and busy searching for birds. Two men closer to her age were behind her.

April half-turned to the men. "Hi. How long have you been with the group?"

They half-focused on April while the hikers continued moving.

"Hey there. I'm Steve. This is Corey. We both try to get out more. Sometimes it's hard to get it on the schedule."

"Have you hiked a lot in the area?" April asked.

"We've done this hike before. It's pretty nice. The trail is gradual. The tree cover prevents a person from getting too much sun. How about you? Do you hike often?" Corey asked.

"I just started this year. Most parks are new to me."

"There are lots to choose from," Steve said.

"I'm discovering that."

For the next hour, the men suggested and debated the merits, or lack thereof, of different trails and parks either they or the group had explored. Other hikers added suggestions. April was gifted an extensive list of new destinations. Her heart warmed when various members invited her to join future hikes.

At lunchtime, they sat on logs a hiker had inspected for critter surprises. People ate peanut butter and jelly sandwiches, food bars, and one person had a salad stored in a plastic box. Trail mix and dehydrated fruit were passed around to share. April enjoyed the company and was glad she had taken a chance on the group.

The next morning April awoke to pale lemon sunrise filling her bedroom. She laid in the middle of the firm mattress, relishing the bed holding her body. The white sheets were wash-worn soft, and everything seemed okay. The occasional birdsong complimented the neighborhood's placidity.

What did she want to do today?

April cat-stretched. Her upper thigh muscles had the good-feeling soreness from yesterday's hike.

Had it really been a month since she started preparing for the Chilkoot? There had been some camping bumps. The hiking had gone well. Hope continued to build that preparing for the Chilkoot would be successful. April wanted to go hiking again today.

She left her bed and dressed in polyester khaki hiking shorts and a short-sleeved light blue colored exercise shirt. After breakfast and readying her daypack, she let her smartphone direct her to 'Grand Oaks State Park' thirty minutes away.

It wasn't yet 8:30 a.m., and the main parking lot was half full. Near a stand of shrubby trees with young green leaves were a map sign and trailhead. April took a photograph of the map. She chose a route that went right and then diverged into separate loops.

The first half-mile was asphalt paved before veering into a mowed boomerang-shaped path through the calf-high prairie grass. She kicked up water from a recent rainfall onto her calves. Small birds burst up from the meadows. Others flew from and to erected nesting boxes scattered on the land.

The lofty oaks in the next section had pole trunks that April could encircle with her arms. The grass receded to be replaced by cut back weeds and intermittent patches of dirt and mud. A sporadic breeze made the forest foliage sound like a gentle rain shower and stirred up a damp, fresh scent.

Further in, the old-growth trunks widen to barrel size. A few pine and birch, or aspen as she couldn't tell the difference, had intermixed. Underfoot was a natural runner of browning pine needles.

Somewhere near an hour and a half, April stopped to sip water. She hadn't encountered anyone on the trail. Judging by the number of vehicles in the parking lot, she should have met someone.

Did she go the wrong direction? Is there such a thing on a park trail?

Minutes later, the trail began to descend, flatten, and descend again. Small rocks embedded in the dirt had April looking down. On a steep decline, a trough-shaped rut in the middle required walking on the footpath's border. Checking the map on her phone, the trail continued downhill through the wooded ravine and hooked left at the river.

She noticed the hiking was going well. She was becoming more proficient. Her camping could too. She felt a tiny urge to cross her fingers.

April felt safe in the woods but looked forward to the brighter daylight along the river. At the shoreline, the trail became a dirt sidewalk. Her eyes were pulled to the middle as if she was looking down a tunnel.

She had woken up feeling good. It occurred to her, she was happier.

April considered the last couple of year's mornings. Too many infused with disinterest, dissatisfaction, and disconnection.

She contemplated the floodplain she crossed. To her left was the cliff of the forested bluff that included views of the surrounding region and river. To her right were anchored, tipped, broken, and drowning trees in swampy, dank marsh that merged with the river.

How could April repeat this morning's well-being tomorrow? The day after? April had a fuller understanding of the landscape she wanted to be in.

A mosquito flew into her ear. Another buzzed her forehead. Moving faster, April heard her footfalls smack on the sandy ground.

She asked herself what had gone well this month? She hiked and overnight camped. She had done her own yard work. She wasn't living in her garage. The project at work was going well.

Reaching an intersection, April picked the eastern loop and began to ascend the bluff and past the tree-rimmed edge onto a plateau of wild prairie.

Next, she asked herself what had gone right this last six-months? She chose the Chilkoot, took a tennis class, was trying new experiences. She stopped blaming Justin for her discontent. April's house became 'her' home. Maybe she was finally figuring out her life. April didn't want to pretend she had it all solved. She wanted to repeat the good feelings and pleasantness that she was experiencing.

April was surprised at how hot she was. The trek upland, the cloudless sky, and the absence of tree shade had her sweating. The near-summer temperature had melted spring and made space for summer.

She was looking forward to her next group hike. April desired company other than her own.

She looked at her surroundings. Light and dark green smooth grasses bent in the breezes. Their long blades fluttered like kite tails. White petaled wild daisies with yellow button centers grew in between. When the wind swept the open grass-land, the ground rippled like a flag. The landscape reminded her of French impressionist field paintings.

April was glad to be here. Her heart wanted more moments like this.

CHAPTER THIRTEEN

The camping weekend with Lauren, her husband Colin, and their two kids, 8-year-old Trevor and 6-year-old Callie was days away. April telephoned Lauren on Monday to iron out details and departure.

"It's one tent per site, but our reservations are next to each other. What do we want to take for meals and snacks?" April asked.

"I know it's last minute, but my parents said we could borrow their RV."

"The reservations are for tents."

"Can the reservations be changed to RV?" Lauren asked.

April wanted to say no, but "maybe" was spoken.

"Camping with the RV would make it much easier with the kids. You're welcome to sleep in the RV," Lauren said.

"Don't the kids backyard tent camp during the summer?"

"Sometimes. But if something comes up, they come into the house."

This was not going how April thought it would.

April gave in. "I'll call the park, but it's a long shot. June is high season, plus it's short notice."

"Thanks for checking. When you know, let's talk about food."

The conversation left April discombobulated. She shook her head a few times to erase her annoyance.

April called the park reservation line. An RV spot was available. She reminded herself that this was an opportunity to camp and hike with people who she wanted to spend time with and supported her. April could sleep in her tent or the RV. She had options.

April called Lauren back. "We now have an RV reservation."

"Great! We'll have a kitchen. We can cook whatever. Colin and the kids like burgers and hotdogs."

"Let's do that. There's a firepit at the campsite. We can cook out, too," April said.

"I'll stop by the grocery store and pick up all that and sandwich makings for lunch. And snacks. On Friday afternoon, we can pick you up, or do you want to meet us at the park?"

"It makes sense to carpool."

"Great! We'll pick you up around 4:30."

April looked forward to the weekend. The RV change had been off-putting, but things going forward would be fine. Her workweek exceeded forty hours. She was ready to escape to the park. At 4:15 p.m. on Friday, April set her gear in the driveway. Last night's 'Thursday evening packing' recent routine made the tasks effortless.

She looked around her yard and neighborhood. The late spring day had heated up to the eighties and invited a person to dawdle in the lethargic rhythm. At 4:50, April considered texting Lauren to ask if something had happened.

At 5:15, April watched Colin drive a lumbering RV up her driveway. When it came to a stop, the rig's horn mooed its arrival.

Lauren jumped out and jogged to April, "Sorry we're late. It took longer to pack this beast of an RV than I planned."

"I was beginning to wonder if something had happened."

"Nope, just poor time management on our part. Is this all your stuff?" Lauren regarded April's large backpack and small plastic cooler.

"Yes."

"There's not much of it. That's your big overnight backpack? Did you shrink your sleeping bag?"

April laughed, "Sort of. I compressed it down into a sack. I thought it would be a good idea to use my Chilkoot backpack this weekend."

"You look and sound like the real McCoy."

Taken by surprise, April blinked and stumbled out a "thank you."

"Your welcome. Now let's get 'Big Blue' into the RV," Lauren said.

"Big Blue?"

"I've christened your backpack."

The group made good time and reached the park in a few hours. After parking the RV and applying citronella bug spray, the adults began to set up camp as the kids played tag around the campsite. Sunset was the backdrop to a supper of hotdogs for kids and gourmet sausages for adults.

April sat in a collapsible camp chair next to the house on wheels while Lauren and Colin wrangled their kids for bedtime books in the RV.

Minutes later, the door opened, and Lauren exited carrying a bottle of wine and two red plastic cups.

April giggled. "You brought wine."

"I'm more of a glamper than a camper," Lauren said and sat down in an opposite chair and handed April a filled cup. "Cheers to a fun weekend!"

The ladies toasted and sat back in the silence of best friends and listened to campers' murmurs around campfires, watched older kids riding bikes on the circular road, and allowed nature to cradle them.

"Your tent looks lonely by the trees. Are you sure you don't want to sleep in the RV? There's plenty of room," Lauren said.

"Thanks, but I'm fine. Did you and Colin have an opportunity to look at the email I sent you of the different trails?"

"We did. We thought the Alder trail for tomorrow. It's shorter and flatter. Easiest for the kids."

"What time will you all be ready to hike?" April asked.

"After breakfast. Say 10:30 or 11."

"Starting then means we're unlikely to reach the end."

Lauren finished her cup of wine. "That's okay. I'm exhausted. I'm going to bed. Night."

April lingered. Thoughts about how the next day would progress parked themselves next to April. *We won't be hiking much tomorrow. I don't have to hike the whole trail. This weekend is to enjoy time with Lauren and her family and practice. Tomorrow is an excellent day to overload my backpack and carry more weight. Things will go well—I hope.*

When April awoke the next day, she heard the campground residents moving about. April poked her head out of the tent and saw that the RV was closed and quiet. After a short walk to the bathrooms, April crawled back into her tent to read.

Several hours later, she heard the RV door open and Lauren say, "April, you awake?"

"Yes," April called out.

"Come inside for breakfast. We have bagels and cereal."

It was closer to noon, and the campground was near empty, when they began their hike. April wore her bulky, heavy-weighted Big Blue and prodded and led her friends to the trailhead. Cheery sunshine warmed a sash like path through basswoods with their heart-shaped leaves.

Lauren reminded the group, "Leaves of three, let it be."

"Why?" Callie asked.

"Because it's poison ivy," Trevor said. "It makes you itchy."

"How did you know that?" Lauren asked.

"We learned in school."

Many stops were made to observe vegetation, dump rocks out of shoes, and skip flat ones on two adjacent rivers. From beginning to end, the hike lasted the duration of a movie.

It was burgers and s'mores supper over a rounded metal grill fire pit anchored to the ground. The adults added bottled beer to their refreshment. Later in the evening, Colin and the children went into the RV to watch a movie. April and Lauren stayed sitting next to the campfire grill.

"The sky seems bigger here than at home," Lauren mused. "The stars go on forever. I can see why you like it out here."

"It's nice sitting next to the fire under the sky."

"Colin won't get a fire pit for the backyard because he says it's a fire hazard. He and I will be revisiting that topic when we get home."

"Keeping a water hose nearby might help your case."

Lauren lifted her beer bottle in thanks. "Good idea."

Both stayed quiet and were enjoying the ambience and darkened scenery when Lauren said, "I'm sorry my family and I slowed up your hiking day. I know you wanted more practice. We haven't really helped."

"It's okay. I appreciate the support."

"Have you told your parents yet about your Chilkoot trip?"

"I will soon."

"I wouldn't wait too long. Isn't next weekend your backpacking trip?" Lauren asked.

"Yes. I need to try extended hiking and camping with Big Blue."

"Are you nervous?"

"Yes and no," April admitted.

Lauren pointed her beer bottle at April. "What if there's an emergency?"

"It's only a few miles to get to the campsite. If it's bad weather or something comes up, I won't be too far from the parking lot."

"I'm very proud of you. You're showing up and coming closer to your goal."

April blushed and stammered, "Thank you." She shook her head and chuckled. "I'm glad no one was around to see my first camping weekend. Sleeping in my tent was scary."

"Your camping skills are strengthening along with your confidence."

"They are. I'm not sure what's on the other side of all this. I knew I had to make a change. Show myself I can be someone else."

"You're doing that. Though I liked the old April too."

April poked the fire logs with a stick. "What parts?"

"You're funny, loyal, and a friend I can count on."

While staring into the wiggling flames, April said, "She's still in there."

"I know. The old April would have slept in the RV."

Yes, she would have.

"I'm comfortable in my tent. The irony is I sought out something that made me feel uncomfortable, and scared, and inept. My discomfort has become less and less. I would not call myself a pro, but I'm not a fraud."

Lauren stood. "I like this new part of you, too. I'm off to bed. Sweet dreams."

April extinguished the fire and crawled into her tent. As she laid amongst the slumber of the campground and periodical hoots of forest owls, she thought about what Lauren had said about liking the old April too and wondered, what parts did she like and want to keep?

Sunday was a repeat of Saturday, and when the hiking group returned to the campsite in the late afternoon, there was no delay in decamping.

On Wednesday night, April started packing her gear one day early. Added to her gear from last weekend, she packed her camp stove, fuel, fleece jacket, extra batteries, bear spray, and water filtrating accessories. This was the first time April would carry extra water just in case her attempts at filtrating failed. The water would be her heaviest and most necessary item.

She left work early on Friday and drove northeast for three hours to Fort Ulmer State Park. After checking in at the Ranger Station, April left her vehicle in the overnight parking lot and began a four-mile hike to her campsite.

The dirt-packed trail she walked on was marked and guided by small plastic diamond-shaped decals affixed to tree trunks. The maple and oak trees shading made the lighting dusky, and there were hot air pockets throughout.

After two hours of hiking, April wondered if her plan was too ambitious. To keep her spirits up, she reminded herself, *I can do this. I'm safe. I've only seen squirrels and birds. Maybe I should talk out loud. Let animals know I'm coming.*

Two miles in, she had passed some campers. Now she wished she had stopped and camped near them. She wished there were more people about. Did she? What if those people were dangerous? Isn't this situation dangerous? What did April know about backcountry camping? She was still learning. Maybe this time, she should have taken a class. April was tired, hungry, and cranky and guessed she had at least another thirty minutes until she reached her campsite.

April groaned and kept trudging as daylight faded.

Her headlamp washed over a trail sign that indicated her campsite was behind her. She was a healthy half-mile pass it. Yelling a swear word, she changed directions keeping a sharp watch for a numbered brown campsite post.

At the spot, April unbuckled Big Blue, letting it slide and thump onto the ground. Her shoulders, back, and hips were pained.

April had to set up camp before she could rest. Tent setup was quick. She couldn't wait to go to sleep.

After a stop in her new outdoor bathroom, April pulled a prepared sandwich from in her pack. Her trail fatigue was enough that she chewed slowly, almost too tired to eat. She reminded herself she needed the calories for tomorrow. Plus, April still had to hoist up her food to keep it away from bears and other animals.

April tied one end of a long, thin rope to a hockey puck-sized rock and attempted to throw it up and over a high tree branch. She missed, and the rock bounced off the ground. Darkness made it harder to gauge the needed throwing height. On the fifth try, the rock arced over and hung. She fed out the line, then switched the rock with her smell-proof food bag. April pulled the rope back and raised the sack out of reach of wild animals. Then she looped the remaining length around the trunk and knotted it.

The next morning, she woke well rested. April changed her underwear and socks and added her fleece while stretching sore muscles and discovering new tender body spots.

Out of her tent, April saw bright morning sunbeams cut through the hardwood forest of leaf-loaded limbs and light up the area. After a breakfast of oatmeal with dried cranberries, April cleaned up, then readied Big Blue.

She was feeling good. April wanted to sing on the trail. Her backpack felt almost weightless compared to yesterday's haul.

April spent the next six hours exploring trails. One impressive sight was a monolithic slate gray-colored formation that stacked and tilted like a too-full bookshelf.

In the early afternoon, she came upon a spur footpath of broken natural stepstones fringed with clumps of rough grass that led up to a jutting ledge. April maintained a safe yard from the edge. Nearby signage stated that the area was an eroded rock cliff that had smoothed and faded during the centuries and weather and now displayed rust-red mineral veins. Down below, a river gorge covered the bottom of a tree-lined valley. Rocks had calved from the cliffs and now rested on both of the river sides and submerged in the water. She could smell the gallons of water that rolled and shimmered under the sunbeams.

Entranced by the vista, April removed Big Blue and sat down. She felt luxuriously fatigued. Underneath the bluebird sky, April laid down. She extended her arms, spreading her fingers out, and let her feet flop to their sides, soaking in the restful delight.

As April walked the remaining distance to her next campsite, she thought about the last twenty-four hours.

Happy thoughts bounced in her brain. She had built more mileage. Another first claimed, she slept in the backcountry. Nature scenery was beautiful. Today was a success. Tomorrow, she'd hike more miles in gorgeous country and return to the car.

Back at camp, her camp stove's immediate warmth contributed to April's jovial pleasure. After supper, she removed the outer rainfly canopy of her tent. Minus the external membrane, the netting on top and part-way down the sides gave April a mosquito-proof vision of the forest. The evening crept across the clearing until darkness lacquered the landscape.

At bedtime, no slumber oblivion came. April opened her eyes and stared at the dark. Something flashed in a deep corner beyond her tent.

What was that? April silently whimpered, please let it not be an animal.

Another flash. She tensed. Her heart beat so fast she was having trouble hearing what was out there.

There was a flash above her tent. Then another. Flying lighted insect bodies winked on and off, filling the clearing with their intermittent luminescence as if they were touchable earthbound stars.

Fireflies.

April smiled and watched the squadron of sparks float away. This was a first she would cherish.

CHAPTER FOURTEEN

Back at work, April reflected on the magic of the fireflies' luminescent gold. She hoped the same for her Chilkoot adventure next month.

Her trail hours, along with weekday evening walks, were gifting nature's beauty, increasing her physical and emotional stamina, and creating a bedrock of hiking and camping skills. Lauren had said she liked the old and the new April. Hiking the Chilkoot would not have occurred to the old April. The new April desired to investigate different frontiers.

April put her chin in her palm and asked herself, who is this new April? What if the present feelings were temporary? What if after the Chilkoot, she slid back into the old April?

Having no answers at the ready, she set the questions on the backburner and started working on a budget report.

Later after her evening walk, April rested on the couch, trying to distract herself with television. She surfed the channels, unable to drop into the manufactured dramas. Tonight would be a good night for tennis. Maybe that was it.

April went into the kitchen then searched through her junk drawer for the goldenrod-colored tennis class contact sheet.

Finding Shannon's name, April telephoned. She had wondered why Shannon kept showing up to class when Coach Deborah consistently yelled at her. April judged that Shannon had low self-esteem and resigned herself to the Coach's treatment.

Hadn't they all put up with Coach Deborah's yelling and aggressiveness?

"Hi, Shannon. It's April from tennis class."

"Hi. I haven't seen you at the courts for a long time. What's up?" Shannon asked.

"I took a break from tennis. Are you interested in playing a pickup game? Tonight? Or maybe later this week? Or next?"

"I can't tonight, or this week. I have my kids this week. How about next Thursday after 7?"

"I didn't know you had kids...or an ex-husband," April said.

"I have a daughter who's ten and a son who's eight. My ex and I share custody. Next week is his week."

"How about 7:30 at the outdoor courts near 6th and Adams?" April asked.

"I'll see you there. Thanks for calling. I'm looking forward to playing," Shannon said.

"Me too. We won't run any drills."

Shannon laughed. "Sounds good. See you next Thursday."

That weekend April went on Saturday and Sunday hikes with Gayle's hiking group. The trails, the other hikers, and hours outside continued to build April's trail legs and confidence. On Thursday evening, she met Shannon at the tennis courts.

Shannon called out, "Hi, April! How are you?"

"Good. Thanks again for meeting up."

"It was nice of you to call."

"I was restless the night I telephoned. Tennis would have helped," April said.

"I have those days too. Let's warm-up."

By the third game, summer darkness surrounded the chain-link enclosed courts. The court lights brightened the white boxed green squares.

After the deciding set, April huffed out, "Whew, that last rally was long. I didn't know if I wanted to keep going to try to win or let it go so I could stop."

Shannon laughed. "It was fun."

April walked to the bench and wiped herself down with a small tennis towel. "Thanks for gathering up the balls."

"You're welcome." Shannon sat on the bench next to April. "Thank you for inviting me to play. Tonight has made me nostalgic for summer nights when I was a kid."

"I forgot how much I like tennis. That last class with Coach Deborah soured me a bit," April said.

Shannon leaned back against the chain link fence. "Coach yelled most of the enjoyment out of the class."

"Why do you think we let Coach Deborah treat us so poorly?"

"For me, it was easier to ignore her. The class wasn't forever. I gave myself the option of not going."

"Several people quit," April said.

"Can't say I blame them."

April rolled a tennis ball between her hands. "Me neither. I've been thinking about my future, and my past. I went through a divorce last fall, and I was miserable. It makes sense that I would let someone behave as badly towards me as I felt about myself."

"If you want to talk about your divorce, I'm available to listen," Shannon said.

"I was unhappy in my marriage and my life. I did what I thought I was supposed to do to be happy. I checked the college, career, marriage, and house boxes." April lifted her arms as if she was supplicating to an alter. "Divorce was the only choice I could think of at that time to make myself feel better and move forward. Have you experienced anything like that?"

"Sort of. At times, I've thought other people got happiness, but not me. Experience and growing older has shown me happiness is about what *I* think and feel about *my* life."

April nodded her head. "This spring, I decided that I was going to Alaska in July to do a six-day hike on an old gold rush trail. I needed something new, a sort of reinvention. I had not really hiked or camped before. I've been learning how the last couple of months," April said.

"Sounds like you've been exploring outside while figuring out your inside."

Surprise made April tilt her head. "I like the sound of that."

Shannon picked up her tennis bag. "I'd like to hear about your trip when you're done. That, and occasional tennis games."

April drove away from the tennis courts amazed by the enjoyable evening.

At home, she checked the weather forecast for the upcoming weekend. There was a slight chance of precipitation. April went to the emptier closet next to the front door and looked for her rain jacket. Near the end of the closet rod, she found the blueberry-colored coat.

April assessed the rubbery material. She speculated at the coat's age. Would it keep the rain out?

She folded the rain jacket into a small square and added it to a packed Big Blue.

In Friday morning rush hour traffic, April drove to Staircase Falls State Park. The weekend plan was to hike five miles to her first campsite. The next day hike eight miles to her second site. On Sunday, she would hike seven miles back to her vehicle via a different branch of the trail system. This itinerary would require carrying Big Blue each day.

Arriving at midday, a late June heat sat on the parkland with no breeze to move through and cool down. April lifted Big Blue onto the top of the trunk. She positioned the pack so she could back up and slide her arms through the shoulder straps.

April groused, there must be an easier way to put Big Blue on. She stepped forward and buckled the hip belt and chest strap. She tightened and loosened the straps transferring the pack's weight about the top half of her body and seeking a balance between anchoring the new appendage and carrying comfort.

She said aloud, "This will have to do--daylight's burning."

At the end of the asphalt was a pitched roof wooden kiosk with a map of the park trails and the start of her hike. April's shoes scraped and scattered small beige gravel as she walked by skinny birch and aspen trees whose vibrant green leaves weighed down branches that jutted out at random positions on the white paper bark trunks. Soon the trail became smooth dirt. The scenery and solitude created a peacefulness that flowed about her.

April headed into a wilderness area she'd never been to before. At the moment, she found it amazing that this was her life. Her adventure.

At mile three, a gradual elevation climbed into a wetter ecosystem of dense hardwoods and wet trail spots. A broom-wide silent stream soon paralleled the trail. Further up, the waterway widened to ten feet, becoming a rushing stream. April began to see large gray boulders as if some random geologic activity had dropped them from the sky to decorate the enlarged river. Up ahead, she could hear a melody of splashing and tumbling water. Twenty minutes later, she saw a ten-foot water-fall drop into a cascade pool.

April sat at the water's edge, she removed her shoes and socks and stuck her swollen hot feet into the water. She leaned back onto Big Blue. Eyes closed, April relaxed into her unexpected fortune. When her feet started to numb, she knew it was time to continue walking.

Exposed tree roots grew across the path and alongside sloped rock outcrops whose smaller waterfalls dropped into clear-water shallow and dense blue deep pools. Puddles of standing water coupled with the heating afternoon created a stagnant humidity. Mosquitos supped and hitchhiked onto April. Her perspiration darkened her shirt armpits. Sweat dripped like a waterfall down her temples, neck, and cleavage.

It was a relief when the wetland terrain started to recede. Small pockets of tall leafed aspens and larger clumps of triangular evergreens surrounded the trail.

April estimated she'd covered at least five miles and hoped she was near her campsite.

In the next hour, April came to a tree-height cluster of jagged rocks. In the center of the rock pile was a cave-like opening big enough for a large mammal to enter. April stood to the side of the entrance and peeked in. There were no animals visible in the room-sized space. Ten more minutes of hiking brought her to her campsite trail marker.

She threw her arms in the air and cheered, "I'm home."

With habituated quickness, April set up her tent and camp stove. Her plan was an early supper then sleep.

April sat cross-legged looking at the vistas and eating a concoction of rice and freeze-dried vegetables. There was no house noise, people, vehicles, or airplanes. The songbirds had disappeared. Above the lowering sun was a layer of deep yellow followed by a line of citrus orange. Higher in the sky was a strip of tangerine that blended into soft cherry light.

She decided that today was good and forecasted that tomorrow's trail miles would be a continuation of the nature she would sleep in tonight.

April awoke as dawn was beginning to light up the land.

Far-off acreage was blurry in its shadows. Her upper body had stiff and sore points where Big Blue had hung and clung. Rolling her shoulders and stretching her arms above her head loosened muscle kinks. She again lightened her water weight when she boiled water for her instant coffee and oatmeal. When the sun was up and the distant landscape visible, April took down her tent and repacked Big Blue.

It was time to start walking.

April squatted, then leaned to the side sliding her arm through a pack shoulder strap. When hooking her other arm into the remaining strap, she tottered and had to readjust her balance. In a sudden torso jerk forward, she stood up and finished fastening Big Blue to her.

The bright and clear day promised good weather. Several miles down the trail, browning parched evergreens scattered in sparse threesomes and foursomes. Short wild grasses filled space where they could. The terrain was level and clear of most groundcover debris. Hiking was quiet, and there were no surprises. April slipped into a mellow meditative gait.

Towards 11:00, she decided to stop and eat lunch. April looked up at the sky. She saw dense black and blue clouds in the Northwest.

Was it rain in the distance? It looked far away. Whatever it was, April hoped it stayed away.

She estimated she had an hour or so before reaching her next campsite. The day's heat was being blown away by intermittent wind gusts. She smelled the moisture-heavy air that preceded rainstorms. The stormy clouds were closer. The need to get to camp and set up her tent propelled April into a trot. The weather front barreled her direction.

The thought that maybe she could hike back and sleep in the shelter of the rock pile surfaced. Common sense noted it was too far. She wouldn't make it in time.

April stopped. She dug out her rain jacket and put it on. She wobbled some as she lifted Big Blue onto her back. The combination of exercise, foreboding, and added humid air made April sweat. Another twenty minutes passed, and dark polka dots of rain splattered the trail.

The rubber raincoat, Big Blue pressed against her, and hiking in the rain created a swampy environment in April's clothing. The over warm moisture pooled and collected in between the sticking layers, adding a chaffing quality. As her discomfort built, the rain became liquid tendrils, showering her and the landscape. April was not having fun.

Thirty minutes later, big rain blobs pelted April in the face, soaking her shorts and slouching her socks. The ground transformed into a squishy, muddy slip n' slide. To keep her footing, she had to slow her stride. The temperature dropped, eliminating the July heat. April started to shiver. *Please stop raining became a silent, repeated mantra.*

The storm accompanied her another hour to what she thought was the second campsite. The rain made it hard to discern. After hunting around the small clearing, April located the park trail post.

She looked around and wondered if flash floods happened here? Would she be washed away tonight? April had to prevent a panic starting. She'd take it one thing at a time.

Big Blue was soaked. With porcelain-cold hands, she set up her tent and staked tight the rainfly. April laid her backpack inside. Water leaked onto the tent floor.

She suspected she was hypothermic. Changing into drier clothes moved to the priority task.

Shaking April burrowed into her pack. Her dirty clothes from yesterday were the driest. That was what she put on. The other clothes she draped on Big Blue attempting to dry them.

To distract and reassure herself, April started speaking out loud the gibberish mash of thoughts colliding in her mind.

"That feels better. I should eat something. How am I going to heat water in the rain? I shouldn't do it in the tent. The gas smell will stay inside. One of the camping website's recommended never to store food in the tent because it attracts animals, and the smells can infiltrate the material."

Holding the flap back, she positioned the stove as much outside as she could while keeping it somewhat protected from the rain. With both hands shaking, April wrapped one around the stove's base, and the other pushed the ignition. The stove stayed lit. When April added water to her instant noodles, she was careful not to spill anything in or on her tent.

She didn't bother rinsing her dishes and added them to her smell-proof food bag. April wandered beyond the campsite area looking for a tree to hang the bag from. The rain and her shivering made the camping task take twice as long. April neared the campsite boundary and noted her tent.

Her tent looked bedraggled. She probably did too. Small pockets of water collected on the roof, pushing the tent in.

Back inside, April curled up in her sleeping bag. The tent floor was damp, but her sleeping pad protected her bag.

She pleaded to Mother Nature, please let tomorrow be a better day.

The next morning, April listened to the rainstorm before opening her eyes. Would she have to walk back to the car in the rain?

April groaned long and loud. Using wet wipes, she bathed herself the best a moistened towelette could do on damp skin. She changed into a sodden pair of clean underwear.

She tried to remember how far away the parking lot was. The trail would be worse than it was yesterday afternoon. Maybe she'd stay here forever and be eaten by wolves.

Repeating the supper steps, she made oatmeal and coffee for breakfast. It had a slight pasta taste, but the heat and calories gave her a shot of hardiness and helped to fortify.

April told herself, *I hiked here, and I can get back.*

She kept her head down and began slogging the miserable hours back to the car. She slid and tiptoed on the soppy, muddy trail. Stepping into hidden holes waterlogged her socks and shoes. She still carried the added rainwater that permeated Big Blue. The raincoat somewhat kept the water repelled, but the rubber made her so hot she sweated through her shirt. Raindrops slipped past her hood and rolled down her chin and then onto her neck.

She was numb and miserable. When April passed new waterfalls, she didn't care or stop.

In the late afternoon, April reached the parking lot. She wanted to cry in relief. The rain would have obscured her tears. April let Big Blue fall to the ground. When the trunk was open, she heaved and threw in her gear.

Sitting in the driver's seat, April thought, *I cannot sit in these clothes all the way home.*

She removed her shoes and socks and chucked them into the backseat. The shoes landed near an old sweatshirt. April saw no other vehicles in the parking lot.

No one would be out hiking in this rain.

She removed her shorts and took off her shirt and sports bra. Wearing only the old sweatshirt and underwear, she drove home.

As she exited the parking lot, April asked herself, what if the Chilkoot is like this?

CHAPTER FIFTEEN

April dried out as the car's heater vents warmed and over-whelmed her unbathed stink. Her lank, greasy ponytail stuck to her neck. The rainstorm hike back to the parking lot had taken several more hours than she had planned. April drove home in the late afternoon and wouldn't arrive until evening.

She sagged in the comfort of sitting down. Today, and part of yesterday, had been miserable. Again, *what if the Chilkoot is like this?* banged around her brain, jamming misery further into her heart.

Did April really think she could do this? Instead of bravery, was she full of bravado? Most of her practicing had been in state parks somewhat close to help. The Chilkoot was in big moun-tains of wilderness. Was April ready for an adventure like that? Had she put big-girl panties on or pretended to? Was the charade up?

April was downhearted. Hot tears of disappointment and projected failure erupted and chaffed the corners of her rain-pruney eyes. The tears were not soft, feminine dashes of wetness but large droplets of saline, making streaks of puffy crimson down her cheek and chin. Using restaurant napkins stowed in the glove compartment, April blew her nose. Another napkin mopped her face.

She was so tired. A dispirited fatigue rode shotgun in the passenger seat.

When April's garage door closed, she lumbered out of her car wearing the sweatshirt and panties. The concrete was cool and smooth to her bare feet.

She wanted a shower. She'd unpack later.

April poked her head out of the garage's side door and surveyed the street. Grass blades were bent, and shrub foliage glistened wet from the recent rainfall. The sidewalk and road were empty of people. Her neighbors were probably inside their homes readying for the new week or in their backyards enjoying the rain refreshed evening.

Her strategy was to zip across the walkway into the house without anyone seeing her.

April waited several more seconds. Believing the coast was clear, she started to the house's side door.

"April?"

April halted in mid-step and looked over her shoulder. Her neighbor Bob was standing above the backyard fence line holding garden loppers.

"Hi, Bob."

Bob, with one eyebrow raised, asked, "Everything okay?"

Oh, hell, was what she wanted to say but chose to explain instead. "I was caught in a rainstorm. My clothes got wet."

"I see. It rained here most of the afternoon. I'll let you be on your way. Have a good night."

"Thanks. Night, Bob."

Neighbor Bob just saw her without pants. Was this the outdoor recreation version of the walk of shame? April wanted the day to end so badly.

Once inside, April swung the utilitarian white exterior door shut with her fingertips, being careful not to slam it. Pressing her forehead on the backside, she sighed long. She felt grubby and exposed in the backseat-rescued sweatshirt, underwear, and dirty hair.

Another person has seen her ineptitude. A shower will help. Ugh, more water.

The shower's hot water steamed up the bathroom and fogged the mirror. April stared at the showerhead waterfall.

Unspoken monologue rolled on her tongue:

Get in.

I don't want too.

This is ridiculous. Take a shower.

A different internal voice similar to her mom's fumed, you're wasting water and time. Remember, all your camping gear has to be dried out.

April laid the toilet seat cover down and sat on top of it. Today had been awful. All those outdoor ads and movies showing people strong, healthy, and living more exciting lives. What was she trying to prove? That she could be like them? She had tried something new. Now she wanted nothing to do with it.

April wretched a little in the back of her throat. Did she stop here? Was the Chilkoot for other people?

After showering, April dressed in khaki shorts and chose a lemon-yellow t-shirt as a sort of wearable inspiration. She went into the kitchen. For supper, April nibbled crackers and peanut butter until the mixture was a mush in her mouth. Swallowing around the knot in her throat was a challenge. Not sure what next to do, she called Lauren.

"Hey."

"Hi. You don't sound well. Are you sick?" Lauren asked.

Yes, sick with a dilemma, but instead she said, "Was I chasing fool's gold when I decided to go hike the Chilkoot?"

"You wanted an adventure and to challenge yourself."

"You could have pointed out my idea was nuts," April said.

"It's not nuts," Lauren soothed. "You can do this. That is, if you still want to?"

"Are you saying I could quit?"

"Yes."

"If I quit, people will know."

"This is about you, not them. Go somewhere else. Montana has mountains and cabin rentals. You have time to think about it. You don't leave for a couple more weeks."

When the conversation ended, April considered what Lauren had said.

If she didn't do it, how would she feel about it? About herself? She could go somewhere else. Or stay home.

April walked back to the side door and peeked out. Neighbor Bob was gone. She returned to the garage. The soaked Big Blue had darkened to a navy color. When April leaned down to pick it up, she grunted a little from the exertion to lift the clammy water weighted pack. Stooping at her shoulders, she carried the pack away from her body and into the kitchen. The backpack and its contents dripped water over the concrete walkway and the house floors.

Next, she retrieved the hiking clothes and trail shoes from the backseat. Water sloshed inside the shoes. April emptied teaspoons of water onto the grass. She held the rain jacket at arm's length and grimaced.

You're going into the trash.

She added her hiking clothes to the washing machine, and then tossed leftover dry snack bars and trail mix onto the kitchen counter. The camp stove, headlamp, and other gear joined the food. Then she hung the sleeping bag next to the washer and dryer. April took her tent into the garage and set it up.

Cleaning up and drying out her gear went late into her Sunday. The physical and emotional exhaustion caught up with April. When she yawned wide and popped her jaw, she knew it was time for bed.

The next day at work, April kept her head down and focused on email and project tasks. She didn't want to think or talk about hiking, camping, or the Chilkoot Trail. For a short time, she pretended it didn't exist. The strategy went well until Tuesday morning. While she was in the breakroom filling up a water bottle, Kari bounced in. "Good morning April."

"Morning, Kari."

"Did you go camping this weekend?" Kari asked.

April mumbled, "Yes."

"How was it? There were thunderstorms here over the weekend. Did you have rain, too?"

Annoyed, April lied. "A little." *Please go away*, she silently wished.

"Did you get wet?"

April bleated. "Yes."

"I'm sure it was no big deal to you. You're so practiced at all that. Your big trip is almost here. Are you getting excited?" Kari asked.

Excited was not April's current word of choice. "The trip is coming up."

Was she going?

"Were your parents surprised when you told them?"

"My parents like to travel," April punted and turned off the faucet.

Kari pointed at April's water bottle. "Hey, wait. Your water bottle is only half full."

"I'm watching my water intake." April hurried out of the room before Kari asked anything more.

Walking down the corporate corridor, she wondered what she was going to do.

Was she going again this weekend? Maybe. She didn't have energy or excitement in her. Last weekend was too miserable. Plus, it was the Fourth of July holiday.

April's phone alarm went off.

Thank goodness, a meeting to go to.

April celebrated the holiday with her family barbequing burgers at her brother and sister-in-law's home then gathering at a local park to watch city fireworks. Because of the holiday, her packing routine was pushed to Friday night. She would only be able to hike Saturday afternoon and Sunday morning with a night of camping in-between.

What should she do?

Looking at her camping gear scattered on the kitchen countertop and the clothes, now clean, waiting in a laundry basket, she rubbed her eyes.

Make a decision. Should she call Lauren? It was too embarrassing to explain. April decided she wasn't hiking this weekend.

April waited for the feeling of dismay to arrive as it had last time. It didn't.

She felt okay. More than okay, relieved and free.

Doing some Latin dancing wiggles, she pivoted the opposite direction.

April texted Shannon to see if she wanted to play tennis this weekend. She'd call Lauren for coffee or brunch.

Shannon was free for tennis on Saturday morning, and Lauren was available on Saturday afternoon. April enjoyed the time with her friends. There was no carrying a backpack for either occasion. Both women asked how hiking and camping were going.

April replied to both inquiries. "I've seen beautiful scenery. I can set up my campsite with some skill. Last weekend it rained, and, pun intended, it dampened the fun." Both women laughed at the diverting humor. April's mother called that evening.

"Hi honey, why don't you come for supper tomorrow night? It will be you, me, and Dad."

"Mom, you didn't ask if I already had plans."

"Do you have plans tomorrow at six?"

"No."

"If you need us to push back the time, we certainly can."

"That's not the point," April said, trying not to snap at her Mom.

Her mom, Sue, moved on. "Does six work?"

April closed her eyes and took in a deep breath and let it go. "Yes."

"Wonderful. We're having lasagna."

On Sunday morning, April woke at dawn. There was no reason to get up. It wasn't necessary to lower her food bag from a tree, boil water for coffee, or pack up stuff. No peeing on the ground. No observing 'leave no trace' and saving her toilet paper to throw away when she was back at home.

April lounged but didn't fall back to sleep. She wanted to know what the sunrise looked like.

Moving to the window, she looked out. The neighborhood houses and trees blocked her view of the sunrise and the horizon.

After coffee and avocado toast, April noticed she was looping around her house.

This was ridiculous. When had she become habituated to needing to walk on Sundays?

Dressed in gray walking shorts, a lavender tank top, and blue running shoes, she left her house. The sidewalks, clear of debris, were flat or a dependable undulation. There were no tree roots to step over. Nothing obstructed her path view. It was early. Many people were still asleep or snuggled indoors, having breakfast or easing into their Sunday of choice. The quiet was familiar and comfortable.

April kept walking and looked at the urban houses painted unobtrusive beige, gray, white, or yellow with an occasional color such as teal breaking the unspoken compliance of exterior house paint. Mowed front yards, lopped shrubs, and planted flower beds and pots with tall decorative grass in the background and multi-colored relaxed pansies; robust, velvety petunias, or more-is-better petal-stuffed dahlias in the foreground. The flora was lovely, deliberate, and tame. She appreciated the supervised beauty and charm of the yards, yet she desired to see expansive views of parklands and bluffs, streams crawling around rocks and trunks, and old trees that grew where they anchored in.

She didn't know she would miss it.

April looked at her phone. She'd been walking for an hour and a half and wasn't ready to turn around. She kept going.

The next hour took her into a business district of parallel lines of white concrete situated on either side of black asphalt by strip malls of restaurants, digital telecommunication branches, and clothing stores. At the three-hour mark, April decided to find an alternate route home.

When her neighborhood's outskirts came into view, people were moving outdoors. Other walkers, runners, and bike riders were out and about enjoying the day. April smiled big and genuine and extended good mornings to those she passed. Once at home, she went to Big Blue and began repacking for her next hiking and camping weekend.

April wanted more.

That evening on the drive to her parent's house, April reminded herself that she had to tell them about the Chilkoot. At first, when she told Lauren and the outdoor recreation store sales clerks, April hadn't been certain she could travel so far on her own and hike the trail, plus learn the new required outdoor skills. Not telling many people had been a sort of safety valve while the aspiration was shaky. She had decided she wasn't going to tell her parents until she felt on firmer ground with the adventurous decision. After the post-brunch family intervention last fall, April was not interested in having to convince or defend this trip.

April did a slow shuffle into her parents' house and called out, "I'm here."

Her dad, Duane, replied, "In the kitchen. Good timing. I'm taking the lasagna out. Will you fill the water glasses?"

"Sure. Where's Mom?"

"In the backyard watering her flower pots. I'm going to let her know the lasagna is done. If the timer goes off, pull the garlic bread out, please."

April heard her dad jabber, "Hey, Sue, supper's ready."

When the three of them were seated around the dinner table and started eating, her mother asked April, "So, how are things going?"

"Things are fine."

"How's work, how's Lauren and her family, and all that?"

"Work is fine. The big project is moving along and will launch in August. Lauren and her family are busy with summer activities. They're going to a family summer camp next month for a week."

Duane chewed fast and swallowed. "What's that? Like a kid's summer camp but for the whole family?"

"That's it. Sleeping in cabins, canoeing, and crafts and such."

Sue piped in, "I think that's wonderful. What plans do you have for the rest of the summer? Maybe another tennis class?"

"Actually, this summer I've played tennis a few times with a former classmate."

Sue leaned across her plate. "New friend or a nneewww friend?"

"Mom, I'm not dating anyone right now. Shannon plays tennis and is also a divorcee."

Duane took a sip of water then asked, "Are we allowed to ask how you're feeling now that some time has passed since your divorce?"

"Yes. I'm well. I've worked through my issues with Justin and our marriage. We grew apart."

April's parents stared at each other and sent silent messages.

Sue began again. "Honey, are you happy?"

"Happier than I have been in a long time."

More silent messages passed between Sue and Duane.

This time her Dad went first. "We want you to be happy. We're not trying to pry, just wondering how you're doing."

"I know." April's conscience demanded she tell them about the Chilkoot.

"If you need anything from us, we're here for you," Sue added.

"Thanks. Do you have any summer or travel plans lined up?" April asked.

"Your mom and I are planning a trip to the Albuquerque Balloon Festival in October."

April's gaze swiveled between her parents, "I didn't know either of you liked hot air balloons."

"The Richardsons did it last year and recommended it, so we're going this year."

Now. Tell them now. "Speaking of new experiences, I'm going on a trip in two weeks."

Sue smiled. "Really? Where to? Is it a girl's trip? What do you have planned?"

Nerves tightened April's throat and saliva pooled in the area. Say it fast, don't stop.

"I'm flying to Whitehorse, Canada and then driving to the southern coastal town of Skagway, Alaska so I can hike the Chilkoot Trail. The thirty three-mile trail starts at Dyea; an abandoned town ten miles north of Skagway. At the trail's end, I take a train back to Skagway."

April pursed her lips and looked passed her parents to the framed and faded riverscape print hanging on the opposite wall. She could see their surprised expressions in the glass's reflection.

They were shocked.

Duane held his lasagna filled fork in mid-air. Sue lowered hers. Each stared at their daughter.

Sue began, "When did you decide this? That distance would require time and planning."

Uh-oh. She's upset.

"I learned about it from a television show last winter. The idea of the experience had a compelling quality."

Duane inquired, "You were persuaded by a show?"

"You were persuaded by the Richardsons about hot air balloons," April pointed out.

"We know the Richardsons and do not have to exit the country to get to our destination. Your mother and I are still discussing whether we want to drive or fly to New Mexico."

Sue inserted, "April, I think the idea of an adventure is fabulous, but that's a long way to go on your own. Has this trip been why you've been going camping on the weekends?"

"Yes. I've become more adept at camping and hiking."

"Honey, couldn't you go on a similar trip closer to home?"

The second intervention began. "I could. I did an overnight backpacking weekend recently."

Sue tacked an alternate direction. "Maybe you could hold off until you and a friend could go together?"

"My work leave time has been requested, the plane tickets are bought, and my trail reservation is made."

"Your mom and I are surprised by your news. We need a little time to take it all in," Duane said.

'Taking it all in' meant conversation for the rest of the meal orbited safe topics and complementary opinions. Her parents gave the leftovers to April. As she was leaving their house, her mom called out, "Why don't you come next Sunday for supper? You can tell us more about this trip."

"I can't. I'll probably get home late on Sunday night."

"Why don't you keep it in mind and call us on Friday and let us know."

"Okay. Bye."

April knew her mother stood in the driveway watching.

I should wave goodbye. I should be grateful they didn't try then and there to persuade me not to hike the Chilkoot.

She glanced up and waved goodbye to her mother, whose replying wave was prompt.

They're going to want to talk about this more.

CHAPTER SIXTEEN

The inside of April's car smelled like tomato meat sauce and oregano seasoning as she drove home.

That went well. She guessed her mom would call tomorrow.

April was wrong. Her dad called the next day.

"Hi, honey," Duane said, infusing his words with parental cheeriness. "How was work today?"

"Work was fine. What's up?"

"Your Mom and I were talking. We'd like to hear more about your trip."

April pursed her lips.

"You still there?" Duane asked.

"I'm here."

"Why don't we all go out for supper on Wednesday night? That is if you don't have plans?"

Go and get it over with. "Okay," April said.

"How about Greek? Or Thai? Or pizza..."

"Greek," April interrupted.

"Great! See you Wednesday."

What was she going to tell them? Tell them more about the Chilkoot.

In her Chilkoot trail research, April viewed photographs of bogs where vibrant green moss and lichen carpeted and cloaked ground and cottonwoods. Mountainous wilderness dropped into tight and wide corridor valleys and climbed toward white ice cream mountain peaks. The enticing challenge of something beyond what she would have sought out previously. How would April explain this? To speak it aloud sounded more whim than wonder.

April arrived early at the Greek restaurant. Seated at the table, she ordered a preemptive bottle of red wine. After a few sips, she set the wine glass down and pushed the stem in fidgety lines ironing the checkered Greek-flag blue and ivory tablecloth.

She felt strange sitting alone at the table. April knew she was nervous about her parent's responses but also realized she couldn't recall a time she had supper by herself in a restaurant.

Had she avoided this?

She had eaten lunch alone in restaurants, blending in with the other varied diners accompanied by paperwork and devices. April perused the restaurant's occupants. There were huddled couples merging personal space, families immersed in their chatter and clatter, and a pair of food-focused dining partners who occasionally spoke. April acknowledged she had unknowingly reserved the evening meal out for couples, families, and friend gatherings.

How did April appear to the other customers? Did they pity her? Was she background scenery? Was it worse if no one noticed her? This contemplation was not helping her courage.

Sue and Duane walked into the restaurant. Duane removed his Roy Orbison black plastic sunglasses and Sue her brown, large owl-eyed Jackie Onassis frames.

April waved to her parents, and they hurried over. Each gave April a quick hello hug.

Sue sat down first. "Hi, honey. Are we late?"

"No. I was early. Wine?" April asked.

"Yes. How was your day?"

"Work was busy."

"That's good," Sue said as she filled her and Duane's wine glasses.

April saw her Dad ignore his wine and fold his hands in front of him. He was ready to get down to the business of learning about her trip.

"What are your trip dates and itinerary?" Duane asked.

Both of April's parents lasered in on her. April pressed her back into her chair, squaring her shoulders.

"Don't you want to look at the menu first?" April asked.

Sue pointed to the menus on the table. "I'm getting the salad and your dad the gyro. And an antipasto plate to share."

They meant business.

The server approached them. In fast minutes the order was taken, and her parents refocused on April.

She swallowed and cleared her throat. "I leave in late July. I'll be gone for a week."

Sue's index finger tapped her fork. "How long will you be hiking?"

Duane asked, "How are you getting to the hike?"

"On Sunday, I take an overnight flight to Whitehorse, Yukon, where I pick up my rental car. Then I drive a couple of hours south to Skagway, Alaska. I have to check in at the Trail Center in Skagway and attend a safety orientation. The Inn I'm staying at will drop me off at the trailhead on Tuesday morning. I'll hike for six days. My hike ends on Sunday at Bennett, British Columbia. There, I'll catch a train back to Skagway. I spend a night there again and then drive back to Whitehorse to catch my flight home."

"It sounds like you have it all planned out," Sue said.

"I do."

"Your dad and I were taken off guard by your news. We're not trying to tell you how to live your life. We just want to know how you're doing and what you're up to. And help where we can."

April's shoulders dropped an inch, "Thank you. I thought you'd try and talk me out of going."

Sue and Duane darted looks to each other.

"We considered it," Sue said.

Duane took a sip of wine. "Your mom and I went on the Internet and started reading about the Chilkoot Trail. The trail was originally a trade route. Did you know that during 1897, 20,000-30,000 people traveled the Chilkoot Trail?"

"I didn't know," April said.

Sue went next. "Most of the Stampeders, that's what the miners and other gold seekers were called, went over the Chilkoot Pass because it was shorter than the other route, but much more dangerous."

"That I did know," April said.

Sue beamed a smile. "The history of the trail is fascinating. Miners, showgirls, gambling, and of course, empty dreams and wallets."

The server set the antipasto plate on the table's center. Each person chewed in companionable calm.

Duane waved his hummus-slathered pita slice, dropping Kalamata olives onto the table. "I can only imagine the determination it took for an individual to traipse through the wilderness and go searching for gold. A miner had to transport one ton of supplies to set up a mining claim. Weighed each allotment at the Scales checkpoint before climbing Chilkoot Pass."

Sue speared Duane's dropped olives with her fork then said, "That Chilkoot Pass is a steep climb. It was hard for both miners and packhorses. One website noted that over 3000 horses died on the trail."

"I'll be carrying my own gear," April said.

Sue leaned forward. "In a backpack?"

"Yes," April mumbled while chewing a cucumber.

Sue queried, "How much will that all weigh?"

April swallowed, "I'll try to keep the weight under thirty-five pounds. There are water sources along the trail, so I won't have to haul a large supply. A couple weeks ago, I carried my loaded backpack most of the weekend."

"April, your mom and I are nervous about you doing this hike by yourself. Several websites suggested hiking with a friend or group."

Before April could reply, the server set the ordered entrees on the table.

Duane continued. "Many people are hiking the trail each day as well as park rangers if you need assistance. Sue, what do they call the rangers in Canada?"

"Wardens," Sue said.

"I know this hike sounds dangerous," April said. Sue opened her mouth to speak, but April kept going. "I'm not making light of the risks. I'll be trail-ready and aware of my safety. Hikers are required to camp overnight in one of the nine Chilkoot campgrounds. I'll be sleeping in a tent community. Plus, it's the land of the midnight sun. The daylight is longer to hike in."

Sue pointed her head, so she looked into April's eyes. "We don't mean to overstep. This last year has demanded you take on new and additional responsibilities."

"It has. I'm doing what I need to do to take care of myself." April gave her parents some reassurance. "I'll check in with you and let you know when I've made it to Whitehorse, to Skagway, when I finish the Chilkoot, and when I return to Whitehorse to fly home."

"Thank you," her Dad said. "I never thought we'd be talking

about you heading on a trip to Alaska and the Yukon, especially a year ago."

April realized the anniversary of her divorce asking was near.

Had April subconsciously known and planned this? Or did it just work out this way?

Duane interrupted her thoughts. "You know the Bosch's went on a cruise to Alaska."

Sue corrected, "It was the Sanders. They did a land and sea tour. Said the scenery was beautiful. I don't think they went into the Yukon."

Her parents continued their tangential conversation. April exhaled.

Things were working out.

Sue turned back to April. "Your Dad and I want to take you to the airport and pick you up. Could you text us your flight details?"

April nodded. Later in the restaurant parking lot, her parents hugged her goodbye, her Mom giving an extra squeeze and her Dad double-patting April's shoulders.

Driving home, April thought, *my parents, want me to succeed. I need to finish packing for my weekend trip. I'm preparing for the Chilkoot.*

The mid-July hiking and camping weekend in the North woods had bluebird skies with comfortable sunshine and daytime breezes. Dried up water holes and bug repellant kept the mosquitos hampered but not completely deterred. On trails that wiggled between aspen and birch and stands of broadleaf maples and conifer white spruce, April encountered more people traffic. At dusk on Saturday evening, tall trees half obscured the sunset, the tails of sunbeams colored the lake in a pink-orange glow.

April heard a loon's high-pitched call float across the lake. A shorter and wobbling yodel replied. The black-headed lake bird with its upper body white-dotted-black plumage glided into April's view. The underwater web feet cracked the glasslike surface and sent back a rippling wake. A matching mate thirty yards behind quick-paddled after. The waterfowl conversed late into the evening.

On Monday morning, April was in high spirits and moved in a satisfied, quick stride. She greeted the colleagues she passed in the hallways. Data research commandeered the work hours until lunch. At 1:00, April strode across the concrete sidewalks enjoying the natural light of sunshine and fresh unconditioned air. Fifteen minutes in, she heard her name called.

Oh no, it was Kari. *Don't turn around. Keep walking.*

Kari didn't give up. Soon April heard Kari's footfalls dog her heels.

"Hey April, I've been calling you. You must not have heard over the traffic."

"Hi."

Kari walked next to April. "It's such a nice day today."

"It is," April agreed.

"I saw you leave for a walk. It's good to get away from my desk and take a break."

April stayed quiet and let Kari gabble on about the current status of the department's projects.

When Kari was silent, April wondered if she missed a question?

Kari started up again, "In a week, you're headed on your big trip. Alaska is a long way to go hiking and camping."

April told herself to ignore Kari's cheekiness. "It is. Hiking the Chilkoot Trail is something I want to do."

April didn't need to explain herself to Kari.

"You know, April..."

April would bet money Kari would tell her.

"What you're doing is brave and exciting. I wish I could do something like that," Kari said.

April stumbled as she cranked her head to stare at the other woman. In Kari's aviator sunglasses, she saw a surprised version of herself reflected back. "You think I'm brave?"

"Yes. I don't think I could do something like that. Plus, you've been practicing all those weekends getting ready. I imagine it wasn't always easy."

"No, there were times I struggled. One weekend it rained so much that myself and all my gear was soaked. I was completely miserable by the time I reached the end. There's also tripping hazards, ticks, wildlife, and being alone and far from help."

"That's what I'm talking about. Uncomfortable and scary stuff and you kept working towards your goal," Kari said.

"Thank you for saying that. My goal sometimes sounds strange to others."

"You're welcome. I suspect your goal sounds strange because what divorcee decides to go hike the Chilkoot Trail on her own?"

Oh, Kari, we were so close to maybe being friends. April said, "I guess."

"I don't mean to offend you. It's just different is all."

"It is," April said.

"I'm cheering for you."

"Thanks. I'll tell you about it when I return."

The corners of Kari's smile almost reached her sunglasses. "I'd like that."

The days before departure moved with a swiftness intertwined with increasingly long hours of work wrap-up, house chores, packing, neighborhood walks, and quick trail hikes slipped in. April purchased a cardinal red rain jacket, black rain pants, and a rainproof backpack cover that advertised protection against drizzle and deluge. The helpful sales clerk recommended that April line the inside of Big Blue with a garbage bag for extra protection. Plus, she purchased trekking poles. The elongated support would have helped April hike the muddy trails of the rainstorm weekend.

After exiting the outdoor recreation store, April sat in her car. She mentally jumped into a tangle of concern and quandary.

Did she have what she needed? What if she'd forgotten something? What if something happens while she traveled or hiked? What if April was knocked on the head and kidnapped? Or broke an ankle and was unable to get help. What if her flight was delayed and she missed her orientation class? What if there was bad weather on the trail or traveling? What if at the trail-head she changed her mind?

What if the Chilkoot Trail was a wonderful, satisfying adventure?

CHAPTER SEVENTEEN

April and the Canada-bound jet waited on the tarmac. She looked out her window, watching the ground crew's orange batons marshal the aircraft backward.

She had a sudden urging for someone to guide her. To the car rental place. On the drive to and around Skagway. Throughout the Chilkoot Trail. A person to tell April where to go, when, and how to get back home.

The plane entered the takeoff lineup. April's chest contracted, making her breathing shallow.

Why didn't she go on a Canadian practice visit? April needed to relax. *It's Canada, not outer space.*

The jet rumbled, roared, and soared. A sigh lifted out of April. The removal of choice relieved her. She put on her headphones and reclined her seat. Her mind slipped into the memory of trip packing three days ago.

April inched pass the camping items laid out in rows and columns on her living room floor. It was her third cross-check with the crumpled list in her hand. Penciled checkmarks partnered with trail shoes, hiking pants, thin gloves, a floppy-brimmed hat, sunglasses, and more. She mailed ahead her camp stove and a pocketknife to the inn in Skagway. April would buy the stove fuel there.

She must buy bear spray, too.

April opened a black garbage bag making the plastic balloon with air. Then she inserted the bag into Big Blue to line the inside before adding her gear. She stuffed folded and rolled wicking clothing and wool socks around her tent, sleeping bag, dehydrated food, and hiking poles. As she cinched down the straps, compressing the bulk caused the pack to release a whiff of dirt.

It all fits.

She propped Big Blue against the kitchen table and stood back. Excitement spread across April's torso, then ran up her head and made her scalp tingle.

She was ready.

On departure day, car engine sounds alerted April that her parents had arrived early. The locked side door stopped their entry.

April shouted, "I'm coming," while she hoofed it to the door. "Hi, come in."

"We're early," Sue said.

"I'm almost ready. I have to finish locking up the house."

"We'll help," Duane said.

April ticked off her fingers. "The windows need to be checked and locked if they aren't already, my thermostat reprogrammed, the light timers need to be turned on..."

Her Dad interrupted, "I'll start with the windows."

"I'll take the thermostat and timers," Sue said.

April's parents rushed to their tasks.

They were sincerely helping her.

Her cell phone beeped. Lauren's text said, "Have fun hiking the Chilkoot. Stay safe. Call if you need rescuing." Followed by a second message, "You'll be fine."

At the airport curb drop-off, her Dad said, "If it's too dangerous or there's bad weather or anything else, you don't have to hike the Chilkoot."

"Let us know when you're done hiking," Sue said.

Her parents looked down at the concrete road, then at each other, and then back at April.

"I'll be okay. Thanks for dropping me off. I'll let you know when I land," April said.

During the group goodbye hug, Big Blue was also encircled.

"See you in a week," April said. Wearing her trail hiking shoes, she walked into the glass and concrete terminal.

I'm coming Chilkoot!

After hours of community sleeping on uneventful flights, April landed in Whitehorse. While waiting to process through customs, she texted her parents. In not much time, April stood in front of a red rental sedan in mountain country.

She was having a hard time believing she was there. April considered pinching herself.

When April exited the Whitehorse airport parking lot, she let out a thrilled whoop. Excitement flowed in her body. She was in Canada on her way to Skagway, Alaska.

April turned onto the Klondike Highway, driving into a land of mountains. The geological monuments were grand in their stature, spread, and constancy. The vast space made April feel free and daring.

In her second hour of driving, it began to mist becoming rain showers. Her sunny mood dried up and her armpits began to perspire. An leaden cloud mass lowered concealing the range and socking in the pass. The precipitation stopped, and fog took its place. Visibility was a car length ahead and behind.

Maybe April should pull over and wait out the fog? Was it safe to do that here? What if she couldn't find a pullout?

April glanced at the car clock.

She must be close to the U.S. border. It sat near the top of the pass before descending into Skagway. April would keep going but go a little slower.

Several vehicles going the opposite direction bulleted out of the fog, making April's heart jump and her arms lock each time. No cars came up behind her or appeared in front. Twenty minutes later, she saw the outline of a building the size of a double-sided garage bisecting the road.

April braked underneath an extended roof that crossed the lane. A middle-aged man wearing a button-up shirt and border control badge approached April's car. After assessing her and the vehicle, he asked, "Passport? Where are you coming from, going to, and why?"

No "hello" or "please." Wasn't Skagway the only place down the road?

"I flew into Whitehorse this morning. I'm headed to Skagway. I'm hiking the Chilkoot," and before April could mute herself, she started to babble, "I've never hiked it or hiked in Alaska or Canada before. This is a big deal for me. Have you..."

The border guard stared at April with the habituated disinterest of someone who is required to listen and has probably heard a similar narrative countless times. "Are you bringing in any weapons and or food?" the guard asked.

Surprised and disappointed by the man's continuous protocol questioning, April stammered, "No."

"Open your trunk, please," the official said.

April twisted towards the driver's door, searching for the trunk release. Finding nothing, her eyes skipped to the dashboard.

The border guard spoke from above April's bent head. "Ma'am, the button is near the steering wheel."

April squeaked, "Oh. Thanks."

The guard looked inside the empty trunk then pronounced, "Ma'am, you're free to go."

April drove further into the lifting fog. The highway sloped down the pass. In minutes the afternoon sunshine burned away the fog. The highway and mountains were in full impressive view. Houses and outbuildings appeared along the road.

She recalled what she knew of the town. At the end of Lynn Canal tucked between coastal mountains, sits Skagway with a population of a thousand, census generous, full-time residents, but when the summer cruise ships' steamed into port, the population boomed.

It still brings in the seekers, April thought.

She navigated to Broadway Street. Tourists dressed in shorts and light jackets wearing sunglasses mingled on sidewalks with other visitors wearing slacks and heavier fall coats.

April had time to check in at her hotel before her safety class at the National Park Service Trail Center.

She drove several blocks until she saw the robin's-egg-blue historic Queen Anne corner house. A path of paved stepstones crossed a tiny lawn halting at three steps leading to a glossy, ornate scrolled wood front door. In an attached side yard facing the street grew exuberant bright pink and yellow dahlias and double-blossom bushy red begonias sharing space with distressed wood plank raised vegetable boxes containing clusters of chives and top-heavy tomato plants.

The inn's website relayed the building's gold rush brothel history. April liked the racy past. She wished those long dead working women who risked the Klondike's wilderness and wild ways would somehow share their gutsiness with her.

April slung Big Blue over one shoulder. With a lopsided gait, she entered the lodging. The thin-striped polished wood flooring creaked inside the yellow regalia brocade wallpapered room. Ponderous Victorian chairs and a chaise were positioned opposite a gilt-edged rectangle mirror above a table with a computer, Wi-Fi box, and a twentieth-century cordless telephone.

No one was about, and April waited. To the side of a staircase was a "take a book, leave a book" bookshelf holding a selection of paperback vacation-read thrillers, mysteries, and James Michener sagas.

April went into a tight, narrow hallway. She tried not to bump into the numerous framed black and white photographs and a collection of dried flower miniatures. Entering a commercial kitchen, she found a woman unpacking warehouse club sized boxes of groceries.

"Hi, I'm April. I'm here to check in."

The woman's head flew upward in surprise. "Oh, hi. I didn't hear you. Welcome. Let's get you checked in." The woman glanced at April's backpack before she started down the hallway to the front desk. "You're doing the Chilkoot" was more a statement than a question.

"Yes. I have a shuttle ride reserved for tomorrow morning," April said as she hurried to catch up. "I return on Sunday for another overnight here."

"No problem. I'll need your credit card and ID. You need to fill out this form." The innkeeper continued rattling off information as if giving a well-memorized speech. "Breakfast starts at 6 a.m. Your shuttle departs here at 8:15. You'll be at the Chilkoot Trailhead in Dyea about 8:30."

"Okay." As April dug in her wallet, she memorized tomorrow morning's timeline.

"Here's your room key. Up the staircase, go left, then walk to the end of the hallway. Your room is on the right. The shared bathroom is at the top of the stairs."

April shifted Big Blue, so it didn't fall off her shoulder. "Thanks. I mailed a box ahead of my arrival."

The innkeeper started back down the hall. "It will be in the office. I'll go get it."

With the addition of her mailed box, April went upstairs. The hallway had white painted wainscoting below hydrangea blue upper walls with framed glossy photographs of local sea, sky, and mountains. She looked behind her and reaffirmed no one else was in the hallway and unlocked the room. The matter-of-fact sound of the deadbolt tunneling into its housing case reassured her.

A double-hung window facing an alley allowed cheery afternoon sunlight into the petite, basic room. The pressure of the backpack's angled load was crushing April's shoulder blade. She leaned, letting Big Blue slide and soft-bump onto the gray-blue carpet.

Next April texted her parents, 'In Skagway. Going well."

It was a couple of hours before her orientation. April could buy the stuff she needed and explore the town.

Glancing around the room, she spotted the garbage can. Removing the liner, she placed her camp stove inside.

She'd look strange carrying this.

Patting Big Blue, April said, "I'll be back soon."

On Broadway Street, tourists spilled off sidewalks and into the road as they strolled and window shopped the two-story merchant buildings whose wood-trimmed frontier facades linked to the Gold Rush past. Mixed in with American English, April heard French, Chinese, German, and several languages she couldn't identify.

She saw an outfitters store sign and wandered in. If a person wanted a t-shirt printed with 'Skagway, Alaska,' or 'Gold Rush,' a bounty was here. A young woman folded t-shirts at the back.

"Excuse me, can I ask you a question?" April asked.

The folding did not pause. "Sure."

Holding up her garbage liner, April asked, "Can you give

me directions to an outdoor recreation store? I need to buy camping stove fuel. I'm hiking the Chilkoot."

"You'll like the hike. I did it earlier this summer. There's a camp store down the street."

April felt torn between asking more questions about the woman's experience and buying her supplies. "I start tomorrow."

"Weather is supposed to be good. You'll see rain at some point along the trail. Do you have a backpack cover?"

April cringed inside. "I do, plus a rain jacket and pants."

"Good. Enjoy your Chilkoot."

In minutes, April entered the camp store. A female and male employee stood near jackets and walking sticks. They appeared outdoor savvy in their earth tone pants, long-sleeved quarter-zip shirts, and multisport webbed sandals. The male clerk approached April with a relaxed smile. "Hey, can I help you?"

April lifted her plastic bag and said, "I need camp stove fuel and bear spray."

The clerk reached for the bag. "Sure thing. What size canister?"

"Medium, please. I'm hiking the Chilkoot. I'll be on the trail for six days."

"Cool! That's such a great hike."

April preened, "I start tomorrow."

"What's your plan to treat water? You don't want to get giardia on the trail," the clerk said.

"I have a water filter system and iodine tablets."

Thank goodness, April didn't sound like an idiot. "Do you have another suggestion?"

"Nah, that'll do."

Foreboding interjected April's mind. How would she hike if

she was doubled over with cramps and messing her pants because of giardia?

April realized the clerk was staring at her. "I'm sorry. Did you say something?" she asked.

"You mentioned needing bear spray."

Oh jeez. She had forgotten. "I'll need that, too. What do you recommend?"

The salesclerk pointed to a display next to the cash register. "That one there. Do you have a bear bell?"

"No, should I get one?"

"It's a good thing to have on your pack. It prevents you from surprising bears and making them mad."

"Should I get two?" April asked.

He grinned. "Nah, one will do. Do you need anything else?"

More confidence, but she didn't say that.

"That's it. Oh wait, can you give me directions to the Trail Office?"

The clerk pointed further down the street. Soon April stood on a planked boardwalk in front of a squat, windowed storefront that looked less federal and more friendly.

April muttered under her breath, "Here I go."

Inside, topographical maps and blackboards of chalked information were attached to the walls between hanging black and white photographs of Klondike stampeders and colored nature photography. Joining the counter line, April surveyed the people in front of her. There was a young couple who looked like college students, an older couple carrying trekking poles and slim wraparound sunglasses pushed up on their heads, and a family of four with two elementary school-aged children.

April's Dad was right; they're all hiking with another person.

Her shoulders began to tense. A park ranger wearing the official stone-colored buttoned-up shirt with the arrowhead patch and olive-green trousers explained to the family about snow on Chilkoot Pass. April folded her hands into prayer position and rubbed her thumbs. She tried to hear more, but the background noises were interfering.

"Five minutes before the next orientation class," a similarly dressed park ranger sporting a Smokey the Bear hat announced.

April left the line and entered an adjacent room with metal folding chairs. She and six other hikers listened to the hat-wearing park ranger give a brief history of the area and trail. Then came the warnings: do not touch any artifacts, drink only treated water, pay attention to surroundings and weather, stay on the trail, observe wildlife safety, and store food in the campground bear boxes.

The last left April silently repeating, *I won't see a bear. I won't see a bear.*

She had her new bear bell to alert bears that she was in the area, plus her new bear spray.

The ranger added one last directive: "Take a credit card with you. If you are involved in an emergency and need to be airlifted from the Chilkoot, you will need your credit card."

As the class concluded, the ranger handed everyone their permits. Nervousness had dried April's mouth. When the other hikers shared thank yous and good lucks, she nodded, unable to speak.

What was April supposed to do next?

Uncertain, she exited the park office and lingered on the sidewalk. She watched tourists carrying plastic bags of Skagway souvenirs amble back to their docked cruise ships.

April would eat, shower, and turn in early.

Her own stroll through downtown led April to a grocery store where she purchased a takeaway supper sandwich, cheese sticks, apples, and snow peas. She continued on until she saw a green lawn park with picnic tables. The departing visitors allowed Skagway's volume to lower to small-town ease. The abundance of extended daylight contradicted the clock time. The mountains surrounding Skagway were like a jagged rock wall whose portentous height and stretch felt both protective and isolating.

April chewed and looked at the scattered empty historic buildings and a log cabin that fringed the park, their preservation creating an isolated loneliness that she understood. Evening breezes chilled her, prompting April to wander the adjacent neighborhoods another hour as she wound her way back to the inn.

After showering, she set aside her 'before' hiking clothes along with her 'after' wardrobe that she'd store in the rental car trunk. Referencing her checklist, April concluded she had what she needed, she hoped.

She propped a loaded Big Blue against the locked guest room door. Full of gear, it stood like a sentry. April attached her bear bell to the front of her pack. The jingling sounded like a holiday sleigh bell.

Time for bed. Tomorrow's a big day. Today and yesterday were big days too.

While lying in bed, April's hands cupped her neck, and her forearms rested on her torso. She asked herself again, was she really doing this?

The brush of an internal yes answered, and the fatiguing combination of jet-lag, anxiety, and excitement pressed April into sleep.

CHAPTER EIGHTEEN

April awoke to her 6 a.m. alarm. Lying in bed, a giddy impulse propelled her to throw up her arms as if she was high-fiving the air. Today April would start hiking the Chilkoot!

Her hiking pants swished as she moved about the room, gathering up her travel toiletries on her way to the bathroom. While brushing her teeth, April smiled big. Minty toothpaste foamed and dripped down her chin, landing on the sink bowl. Grinning, she filled her water bottle and plastic storage reservoir.

Then April wound her way downstairs to the dining room. The room had the square box shape of a building addition and vinyl windows. Hanging abstract canvas paintings added color and energy to the space. A continental breakfast and coffee were set out for guests, yet no one was there. She sat down at a table near the food and waited. Several minutes passed, and no one appeared.

Knowing today she would hike seven and a half miles to the Canyon City campground, April served herself larger portions of eggs, bacon, and toast. It occurred to her this was the second meal on this trip she'd eaten privately in public.

April glanced at her plastic wristwatch, bought especially for the Chilkoot in case her phone battery failed. It was 6:55. There was over an hour before her pickup shuttle. Uncertain what to do, she refilled her coffee. A man wearing a long navy pinstriped apron and resembling the bald shiny Mr. Clean mascot came into the dining room.

He saw April and said, "Good morning. How are you? Sleep well?"

"I'm well. Thank you."

The fellow removed April's dirty plate. "Excellent. Call if you need anything."

Not knowing what to do next, April went outside to check the weather. The chilly morning was clear. The mountain peaks towering above Skagway were hidden in a rolling fog. She inhaled deep to taste the air and settle her nervousness she could feel building. April wanted to walk off the tension, but a reminder of the trail mileage ahead of her made her turn away from the coastal beauty and return to her room.

She lay on the bed, killing time while her hiking shoes hung over the edge preventing duvet dirt smears and sprinkles. Her ankles flexed in a rapid frequency of nervousness. Lying down was not discharging nerves and reaching calmness. Maybe combing through her backpack to double check was a good idea? On the heels of that thought was the anxiety-stuffed question of 'what if she accidentally left something behind?'

April poked her head under the bed and walked her eyes over the room's crannies and carpet. Everything was packed and bundled, ready for the Chilkoot.

After stowing her other luggage in the rental vehicle, she was back in her room. In her boredom, it occurred to April to text her parents and Lauren. 'I leave for\\ the Chilkoot shortly. I'll text you on Sunday when I'm back in Skagway.'

Internet browsing filled the time until her phone chimed its departure shuttle alarm. She lifted the pack to the bed. Squatting down on her hunches, April slid an arm through one shoulder strap and then the other. Using her thigh muscles, she boosted up and stood with the readied pack. The gear's weight pressed into her shoulders, causing her body to sway. April wondered if she looked capable of hiking the Chilkoot.

She waited at the inn's front door. Minutes passed. Again no one appeared. She walked to the kitchen. It and the dining room were empty of people. Panic pumped her heart. Had she missed her shuttle?

Perspiration dampened April's long-sleeved gray wicking shirt. She bustled out the front door to search outside. She saw the man from earlier lounging against a white minivan.

Hurrying toward him April all but hollered, "Are you my Chilkoot shuttle?"

"That's me. I'm Jasper, by the way. I'll take your pack."

April's dry throat croaked. "Thanks."

"You'll like hiking the Chilkoot," Jasper said.

"Have you hiked it?"

"Several times."

Several times! April wanted to survive it at least once.

"Any recommendations?" April asked.

"The Chilkoot is beautiful. Enjoy it and the people you'll meet. You'll be walking in the steps of history."

In less than twenty minutes, Jasper turned into a parking lot a little bigger than a tennis court and said, "You're here."

As a courtesy, Jasper held Big Blue up for April to slide her arms through the shoulder straps. She buckled and tightened the straps until she and the pack moved as one.

"Enjoy yourself," were Jasper's departing words.

Alone, April watched him drive away. A rectangular sign displayed sunflower yellow painted letters that read 'Chilkoot Trail Unit Klondike Gold Rush National Historical Park.' The upper left corner showed silhouettes of miners climbing on a faint blue backdrop of the Golden Stairs in winter. Adjusting the zoom on her cell phone, she centered the sign and took her first trail picture.

She started on the sole path and pondered the forthcoming adventure she had chosen. April's gut quivered. Beside the opaque moss green Taiya river, chiseled into a sign the size of a kitchen cutting board, were the words 'Chilkoot Trailhead' with an arrow pointing toward graded gravel. There was no fanfare with the easy-going first steps onto the Chilkoot Trail. Her stride lengthened in positive forward momentum. A happy feeling whipped up her spine.

April had not gone far when she saw the moss-draped overhang roof of a kiosk. Glass protected maps, rules, and park information. Underneath, a closed cubby held a chained trail registry. She turned the dirt-smeared front cover and saw pages of listed hikers. Using the blunt, stubby pencil, April added her name.

The trail shifted into a stone staircase covered in twigs, dirt, and decomposing leaves. It was like climbing a bunched stone zipper. The sharp-ridged gray rock steps were wide and flat enough that April could step up and push off while keeping balance with her heavy pack. The forest solitude amplified the rhythmic thunks of her shoe soles on the hard-surface.

Stones gave way to hard dirt. Spreading ground moss covered and cloaked half-buried rocks and semi-exposed tree roots of lofty cottonwoods. A winded April sipped water. A sign displayed 'Trailhead 1.6' miles back to the beginning.

The Chilkoot wiggled through bogs. Split log footbridges, whose width was a bit wider than April, crossed the marshy ponds.

Don't fall in. Don't think about falling, she told herself.

The darkened water was like a stained-glass image as it

reflected the sky, trees, and ferns that grew from the banks. April had seen a version of this landscape in her online research. The pictures had been incredible, but she was intimidated by this section. As April stepped onto and shuffled across the rough-hewn bridge, the wood bounced and dipped, and she wobbled.

Time to use her poles.

Reaching behind her, April pulled back the Velcro straps on one trekking pole and lifted a pole up and out of its mooring. Then the other. Extending the poles to a helpful length, she then locked their position. April stabbed a pole point into the timber walkway, stepped forward, poked the other pole into the wood, stepped, and repeated. Across the bog, she cycled her arms and her feet like a slow train in an attentive progression.

She'd take it slow.

Further in, the bog dampened into a rainforest. Mosquitos started to bite. At a solid-ground gap, April took off Big Blue and applied a bug spray that smelled similar to citrus furniture polish. Newly perfumed, she leaned down and hooked her arm through the shoulder strap and tried to swing the backpack upward. The pack dropped to the ground. Next, she squatted down and put her arms in place and with her legs thrust up to standing.

She hoped this would get easier.

April heard people's voices behind her. It had been a couple of hours since she had spoken to Jasper. The chatter grew louder and nearer.

She shuffled to a pull-off, and in minutes a hiking party of five young adults reached her. Swift greetings and relaxed smiles were exchanged. April watched the smooth stride of the group move up the trail.

Hiking close to their talking would help keep the bears away.

The group was faster than April. Soon she lost sight of them. April looked at her watch and guessed she was close to the five-mile mark of Finnegan's Point campground. Twenty minutes later, she walked into the campground clearing that included a warming shelter and two olive-green colored bear-proof locker boxes.

Near the shelter was an enormous tree whose circumference gave privacy to anyone on its other side. Similar to a jumbled fabric-looped mop head, the above-ground roots were the size of average tree trunks and created nestled seats.

April unbuckled Big Blue and set the pack on a barrel-sized root. Minus the bulk, her back felt released and unencumbered. Unzipping the top pocket, April withdrew a bag of mixed nuts, cheese, crackers, and an apple.

It pleased her to be sitting on a Chilkoot Trail tree root. Reflection on and of the beginning miles had been sidelined while she concentrated on steps, prevented injury, and managed her jet lag. April would have opportunities in the miles ahead to understand more of the meaning of her Chilkoot adventure and inner exploration.

As she chewed, April watched a pair of hikers set up their camp. One hiker pushed poles into tent corner grommets while the other blew up the sleeping pads. In minimal time they centered the rainfly over their standing tent.

April reminded herself to put her rainfly on tonight.

After lunch, she wandered to the banks of the Taiya River. Beyond, the Irene Glacier's blueish snow and ice draped and pushed between green-treed mountains.

Back on trail, April encountered boardwalk bridges. These bridges did not have sides, but the width of the planks was at least a yardstick wide. As she thudded across the smoother-planed boards, ferns and foliage rustled, birds called, her bear bell warned, and the rest of the backcountry stayed quiet.

It wasn't long before April needed a bathroom break.

Why hadn't she gone at Finnegan's Point? She must hike smarter.

Stepping off the trail, April ducked behind a thick clump of trees. Dropping the pack to the ground while avoiding the pointed and poisonous maple-tree shaped fanning leaves of devil's club, she attended to her waste management. When she finished, April folded the used toilet paper and placed it inside her designated trash bag. She'd be carrying her trash on the Chilkoot and into Skagway.

The trail cut through pine stands that didn't have the height and cast of the cottonwoods, allowing sunlight to dapple the path. In five hours, April arrived at the Canyon City campground by mid-afternoon. Canyon City was a larger version of Finnegan's Point. She selected the flattest tent spot possible and unloaded her pack. Food, toiletries, water filtration system, and camp stove were cached in the shared brown bear box that looked like an overlarge metal toy box.

Time to set up her tent.

She looked around to see if anyone was watching her.

That was dumb. Why would anyone be watching her? She had watched a pair of hikers at Finnegan's Point.

April took in a belly breath and laid out the footprint of her tent. When she began attaching the black clips to the tent poles, the poles slipped in her sweaty hands. In minutes, her tent was up. When the rainfly was anchored April pulled her shirt away from her sticky chest. Next, she blew up her sleeping pad and arranged the gear inside her fabric house.

With time before supper, she decided to check out the nearby Canyon City Historic Townsite.

April started on a spur path. She came to a placard that described the Klondike Gold Rush settlement. Next was a suspension bridge anchored to the banks with steel footings. Its handrail was the middle cable in an open grid on either side. Her hands skimmed along the nearest in the event of a needed quick grab. A meter or so underneath, cloudy, light-teal colored easy rapids flowed. The bridge's rickety springiness responded to each of April's steps.

Once over, April negotiated the bank boulders and continued on a looping path. She looked over a rusted, disintegrating ochre steam boiler the size of a compact car. Above the furnace door, 'Union Iron Works' was cast in the metal.

How in the world did someone get this enormous piece of equipment all the way out here?

Next was a cabin that was now, like the boiler, more ruins than relic. Other rusting metal scrap artifacts were scattered amongst the brush. The desire to continue exploring was superseded by hunger.

It was time to head back to camp.

At the bridge, April whooped, "I've met you before."

This time, she capered across using the bridge's giving bounce to lift her. Laughing, April skipped off the bridge. At the campground, she saw new hikers had arrived.

One hiker sat at a picnic bench writing in a notebook, and others headed down the spur trail.

At her tent, April changed into closed-toe webbed sandals with plastic soles. Her feet and toes stretched and luxuriated in the roominess and cushioning of different shoes. Carrying her water bottle, April went to the bear box and pulled out her camp stove, a sealed pouch of dehydrated pasta and sauce, and her spoon. Then she opened the screen door to the canvas-roofed warming shelter and cookhouse. It was more hut than house. The interior was dim. Previous years' stale smells had fused into the structure.

Inside, a hiker heated up water and said, "Hello. Supper time for you, too?"

April guessed the woman was in her sixties. A tie-dyed headband held back wavy silver curls.

"I'm ready to eat," April said.

With a tired, happy smile, the hiker said, "Well-earned today. Loved the scenery. How about you?"

April put together her cook stove. "Good for me, too. Those stone steps in the beginning kept going and going."

The woman poured water into three food pouches. "Nature's own Stairmaster. I'm Rita."

"Nice to meet you. I'm April. Are you headed to Sheep Camp tomorrow?"

"Yes. I'm hiking with two friends I met in college during the late '60s. We wanted an outdoor adventure retirement reunion."

April started her stove. "The landscape is almost indescribable."

"Agreed. See you at the picnic table?"

"Yes, thanks."

April was gladdened by the invitation. She had been uncertain of the number of hikers she'd encounter on the Chilkoot and was prepared for many hours of solitude. Boiling water neared the lip of the pot. April shut the propane valve. She poured hot water into the food pouch, and it began to heat and plump. Gathering her portable kitchen, April went to the picnic table.

Rita called out, "Come on over."

"It feels good to sit down. And eat," April said.

"It sure does. This is Dot, and that's Claire."

The college friends each had curls. Dot's curls were a cap of tight ebony afro curls accessorized with Zuni earrings. Claire's springy soft red was gathered in an unadorned black hair tie.

Dot asked, "What did you think of the rushing water underneath some of those bridges? Snow must be melting further up the mountains."

"As long as it doesn't melt too much and create an avalanche," Rita said.

April gulped. "I thought the avalanche situation was safe? That's what the orientation ranger said."

Claire spoke up. "I imagine it's safe enough if the rangers are letting people on the trail. We heard from other hikers that the rangers are recommending people leave Sheep Camp early because of the snow on the Pass."

"Tomorrow's short hike to Sheep Camp will be good elevation practice before the climb up the Stairs and over Chilkoot Pass," Dot said.

April nodded in agreement.

"There's the ranger talk tomorrow night," Claire reminded.

They spoke of traveling to the trail and the scenery they hiked. The sun moved to the far side of the mountains. The forest shadows created a dusky evening in the land of the midnight sun.

Rita stood up. "I'm tired. Goodnight everyone. Happy trails."

A good night chorus replied. After stowing her cooking supplies and garbage in the bear box, April strolled to the river with her water treatment system. She filled the filter pouch, then inserted the drip hose into her plastic storage reservoir. April sat on the riverbank to wait. She pulled her knees up and rested her chin. The evening was serene, including the easy-flow river rapids.

April felt lucky to be here. There had been no urban noise since this morning or a plane overhead. Just the sounds of leaves moved by a breeze, birdsong, and her footsteps.

When she jerked awake with a start, April realized she had drifted off. Her drinking and cooking water was treated and ready for tomorrow. Back in camp, she saw a straggling three-some arrive late.

"Good evening," April said.

A slim man not much taller than April chimed back, "Good evening. How was your hike today?"

"Excellent. Yours?"

The man swung his arm out to include his companions, a shorter woman who appeared to sag under a mix of tiredness and her backpack, plus a lanky older adolescent teen. "It was good. We're ready for supper and sleep."

The hiker's cheerfulness had April responding in kind. "Well deserved. Enjoy your supper. Happy trails tomorrow. Good night."

"Night," the others replied back.

April set her watch and phone alarm for 7:00 a.m. Then she listened to the forest quiet as thoughts of the day floated in. Today went well. She had met friendly people. The ladies with the curls were jovial and friendly. April decided to nickname the women the Curlies. She guessed she'd see the Curlies at the Sheep Camp campground tomorrow.

Tomorrow's hike was a little over five miles. The shorter distance put April's arrival time around mid-afternoon, creating a longer rest period before the hiking day to the Scales, up the Stairs, and over Chilkoot Pass before stopping for the night in Happy Camp. Happy Camp sounded pleasant. The name "Scales" had an ominous sound. As if the hiker would be judged. The only judging April wanted to do on this trail trip was of distance and time. Hiking day one was done and five more to come.

CHAPTER NINETEEN

April's muffled telephone alarm woke her. Her sleeping bag's nylon rubbed her face. Reaching down into the bag, she withdrew her phone to stop the noise. The sounds of tent zippers, the pit toilet door banging closed, and hushed conversations of readying hikers floated about Canyon City. April wiggled her toes and rolled her ankles. A mild soreness vibrated up and down her legs.

Sitting up, her lower back twinged. April shivered in the mountain morning. She dressed in clean underwear and socks, a short-sleeved petunia pink hiking t-shirt that smelled of an outdoor scented dryer sheet, and yesterday's sports bra and pants. A hooded zip-up fleece was needed before crawling out of her tent and jamming her socked feet into her shoes.

The crisp air smelled like wet leaves of late fall, not July, and dew streaked her tent. After using the bathroom, April refilled her lungs with fresh air. Her stomach grumbled. She gathered her breakfast makings from the bear locker and went inside the warming shelter. Dot of the 'Curlies' was inside. Today Dot wore hammered metal dangling earrings.

"Morning. How'd you sleep?" April asked and started her water to boil.

"Morning. Out like a light. You?" Dot asked.

"The same. I'm a little trail sore."

"Me too. I've already taken Ibuprofen. You need some?"

April considered, "I'm okay. Thank you for the offer. I'm starving."

"The hiking we did yesterday plus the fresh air makes a big hunger."

April craved eggs and toast. Her sigh pined for what was not available, and her shoulders dropped in acceptance.

"I have oatmeal and raisins. I seem to eat the same breakfast when I camp. I'm ready for a cup of coffee," April said.

Dot chuckled, and her earrings swung. "I'll see you at the picnic tables."

As Dot exited the gentleman from the previous night's late arrival entered. April said, "Good morning" over her shoulder.

In the same cheerful attitude as last night, the man sang out, "Good morning. Beautiful day out there."

April tore open an oatmeal packet, and a cinnamon cloud puffed up, "Once I've eaten, I'll be ready for the trail and can enjoy it."

"There's nothing like a camping breakfast. My wife, Merri, and I want to take it easy today. Our teenage son, Conor, has the energy replenishment of the young. He's being patient with his parent's speed. By the way, I'm Rob. Nice to meet you."

"I'm April. Nice to meet you." April ripped open a peanut butter pouch and restaurant jelly packet and smeared both onto her lunchtime bread.

"How many days are you hiking?" Rob asked.

"Six days. I catch the train at Bennett on Sunday."

"Us too."

April gathered her cooking gear. "Enjoy your breakfast. See you at Sheep Camp."

"Thanks. Have a good hike today," Rob said.

April saw the Curlies talking to the group of young adults from April's marsh meetup yesterday. She walked to them.

The breakfasters exchanged good mornings. The Curlies were finishing up, and the others had dirty breakfast dishes in front of them. As April sat down, Rita said, "Morning April. How'd you sleep?"

"Good. I'm hungry this morning."

The assorted hikers laughed.

Rita's pink swirled headband matched the brightness of her chortle. "My body was yelling for breakfast early. I am stiff this morning. At my age, a little stiffness is nothing new."

A young man sporting a black hoodie said, "I think it's excellent that you ladies are hiking the Chilkoot."

April tacked on, "I agree."

Rita glowed. "Thanks! That's nice to hear."

Hoodie Hiker said, "You ladies rock."

"Thank you," Dot said, then added, "These ladies need to be rocking down the trail if we're to get to Sheep Camp. See you all later."

Another female hiker wearing a purple puffy vest and matching earband said to Hoodie Hiker, "We should visit the old townsite before leaving camp."

"I was there yesterday. It won't take long to get there, see the Stampeder's artifacts, and be back on the main trail," April said.

Hoodie Hiker stood up, "Nice. See ya," and he and his friends headed to the remains of the abandoned gold rush town.

Canyon City's temporary population dwindled as hikers headed north to Sheep Camp, leaving behind a deserted and tranquil campground. April spooned and chewed the last mouthfuls of congealed oatmeal and tipped back her cooled instant coffee.

She'd better get going too. The morning had started well.

April put on her wool beanie and thin gloves for warmth. Her muscle tenderness was ignored, stretched, and assuaged while she decamped.

Her soreness was minimal. She was doing well on the Chilkoot.

April slid on, buckled, and quick-cinched Big Blue. The now-familiar weight and expanse pressed into several tender spots at her shoulder blades and hip bones. April walked out of Canyon City and started her next five miles. Similar to yesterday's rock steps, this section reminded April of an unaligned spinal cord as it snaked steeply upward. She shifted and leaned forward to prevent tree limbs from catching and grabbing her pack.

This is preparation for tomorrow, she thought between breathing huffs.

On a ridgeline in a compact clearing, April saw a panoramic undulation of leaf and needle trees covering the valleys and mountains and eventually merging into the white cape of a distant glacier before vanishing into the matching sky.

It's magical here.

The Chilkoot coyly flattened into soft dirt before a winding descent into a deep green valley. Moss wallpapered itself onto the rough bark of the light pole pillar trunks whose upper-story long, thin needled branches were like nature's version of a cleaning duster. Most lowered branches were gone. April suspected years of voluminous snow weight had snapped these. Dulled green moss carpeted the ground's rippling mounds and holes.

She hiked through the valley and up a section that was lower on the left and higher on the right. This made April walk lopsided. She adjusted her hiking strategy and moved along the unstable, muddied shoulder. The bordering ferns were becoming fewer. April realized the wet sheen of the coastal rainforest was being supplemented by alpine forest. Trees arched over trampled trail of dry needles, and twigs snapped under April's feet. Several waterfalls appeared on either side of the trail.

When she reached a lofty viewpoint, the daylight was brighter. April could see another forested canyon further down the trail. On the right side, the acreage moved up the mountain giving the impression of the trees being taller.

April stood on the Chilkoot Trail and had a 360-degree view of miles of forested wilderness. It was breathtaking.

She took out her phone and attempted to capture the postcard-picture wilderness without regard to photo roll count.

My parents and Lauren would love this.

A dart of loneliness pinged April's heart.

She wished they were here. Sharing this. April could have asked someone to come with her. Who would she have asked? Her parents? No. Lauren had her family, job and wasn't interested in this type of camping. Kari from work? Nope.

Part of April wanted to show herself, and others, that she could do this on her own. This was her adventure. Solo traveling meant she was the one to make the final itinerary decisions of where, when, and how. Plus, April could choose how she spent her time without having to negotiate or cajole a travel companion. Not having an immediate travel partner or family about was propelling her to meet new people she might not have engaged with had she invited someone to join her Chilkoot hike.

Further down the trail, the forest floor looked like a bumpy, electric-green moss blanket. April found a perfect seat in a dipping hollow. Minus Big Blue, she sat and reclined with a snack bar. The moss underneath poked her bottom until she squished it down to comfort.

She was like a woodland creature.

April giggled. She heard voices and laughter coming up the trail.

Must be the college kids from Canyon City.

Soon April could see them, but they, not her. She closed her eyes. When April awoke, she checked her watch. The nap had maybe lasted twenty-minutes, but it was a short rest in paradise.

She'd better start moving.

April was almost to mile ten when she came upon Rob, his wife, and son standing near a suspension bridge. The bridge's treads were planks bolted to a cable gird system that was open-sided. It crossed several stories above whitewater river rapids that waterfalled down a hill.

April slowed and said, "Hi. That's quite a crossing."

"This is not the bridge to be tippy on," Rob said, then turned to his wife. "Merri, why don't I take your pack over, and then you and Conor cross?"

Merri shook her head. "Thank you, but I can manage. I won't fall into the drink." Then turning to April, "Sorry to hold you up. Feel free to go around us."

April stepped onto the bridge. It swayed and waggled. She grasped the cold metal cables near her hands. The water radiated similar temperatures of its snowmelt and glacier source. Concentration and caution moved April's focus and feet making sure to not step into the gaps between planks. The wind, following the river, flew around, over, and under her.

Her tongue pressed the top of her mouth. *Look at the planks, not the water. They're watching me. All the more reason not to fall in.*

April stopped mid-bridge. She gaped at the rushing river as

its white caps licked and curved around boulders and whipped past the riverbank.

This isn't too bad.

At the bridge's end, April heard Rob call out, "Good job. See you at camp."

April waved goodbye and continued on.

In five and a half hours, she arrived mid-afternoon into a semi-empty Sheep Camp. As she loped into camp with satisfying ease, April wanted to shout "I did it!" She was safe in Sheep Camp. A posted sign notified that there would be a 7 p.m. required ranger talk.

Instead of the ground, between thickets of brush and shrubs were elevated wood platforms to pitch tents on. April chose a platform positioned on an elbow of the campground walking loop. She repeated her setup routine from yesterday, bathed herself with cleaning wipes, carried her kitchen, toiletries, and trash to the bear lockers, plus filtered water for later use.

April wasn't sure what to do with the several remaining hours before the ranger talk. It was too early for supper. Kicking off her shoes, she crawled into her tent and laid atop her sleeping bag. The warmed air inside induced her to close her eyes.

She woke and looked at her phone. She'd been sleeping for an hour.

Again April was surprised by how tired she was. The extra rest would help tomorrow.

The next day's section was almost an eight-mile trek with a 3000 foot elevation gain. It included traversing the Stair's boulder field up a mountainside to the top of Chilkoot Pass, then hiking down and across snowfields that buried the other mountainside before continuing onto high alpine trail and into Happy Camp. Hiking time estimates ranged between eight and twelve hours.

Tomorrow would be hard. April would be relieved and pleased when she reached Happy Camp.

Fear tightened her throat and slid down to her stomach that cramped in protest.

Getting herself worked up was not helping. She needed a distraction.

April went for a walk. Sheep Camp had transformed into a boisterous campground as hikers moved about completing personal tasks. While she had rested, most of the tent platforms became occupied.

Where did everyone come from?

April had been passed by several pairs and groups of hikers, but the number of people in the campground was larger. She saw the Curlies setting up their tent and wandered over. "Hi, how was hiking today?"

Claire stopped blowing up her blue sleeping pad and heaved a little. She sucked in air and said, "Today was good. What'd you think of that long bridge crossing?"

"It was okay. We had plenty of practice crossing all those bridges yesterday."

Claire smiled around the valve she resumed breathing into. Dot held silver tent poles and added, "Today's going to look easy after tomorrow's done."

"We may be slower, but we're ready. Right gals? You're ready too, April," Rita said.

Happiness at the inclusion made April's heart shine, and she agreed. "We're ready. I'm going to walk around. See you at the ranger talk."

April looped the campground surveying the other hikers and their platform setups. She didn't see Rob, Merri, or Conor.

She hoped they were okay. Rob said they were taking it easy.

April saw a group of five laughing and chatting women of

similar age to her strut into camp wearing bulging day back-packs with accordion-folded tangerine-colored sleeping mats lashed to the bottom.

Day packs? Where were their big backpacks?

Curious April moseyed behind them as they looked for open platforms. April pretended interest in a line of scrubby trees on the perimeter so she could eavesdrop on the group. The women chose two sites, then unbuckled and opened their packs, withdrawing minimal gear. April was astonished.

Did they start the Chilkoot today and hike to Sheep Camp? It was possible. They were probably hiking the trail in three days.

As an organized team, two women began putting up two tents, another woman rounded up food and toiletries and sought out the bear boxes, and the last pair went to fill the water containers and bottles. April was impressed and envious. These women were capable and confident.

She'd bet money they didn't fear tomorrow. Why hadn't April realized there'd be cool kids on the trail? Comparing herself to them was not helping her.

April decided to head to the warming house and make her supper. The shelter was full of hikers cooking before the ranger talk. Hikers greeted each other and asked how the Chilkoot was going. April joined them and went to work boiling water for her dehydrated pouch of turkey casserole.

When the food was a chewable mush, April ate the entire packet. An hour remained before the Ranger talk. She felt moody and jittery. After storing her supplies, she headed to the Taiya River.

Maybe the view would make her feel better.

The glacial river was swollen with melted mountain snow runoff and flowed fast. April walked downriver, stepping over

and around bleached and smoothed limbs strewn on the beach
riverbank.

Again the river soothed April's ruffled feelings. The idea of
this hike was a faint fantasy last spring. She'd hiked miles and
hours to bring herself here. Things were going well. She
reminded herself to appreciate how far she had come.

April hugged herself. Maybe she'd even find gold. She
laughed out loud at that.

The flat bank was interrupted by fingers of steeped earth
that jutted into the river. In the middle was a naturally cut cave
that created a roofless shelter. A pale tan log lay inside. April sat
down on the smoothed wood whorls and watched and listened
to the river. Minutes later, she heard women's voices. April was
unsure whether to let them know of her presence or stay silent.

She peeked around the corner. It was the expert hiking
women from Sheep Camp. They were in the upside-down
triangle of the downward dog yoga pose.

Seriously, they do yoga too? Maybe she could sneak behind
them?

Then one woman said, "Take long deep breaths in and then
out."

April felt awkward and didn't want to creep out of her
hidey-hole.

Might as well join them.

"Ladies, we'll begin with a similar sequence to yesterdays.
Adjust balance and footing on the uneven ground as needed."

The group remained unaware as a still hidden April
listened to the teacher's instructions and did the best Chilkoot
wilderness yoga she could.

CHAPTER TWENTY

April heard, "Namaste," followed by retreating footfalls stepping on beach rocks.

When she was sure the group was gone, April rose. A serene gloaming softened the Taiya River to a wavy swath and colored the trees and shrubs a blurred green-black. Gentle winds dipped and nipped. April wrapped her hands around her shoulders and followed the departed yoga hikers.

Near the warming shelter was a seating area of tree trunk-legged benches and freestanding stump seats scattered about like forest mushrooms. Thirty-five or so hikers dressed in the unofficial trail outfit of earth toned multi-pocketed hiking pants; colorful, lightweight jackets; and pulled on hats or hoods conversed while waiting for the required ranger talk to start.

April found an empty seat on the perimeter by the young hikers she had met in Canyon City. Puffy Vest waved to April. "Hi. How was hiking? Heard any new news about the snow conditions on the Pass?"

April's insides squirmed at the last question. "Today was good. No new news."

"Did you see any signs of bears?" Puffy Vest asked.

"No, thankfully. You?" April asked.

"We saw a couple of scat piles off-trail, but no bears."

Hoodie Hiker added, "If we see a bear, all the pepper spray you brought will make the animal smell like cayenne pepper for months."

"Better safe than sorry," Puffy Vest said.

"You're packing your fear."

That idea perplexed April. She asked, "What do you mean?"

"Whatever you're afraid of, you compensate by overpacking. Worry about running out of food, then you bring along double or triple food needed."

April considered. "My fear is being caught unready in a rainstorm. I have a pack raincover, rain pants, many extra socks, rain jacket, and a poncho. I considered bringing a small umbrella."

"Bringing some extra gear is smart, but overdoing is burdensome," Hoodie Hiker said.

"What's your fear?" April asked.

"Losing or breaking my camera. I have a backup camera, a second lens, and my phone."

April suspected this trail wisdom applied to other areas of life.

"Hey there," boomed Rita as she and the Curlies joined the group. "Has the Ranger arrived?"

"Not yet. I heard yesterday's ranger hiked out. A new ranger is hiking in. I hope there wasn't a problem along the trail. How was your hike?" Puffy Vest asked.

The Curlies mentioned the waterfalls and elevation gain. April saw Rob, Merri, and Conor arrive.

Rita waved to Rob. He led his family over. "Hi!"

Hoodie Hiker stood and beckoned Merri. "Have my seat."

"Thank you," Merri said and dropped down in an exhausted slump.

"Wasn't today's scenery unbelievable!" Rob said.

"The elevation gain was tiring, but when we reached this one clearing the mountain view took our breath away," Claire said.

Dot added, "I couldn't get to my camera quick enough."

While the group chatted, April's interest skimmed over Merri. Expert mahogany highlights blended Merri's pixie haircut and covered any early-fifties graying. Her clothes looked like the other hikers, but Merri's body type wasn't the typical outdoor recreation advertisement of trim and tall. Merri was five feet of roly-poly.

April wondered why Merri was hiking the Chilkoot. Could Rob or Conor have convinced Merri? If they had, what made her agree? Didn't Rob and Conor care for Merri's wellbeing? How was Merri going to climb up and over Chilkoot Pass tomorrow? The question of how April herself would cross the Pass besieged her.

The commotion of April's projective inquiry halted when a ranger wearing a wide-brimmed Saturn-shaped floppy hat and an apple red sleek daypack strode towards the congregated and called out, "Hello! Sorry, I'm late. Business in town held me up. How's everyone tonight? Good day today? Excited for tomorrow?"

"Had to cross the river a few times," a hiker with his hands extended out as if walking a tightrope said, and the assembled laughed.

The Ranger grinned. "Me too," and took a drink from her plastic water bottle. "Before we start, has everyone stored their food and toiletries in the bear boxes?"

"Yes," the hikers chorused.

"Great! Thanks for helping keep everyone and the wildlife safe."

The group quieted and directed an obedient attentiveness at the ranger.

"Tomorrow morning, you'll hike the most challenging part of the Chilkoot. There are snowfields in the canyons before the Scales and on the Canadian side. Avalanche danger is low, but we still advise being cautious. We've marked a path with orange fluorescent poles to assist staying on the trail and climbing the Golden Stairs. Please don't move these poles. We recommend leaving Sheep Camp around 4 a.m. as that will give hikers plenty of time to get to, then up and over the Pass, and down the mountain on firm snow. The snowfields become slippery and softer as the day warms up. Use your trekking poles and crampons if you have them."

The word avalanche prompted April to bite her lower lip. She hadn't practiced hiking on snow, and her shoulder blades contracted tight.

"As you cross Chilkoot Pass, you'll enter Canada. Please follow the Parks Canada regulations. There will be a Parks Canada Warden and day-use shelter on the Pass's Canadian side. The shelter is a good place to take a break and have a snack or lunch. Any questions?" the Ranger asked.

No one spoke.

The Ranger restarted. "I saw a few bear scat piles on and around the trail but no sightings or encounters. Keep your bear spray handy. You don't want to be digging in your pack when you need it. Talk, whistle, sing, or use a bear bell to prevent surprising bears. Any questions?"

April swallowed every few moments attempting to push down her fear. Her mind couldn't hear hikers' questions and the ranger's responses. She told herself to relax and stop panicking. April needed to pay attention.

She unzipped her jacket halfway, and the evening air cooled her stress heat. April reminded herself they were all hiking the Pass tomorrow. The camaraderie reassured her. This recalibration centered April, and she could hear the ranger speaking.

The ranger wrapped up her talk and added, "Klondike stampeders came seeking gold and adventure. As you hike the Chilkoot, enjoy your golden adventure."

April saw Merri's closed eyes and satisfied smile. Beyond the camp, the mountains were indigo outlines.

Rita clapped her hands. "Big day tomorrow, I hope everyone gets a good night of rest. We'll see you in the morning or at Happy Camp."

"Happy Camp is aptly named," Rob offered.

"The happy will be well earned. Rob, pull me up. I'm ready for bed," Merri said.

Hoodie Hiker called out, "Night, everyone. Happy trails," and his friends piled on good nights and left for their tents.

"I'm turning in too," April decided.

"Sweet dreams and sleep well," Merri said.

Under black and navy bruised clouds, April walked to her tent. She heard low pitch conversations, tent zippers, pack buckles unclipping, and boots soft-striking the packed earth. April felt at home. This pleased and surprised her. At her platform, April sat on the planed planks. The land smelled good, like trees, water, and wind. The wind's chill pressed through her pant legs.

April kicked her camp sandals off. She spread her toes and stretched her feet, easing the tired-ache. She wondered what the stampeders thought of this land. Was it a grand wilderness adventure with possible fortune? Danger at any moment? A life escape? Did they get bored by the mining? What kept them going during the hard parts? What made a person give up and go home?

Yawning, April unzipped her tent and crawled inside. The afternoon heat was extinct. Planning ahead, she changed into tomorrow's clean underwear, a mint green hiking shirt, and matching socks. She decided to read one of the books loaded on her phone. She set two alarms on her cellphone. Her phone battery was at least fifty percent strong. The travel charger was in one of her pack's zipped pockets. She would charge her phone tomorrow while hiking.

After an hour, April tightened the bag's hood around her head and drifted to sleep. When she woke, she felt rested. April wasn't warm and wasn't cold. Stretching and rolling her neck reminded her of her sore muscles. Upon opening her eyes, April noticed it was brighter inside her tent.

She pawed inside her sleeping bag, searching for her phone. It wasn't there. April's hands swept the tent floor. Her hand knocked into her smartphone. She grabbed it and pushed a button. The screen stayed black. Her fingers skittered about searching for her backup watch. The glowing teal face showed 7:06 a.m.

April's mind melted. The thoughts "I didn't" and "I couldn't have" crashed into each other.

She crawled across the smooth floor, then slipped and landed on her elbow. April yanked the tent zipper down and leaned out. She saw no tents and heard no people.

April failed. She should have left camp hours ago. She was inept and stupid. Why hadn't April charged her phone last night? How did she not hear the other campers leaving?

The goosebumps on her thighs reminded April she wasn't wearing pants. Flopping back into her tent, she wiggled into pants.

What should she do? Stay in her tent and not come out. Hike back to the start?

April brushed at her tears.

The Curlies, Rob, and Merri would wonder why she wasn't at Happy Camp. Thirteen miles of embarrassment back to the start or seven miles to Happy Camp across rocks and snowfields?

April crammed her feet into her shoes. The campground was deserted, and yet April waited several seconds to make sure no one appeared before heading to the pit toilet. The empty platforms looked like unconnected squares on a checkerboard. A knot of tears crowded her throat. She stopped by the bear boxes and retrieved her food and toiletries.

She wished she had never come.

Back at her tent, April stared at the mountains and wondered what to do.

Everyone was probably close to the Scales. No one would see her late hiking.

As April broke down her camp, she cried, sniffed, and swiped at tears with her fleece-encased forearm. She stored snacks in her pants pockets. April hiccupped sobs and walked to the main trail. She had a choice to make—go forward or go back.

April wanted to finish the Chilkoot.

The trail meandered through thick tree, bush, and brush utilizing an inclusive list of green colors and eventually exited into a long, open-space valley flanked by craggy mountains. The trail flipped between hard-packed dirt and shoe-imprinted squishy mud. Head down and eyes on the trail, her footsteps slid, were sucked into, and broke loose, and her internal recriminations mirrored the actions. She had thought she was prepared, but when she needed to get it 'right' April screwed up big time.

She hiked and cried until there was no tear supply. April increased her speed, and after thirty minutes, she was breathing hard and sweating. She wondered what the use of it all was. April started late, and trail demands would increase into the day.

She yelped her misery as she moved past head-height shrubby trees whose gnarled roots wrapped around stones and trunks.

The 'why' questions flooded her brain: *Why do others have it so much better? Why couldn't I have been content with what I had? Why am I on this trail? Why can't I be happy too?* That last thought slowed April to a slow slouch. The question, *What if I'm never happy enough?* made her heart squeeze. Before she knew what she was doing, she gave a yell that echoed in the valley.

Tired of her thoughts and needing a sip of water, April took a break. She wasn't sure how far or how long she had hiked. There had been no pleasant trail encounters or exchanged hiker banter. She was all by herself. April turned in a circle and saw the overcast morning begin to shift, letting blue sky with an undertone of turquoise show itself. On the mountain ranges, gray-white stone pockets and patches interrupted crisscrossing forest green treelines below frosted snow peaks. The morning's high dew point magnified the musty smell of vegetation and earth.

The Chilkoot pushed up a long hill then crossed a waterfall at the top. The increasing elevation included high numbers of couch-sized rocks on and along the path. Fluorescent orange poles marked the way through tumbled rock gardens. A group of grey granite slabs reminded April of a ramshackle cemetery. Adjacent to piles of winter snow and trickle streams, other boulders were concrete colored with reddish-purple mineral seams and spots like bruises on skin.

Up ahead, April could see interconnected canyons with snow heaps on the ground and in the mountain outcrops and fissures. She halted when she saw the words 'Avalanche Zone' on an arm's length and width sign. According to the sign, the area was subject to avalanches until mid-July. Immediate nervousness made her peer for cracks in the upper snowlines. Much of the trail was covered by snow.

Intermittent posts directed a path over a natural roadway of snow and past low shrubs and a few compact trees up a canyon before traversing into another ascent. A mid-morning fog now shadowed the mountain tops. April knew she was close to the Scales landmark when she spotted a rusted pulley, pipes, and other metal refuse that had been left behind by the Klondike miners.

April followed the dependable line of orange markers and trudged up the mountain past paralleling slopes covered in chipped, loose talus. At the rim of the canyon was the start of the next elevation-building canyon. When April saw the football field-sized sloped mountain wall of jumbled and scattered boulders from ancient geologic rumblings, she knew it was the Golden Stairs. A grim determination commanded her concentration. April reached the bottom of the stairs and saw bright color flashes as people and their backpacks worked upward.

She stepped off the snow and onto a stone porch that became a tilted pathway of hodgepodge rocks that graduated to boulders. April climbed, leaned, teetered, wobbled, stretched, and sometimes crawled following the zigzagging route up the sloping rockpile. Several times her limited focus on the rocks right in front of her meant she missed a pole and required her to backtrack and reconnoiter.

At what April guessed was halfway and at least an hour from the bottom, she rested and looked at the extensive wilderness vista she had traveled. The famous image of the miners lined up the mountain jumped into her mind. The height made her dizzy, but she didn't want to be anywhere else other than where she was.

April grabbed the boulder above and continued to boost, mount, and scoot up. When she reached the false summit more than an hour later, she encountered Merri, Rob, and Conor.

"Hi. We didn't think anyone was behind us," Rob said.

April's cheeks reddened with embarrassment. "Slow start," she mumbled.

Merri, with a tired smile, nodded. "I'm having trouble negotiating the rocks. Please go around us."

"Merri, it's harder for your shorter legs to climb. You're doing good. The rest of us have an advantage," Rob assured her.

April agreed with Rob's assessment.

"I'll get to the top. I'll do it in my own time and way," Merri said.

"Me too. See you at the top," April said.

April long and short stepped to reach the true summit that she found in a snow-filled corridor of salt and pepper stone walls. She knew it was the summit because a sign had labeled it and welcomed her to Canada. April savored her satisfied exhaustion and the view from the top of Chilkoot Pass. In the far distance, clouds socked the range in a silvery-white. She checked her watch. At least five hours had passed. It occurred to April that she hadn't charged her phone or photographed the morning. She closed her eyes and breathed deep from her belly.

Minutes later, she heard Rob say, "Great job! Welcome to Canada!"

April opened her eyes to see the trio walking across the snowfield.

"Hi, April!" Rob shouted.

"We're here!" April cheered back.

Together the foursome walked up a rocky path and paused at a monument constructed like a stone wishing well and dedicated to the Klondike Stampeders. The orange poles were replaced by wooden ones with tipped red triangles on top. A snowfield curved and unfolded into a road. Like an aerie, a diminutive weathered-plank cabin with a peaked faded moss green metal roof sat in the distance.

When they were fifty meters from the Parks Canada cabin, a Canadian warden wearing an orange winter coat walked towards them and called out with a cheerful ring, "Hello. Are you folks heading to Happy Camp today?"

"Yes," April responded for the group.

The Warden's stance was that of an individual used to repositioning on uneven ground. Underneath her gray beanie blond shoulder-length hair curled around her chin. Her bright blue eyes had corner crinkles and were framed by a sun-tanned face. She pointed to the sky. "Heavy weather and fog are rolling in. I'd recommend you stay here tonight. You can sleep in the day-use shelter."

April was content to spend the night on top of Chilkoot Pass.

CHAPTER TWENTY-ONE

A combination of the Warden's recommendation, hunger, and weariness had them all agreeing. They settled into the shelter that was more of a windowed backyard shed. Backpacks were piled near the door. Hooks above a trail sheet map became a coat rack and clothesline.

"I'm glad we ended up here," Merri said.

Rob squeezed Merri's hand. "Me too. How often does a hiker get to sleep on top of Chilkoot Pass!"

They gathered around a small corner table. A lantern and emergency candles were pushed aside to make room for water bottles, plastic bags of food and toiletries, and a tea kettle the size and roundness of a basketball. The warden named Dana had brought them hot water. Tired small talk flitted between settling in and supper.

"If the weather hadn't changed, I bet we'd have made it to Happy Camp," Conor spoke.

"Just as well, we didn't. I'm pooped," Merri said.

"Starting tomorrow, the trail begins descending and should get easier," Rob assured them.

Merri emitted a half-chuckle. "I concentrated so hard getting to and up the Stairs, I forgot to go to the bathroom."

"This has been a once in a lifetime adventure. I'm glad we're doing this," Rob said before eating a handful of trail mix.

"Me too," April agreed.

The row of blue, orange, and lime green sleeping bags lying across the floor looked brighter contrasted to the graying daylight. As her new roommates bedded down early with their heads towards Happy Camp, April stared back at the direction she'd hiked. A glazing frost built up the panes. A languid fog ate the scenery. Winds gusted, sending thread drafts into the room. Amazement brushed her mind. Instead of Happy Camp, she was nested like an eagle in the clouds atop Chilkoot Pass.

It wasn't long before the family's snoring nasal blasts and wheezes filled the room. April was exhausted. She settled into her sleeping bag. Her day's high adrenaline still reigned her nervous system and blocked sleep. She rolled over, pressing one ear into the polyester smoothness and placing a hand over her exposed ear.

April reviewed the day. It started rough. She'd persevered and summited the Pass. But, she hadn't made it to her destination, throwing off her distance timeline. Drips of criticism began to dilute her accomplishment. She should have practiced more, then this delay could have been avoided. She should have remembered to put her phone in her sleeping bag to prevent the cold from killing the battery and set her watch alarm. She should have just stayed home.

She pressed her hand firmer into her ear, trying to muffle the noise. Her muscles clamped stiff. She breathed rapid and shallow. Similar to her post-divorce depression, tonight's recriminations clouded her perspective. April couldn't stop the momentum of the thoughts. Not knowing what else to do, she

let the words and sentences race and swerve until the requirement of sleep was stronger.

The next morning April awoke recovered but not well-
rested. The others were still asleep. The morning light was hazy.
She lay among the muffled snores of her cabinmates. No
demands or urgency swelled up inside her. Yesterday was over.

Today they would hike down the Pass and into the second
half of the trail. Happy Camp was four miles away, Deep Lake
campground was seven miles, and pushing onto to Lindemann
City campground involved a ten-mile hike. April hoped to make
it to Lindeman. Depending on trail conditions and her speed,
Deep Lake would be her backup plan.

It occurred to April that she was thinking like an adventurer. She assessed her situation, the distance, potential terrain
adjustments, and left room for the unexpected. April was
growing in this adventure, and that made her happy. Later,
when she would tell her Chilkoot hiking story, the Golden
Stairs day would cause her listeners to lean in.

She had climbed the Stairs, as had all the other Sheep
Camp hikers, including Merri. Again, April wondered what the
Chilkoot represented to Merri. Had Merri wanted to come?
Was Merri enjoying the Chilkoot? Rob and Conor supported
and cheered on Merri, similar to how Lauren and April's
parents had.

She heard a sleeping bag rustle. The floor planks creaked.

April heard Rob whisper, "I'm going to the outhouse. Then
I'm going to boil water for coffee."

"I'll be up shortly. Get Conor up," Merri murmured.

"I'm already awake," Conor groaned.

"Not so loud," Merri hushed. "You'll wake April."

April kept her eyes closed and pretended the deep
breathing of what she hoped sounded like sleeping. After the
guys left the shelter, the women continued resting.

It wasn't long before April's bladder interrupted her repose. She reached for her hiking pants and attempted to put them on without disturbing Merri.

"Good morning, April!" Merri sang out.

"Sorry. I was trying to be quiet. Good morning."

Merri stretched her arms above her head. "How'd you sleep?"

"Okay. You?" April asked.

"Deep and heavy. I don't recall falling asleep. Goodness, I'm stiff and sore. Climbing over those rocks was a lot of work."

April put on clean socks. "No Stairs today."

Merri stood up and looked out the south-facing windows. "Funny thing, the Scales and Stairs section is almost like a life metaphor. A person weighs decisions, starts up the path, and then rebalances as they make their way."

April stared at Merri. "Sometimes, I think I don't consider the consequences of my decisions enough before acting, then I spend more time trying to get my balance. You did great yesterday."

Merri smiled big. "We all did."

"Merri, why did you and your family decide to hike the Chilkoot?"

"Conor is almost an adult. In a couple of years, he'll be launched out in the world. I thought hiking the Chilkoot would be an excellent family trip that included hours of together time. Plus, I wanted to do it while I physically could. I may not hike fast, but I'll get to the end in time to catch the train back to Skagway."

April felt the radiation of Merri's assuredness and strength. "Yes, you will."

"The guys are boiling water for coffee if you want some."

"Great, thanks! Bathroom first for me," April said.

April left the shelter. In a wintery misty haze, she followed a stone pathway onto a connected ridgeline that held the pit toilet. April returned to an empty shelter and finished getting dressed. She suspected the others had gone to Warden Dana's cabin.

Carrying a camping mug and a breakfast bar, she started for the cabin. To the north, an unending white snowfield unfurled down the mountain, burying the next section of the Chilkoot. April wandered past a pond of darkened clear water half covered by a snow pile. The landscape was more January than July.

April was almost to the steps of Dana's cabin when April saw Dana beckon her inside. Upon entry, April smelled hot coffee and felt cozy warmth from a heat stove, and in addition to Dana, Merri, Rob, and Conor crammed into the tidy space. The steamed-up windows looked out onto miles of rock ranges. Building-sized low clouds overshadowed the peaks. Snow striped the upper elevations, and drifts settled in the lower halves.

Dana lifted the multi-gallon galvanized teapot from a double burner hot plate and spoke to April. "It's a cold morning. How about a hot beverage? I have tea and instant coffee. What would you like?"

"Thanks, I have a packet of instant coffee already in my cup. I'd gladly accept the hot water." April presented her mug, and Dana filled it.

"If you run dry, there's more. How'd you sleep?"

"All right. You?" April asked.

"I generally sleep well on the mountain."

"How long do you stay up here?"

"It varies. Sometimes a week on, then a week off. I'm at the end of this rotation. I'll hike down to the crossing in a few days."

"How long have you been a warden?" Rob asked.

"I've worked at different parks around Canada for twelve years."

For the next hour, the group swapped hiking stories, suggested other trails, and spoke of their lives at home.

Dana stood. "I know it's still early, but the fog will lift soon. It's a good idea for you all to start down. Where are you headed today?"

"I'm going to try for Lindemann City," April said.

Dana tapped her lips with a finger. "That's almost ten miles of hiking up and down and along the edges and rims of the mountains. The first four miles are mostly snowfields and include several short water crossings. Keep Deep Lake camp in mind as a secondary option."

Rob said, "We're headed to Deep Lake. April, you're welcome to hike with us if you want. We understand if you want to hike faster."

A happy heat suffused April's cheeks and chest. "Thanks! Let's start out together."

Dana walked to a shelf next to the door. It held a cracker box-sized black radio with soda can round knobs, handheld two-way radios, folded up topographical maps, and emergency yellow-colored binoculars.

"I'm checking the weather for the day. If you can be packed and ready in twenty minutes, I'll lead you down the mountain," Dana said.

"Sure thing," Rob and Merri said at the same time.

"Thanks," April said.

The foursome returned to the shelter and repacked their gear. April's stomach quivered as she tightened Big Blue's straps then put on her beanie and gloves. It was then she noticed that her hiking partners each wore waterproof gaiter sleeves that protected their shins, calves, and the tops of their boots from snow and water. She may need to think of ways to keep her shoes and socks dry during the water crossings.

Back outside, Dana assessed the group and started to speak. "Glad to see everyone dressed warm. Going down it's best to use your trekking poles. Take small steps and be sure your heel dents the snow before taking the next step. If you fall, push out your poles. If you skid, try to jab your pole into the snow to slow and stop yourself. Any questions?"

They answered "no" in unison.

"The fog is lifting. Little wind. Let's go. We'll be making a footpath for today's hikers," Dana said.

In a human line, the group followed the guide poles topped with red triangles that snaked down the mountain. April's shoes rasped and her trekking poles punctured the snow. The first five minutes on the snowpack was flatter with a slight angle, but then the terrain changed to a steep downward slant. She banged her heels into the crusty snow top to deepen the dents made by Dana. Conor followed her, then Merri, and Rob had the rear. No one spoke as they focused on hiking the sloping snowfield.

Feeling more poised in her steps, April looked down the mountain. She gulped back her fear of the high height. The snowfield they walked on looked like a mammoth pool of spilled cream. The lake at the bottom had an open water middle surrounded by cracked ice edging that extended into snow cover. The actual size of the lake was obscured. If April fell, she wasn't sure she could stop herself from careening down the mountain and into the lake. In the water, Big Blue would pull her under and she might drown. Making the train would be the least of April's worries.

They were past halfway. April slowed her pace and put a meter of distance between her and Dana. She glanced back at Conor. He was too close. Could she politely ask him to give her more space?

April heard boot soles skid. She squeaked out her distress and halted. Her heart hammered. She felt light-headed.

"Rob, you okay?" Merri asked.

"I'm fine. My foot slipped."

April wanted to screech, "Don't let that happen again!" She kept silent.

Sweat moistened her torso and back. April unzipped her jacket. Her back muscles tensed into an accordion shape and pulsed discomfort. She reminded herself she was upright and safe with Warden Dana.

"Let's take a break." Dana stopped and put up her arms as if she was going to bow. "Look at this beautiful scenery. In deep winter, this canyon is filled to the top with snow. It's been a cooler summer, so the snowmelt has been slower, but the ice on Crater Lake has started to break apart. The water's color changes from teal to turquoise to a midnight blue with the sunlight and the season. It's breathtaking."

April took a deep inhale. The forced cold air caused her to feel the expansive lift of her lungs. Her eyes widened. Suddenly everything seemed brighter and sharper. April admired the white, black, and blue colors of the mountains, snow, and space. She heard the clicks of picture taking and withdrew her own phone.

Happiness expanded from April's center. She was in high country looking at mountain ranges of white and black chipped peaks that pushed past the horizon. The clouds were ponderous swathes of down rimmed in sky blue as if a sleeping bag had been cut open and its insides had been thrown up into the air. She was on the Chilkoot and closer to Crater Lake, whose surface reflected the western range.

Dana moved to stand next to April.

"April, I think hiking would be easier for you if you extended your trekking poles a little more."

April hadn't realized she was hunching over her shorter poles. This limited her propulsion forward and contributed to her minor backache.

"I'll do that. Thanks."

The hiking party resumed moving.

"What wildlife have you seen on the Chilkoot?" Dana asked.

"We saw a beaver and some songbirds. No bears," Merri said.

April's mind darted to the serendipitous minutes she learned about the Chilkoot Trail. The images of the Klondike miners hiking on snow buzzed her memory like traffic moves down a street. Then there was the fun memory of gear shopping with Lauren. A giggle bounced inside when she recalled her neighbor Bob's expression when he saw her walk from the garage into the house in her underwear and a sweatshirt after the weekend of rain hiking. April believed the last twenty four hours would be the most memorable of her trip. She savored the Chilkoot beauty, the thrills, the new friendships, and the safety within the group.

At the mountain base was a neighboring hillside of yellowed grass and lichen. Large rocks with striations and pock markings of mineral colors complimented the short stacked stones of the cairn trail marker. This was the first cairn April had seen on the Chilkoot.

"This is as far as I go," Dana said.

"Thank you for letting us spend the night in the shelter and making sure we got down safe," April said.

Merri, Rob, and Conor responded in kind.

"You're welcome. Enjoy hiking the rest of the Chilkoot," Dana said. Then she turned around and started back up her mountain.

April watched Dana's orange jacket and purposeful steps going home. She whispered, "Thank you."

They continued on and came upon a pile of weathered boards, pyramid-shaped rock heaps, and a rusted saw blade larger than April's torso. From this vantage, April suspected if she could tip a skyscraper on its side and lay it next to Crater Lake, the lake would be longer.

Next was a slow climb back up a snow-covered mountain, the top encased in fog. Hiking down the next ridge there was a rock field. Near the middle were multiple streams rushing down, bouncing off boulders, and spraying the area. April stuck her trek poles between the rocks, using the stabilizing leverage for balance to step over and on wobbly, slick surfaces.

Almost an hour later, Merri called out, "I need a break and snack."

The morning's motion and cadence had burned away April's low-grade tiredness. She told the group, "If you don't mind, I'd like to keep walking."

Rob swallowed a swig of water. "If you need anything, we'll be coming up behind you."

"Have fun! We're planning on stopping again at Happy Camp. We might see you there," Merri said.

"Great. Enjoy your hike today. I think today's weather will be good," April said.

Conor waved and said, "See ya."

April moved north across the canyon's snow-covered floor and onto the next slope climb. She was ready for the Chilkoot's next section.

CHAPTER TWENTY-TWO

An energized electricity in April's muscles accompanied a desire to eat up the mileage. The accomplishments of reaching the Scales, climbing the Stairs, and descending the Pass in the last twenty-four hours had her feeling plucky. Looking back, the Warden Station was out of sight and several valleys back. She fretted some at leaving behind Merri, Rob, and Conor.

The trail continued up and down, and hugging the snow mountain slopes absent of trees. At times the Chilkoot wasn't easy to identify. April had to keep an eye out for guideposts, cairns, and prior hiker footsteps. Snow packed the saddles between the peaks. She imagined this is what it would be like to hike in a container of cookies and cream ice cream.

The air didn't smell sugar-sweet. Instead, the cold aired out April and her clothes. She hadn't wiped her body with a moistened towelette or brushed her hair since her evening in Sheep Camp. On the Chilkoot, her appearance was of little concern other than having the outdoor clothing she needed. It occurred to April that when hiking and walking, her body focus was on strength, stamina, and capability. Any concerns regarding body image and weight didn't come up.

Like a backbone, rocks and the trail wiggled up a surprise grassy hillside. On the other side was another snowfield. In the distance, the sky and earth appeared to touch. April wished her friends and parents could see these vistas. She took pictures trying to capture the landscape's grandeur. The panoramic orientation included the vastness but reduced details and colors. The portrait orientation showcased fine points but scrunched size.

By mid-morning, it was late enough that last night's Sheep Camp hikers might be climbing the Stairs. April sent them good luck. It had been amiable to wake up next to friends in their version of an adult slumber party. The coffee and conversation in Warden Dana's cabin were a pleasant precursor to the morning group hike. April decided that when she was back home, she would invite people to hike with her and participate more in a formal hiking group.

Further down the trail, a curved lake carved the valley. The trail wound the rounded base of a peak and then disappeared into a rock field. April knew when she compared several rocks to bread loaves, it was time for a snack. She located a large rock whose top surface would provide comfortable enough seating.

The sound of her chewing peanuts and dried fruit seemed loud without urban and campground noise. She hadn't seen anyone for at least an hour. April checked the time. She hoped Happy Camp and lunch was a mere hour away.

April was done eating, and yet she wanted to stay sitting there gazing at the valley and mountains the Chilkoot Trail crossed, connected, and made into legend. Many Klondike gold miners had been everyday people chasing a remarkable dream and risk. April was an ordinary woman who took steps that culminated in this extraordinary personal experience. Yesterday, she crossed the halfway mark.

In the next valley, the trail moved higher towards the ridge-

line. Down below, chunks of snow bergs, ranging in size from
dinghies to pontoons, had broken off and floated on what April
suspected was Long Lake. Sunshine cut through voluminous
and trailing cotton candy clouds smudged with light blue sky.
April crested the ridge. From her topside perspective, she saw
another snow-stuffed section that made the mountains appear to
shrink. In the distance was an open lake to the left and exposed
ground with wild green grass and evergreens to the right.

It took another forty minutes to reach the summery land.
An established trail gradually rose up and along a dirt embank-
ment fenced by evergreens above and the lake below. The lake
was unlike anything April had seen. An outer ring of dark
brown water gave way to an inner circle of smoky tan that
melded into a ruffled turquoise-teal shade and then into a core
of deep blue. What Warden Dana had mentioned earlier that
morning, April was seeing firsthand.

For the next hour and a half, the landscape alternated
between snow-saturated valleys and canyons and the dry, dirt
trail travel that allowed April to hike faster and make up time.
The hours spent crossing the snowfields meant she wouldn't
make it to Lindeman City. Per Warden Dana's suggestion, April
would camp at Deep Lake campground.

The summer sun rays melted snow, feeding narrow gullies
that populated the path. A wide-legged leap was the typical
response action, and a few times, large rocks became stepstones.
Thankfully, mosquitos did not occupy the numerous water
sources.

Impatience kept pinging April's brain. She had to be close
to Happy Camp.

Twenty minutes later, coming around a bend, she saw her
first destination of the day. Wavy grass, green shrubs dense with
small leaves, and plump, shorter evergreens interwove Happy
Camp. Bright colors of camping gear were scattered on wood

platforms as a handful of hikers readied to start their hiking day. April guessed they were probably heading for Lindeman City or Bare Loon Lake. The peaked metal roofline of the warming shelter poked up.

April couldn't help smiling as she strolled on an easy strip of pounded dirt and gravel into the tranquil camp. At the steps of the shelter, April paused. The ground to her left sloped towards a shallow river with sand bars, half-buried rocks anchored by lichen and moss one could lounge against or sit on, and cheery sunshine. April decided this place was aptly named beyond it being the campground hikers reached after crossing the Pass.

She had stayed warm hiking but knew that the absence of activity would chill her even in the sunshine. No one was inside the cabin shelter. The structure probably wouldn't be used until late afternoon as the hikers from Sheep Camp arrived.

Sitting at the wood picnic table, April chewed salted mixed nuts. They tasted good. She sucked at the salt crystals absorbing the dissolving mineral into her tissue.

It felt strange to be the day's earliest arrival. Another new experience for her on the Chilkoot. After deciding to divorce, she had known there would be 'firsts' in her near future. At times the expected, and unexpected, had been daunting and included surprises. It occurred to her that that rhythm of adaptation was similar to moving about an outdoor trail.

Next, April crunched into a bruised apple. At first bite, the fruit's juice geysered out then dribbled down her chin. She used her sleeve to wipe the juice. It was on her to clean up after herself.

The dirt path out of Happy Camp followed the river into a canyon hugged by bluffs. It wasn't long before the trail became littered with light grayish-white chipped stones that resembled broken floor tiles. The stones wobbled, slid, and clacked as she moved across them. The trail tilted up, skirting the mountain bases, making April lopsided. Half a mile later, snow again laid atop the trail like a dirt-dusted used white bandage providing a surprisingly less slick walking surface. Her motion and momentum adjusted with the terrain.

She stopped at a wider stream whose ankle-high volume and rapidity launched and bounced water off the edges and sides of rocks positioned like a pinball machine's playfield. Her feet would be submerged at this crossing.

Not having any better ideas, April rolled up her pant legs to her knees. Next, she removed her shoes and wool socks. Reaching into Big Blue, she pulled out her camp sandals. The enclosed toe cap would minimize the bumping into underwater rocks. Finally, she tied her trail shoes and socks to her pack.

Immediately the frigid water swamped her shoes. April shivered and curled her toes. She stepped forward. The slippery rocks caused her feet to slide. Her trekking poles helped to steady and balance. After several minutes she was on the other side, squelching water onto new grass growing up between the yellowed-white of last season's growth.

April plopped down and yanked off her sandals. Additional water trickled out. Double-checking no one was visible, April lifted her legs into the air and flutter kicked, shaking off moisture and trying to speed up drying.

When her feet were reshod in her dry shoes and the wet sandals hung from Big Blue, April and the Chilkoot wound through mountain foothills. The elevation level kept diminishing, and she came to the edge of the boreal forest. These canyons and valleys had stubby grass, sparse evergreens, and melting piles of snow. This trail section was hard-packed. April hiked with an easy stride. She had hoped to make it to Deep Lake in the early afternoon, but between the time used to descend the Pass, traverse the snow and rock fields, and cross the different waterways, April wasn't sure what time she'd reach camp.

Thick cloud cover shadowed the land of the midnight sun. A breeze started up and caught her hanging sandals, tugging them in multiple directions. April became annoyed by the jostling footwear. Unbuckling Big Blue, she shoved the sandals into the top of her pack.

At an open plateau, April stopped and completed a full turn. There were small ponds and lakes, outcroppings of boulders, and vegetation that had the look of unattended hedge barriers. The thought that bears could be around here zoomed into April's consciousness.

She completed another turn but slower this time. April searched the landscape for danger. What if there was a bear out there watching her? What would she do? What could she do? If she walked faster, she'd reach Deep Lake sooner.

April began speed hiking. More thoughts crowded in. She didn't know how far from Deep Lake she was. What if she was still out here hiking in the evening? How would she see danger?

Fear made April's hearing hypersensitive. Innocuous sounds had her head whipping one direction and then peering into a different distance for animals or other unseen dangers. She knew her mind was jacked up into fear.

She needed to stay level headed and focus on something positive, pace herself, and maintain her energy. April surmised all the people who climbed the Pass today were content in their tents in Happy Camp. How freaking fantastic for them. She was somewhere on the Chilkoot all by herself. If she got to camp in one piece, she might have to set up in the darker evening, plus filter water and cook supper. Cooking smells drew animals.

April wanted to yell out her frustrations and whine that it wasn't fair. Why wasn't she there already? She should have been there by now. Why didn't April stay hiking with the others?

She kept moving. The cloud cover shadowed the land more. April hoped a storm wasn't moving in.

A spur trail to the left came into view with a wood sign indicating Deep Lake. April blew out air. Relief made her want to jog into camp. The camp was quiet. There was no warming shelter. Instead, she found a communal area with a picnic table that had a view of what she suspected was Deep Lake. Further up a hill were empty tent platforms encircled by needle-heavy evergreens.

April wondered if there were others in the campground. She didn't cotton to the idea of camping alone here. She reminded herself Merri, Rob, and Conor would arrive soon. April hoped.

She spotted two platforms occupied by hikers. Choosing a platform somewhat near for safety and a little distance for privacy, April began to set up her campsite. Indiscernible noises pulled April's attention. A few times, she turned her body in the directions of the disturbances, but no animals came crashing through the bushes.

The memory of April's first camping trip when she slept in the car flitted into her thinking. That was months ago. She had come a long way since then. A quick mental list of her skills and growth buoyed her spirit.

The quilted clouds above darkened the land. April strapped on her headlamp and walked to the nearest creek mouth to collect water. While squatting down, her nose began to drip. She swiped her nose into her shoulder shirt sleeve. The proximity to her armpits made her head jerk back. She smelled like old onions.

April finished her water haul and was walking up the bank when she saw Rob, Conor, and Merri shamble into camp.

"Welcome!" April called out.

The threesome stopped.

Rob said, "Hey there! We're glad to see you at Deep Lake."

When April was a few meters away, she said, "It's quiet here. There's only a few of us in camp tonight. The water is down that way."

Rob turned to Merri and Conor. "Why don't we set up the tents and then I'll go get water. We could meet for supper at the overlook platform with the benches that we passed coming into camp. April, you interested in joining us?"

"Yes. I'll get my food and meet you down there shortly."

April wiped down her body before changing into a clean shirt and underwear. She added a beanie, gloves, and jacket before carrying her portable kitchen to the platform. Her boiled water was rehydrating chili when Rob and Conor arrived.

"Good evening," Rob said. "Merri's tuckered out. She went to bed."

"Crossing the snowfields made today more challenging," April said.

"That it did. The views were great. It's hard to believe we only have two days left."

The fact made April sad. The adventure was in its last hurrah and had a tender, bittersweet quality attached to it. April was turning the new feelings around her heart. She was surprised by this recent sentiment. Before she could inspect the realization closer, Rob asked, "What made you decide to hike the Chilkoot?"

The pat answer was an adventure. April didn't want to give that thin response.

"I saw a show on television about the Klondike Gold Rush. I was intrigued. Not long after that, I was in a coffee shop and saw a guy with a Chilkoot patch on his backpack and asked him about it."

"Serendipity?" Rob asked.

"Maybe. I decided to hike the Chilkoot Trail. I then spent the next several months learning how to hike and camp." April told several of her more memorable learning experiences preparing for the Chilkoot.

Rob and Conor laughed with the supportive snorts of friends. With a thoughtful tilt to his head, he said, "You could have stayed home and shelved the idea, but here you are."

"Yes, I am. And you too. Were you surprised when Merri told you she wanted to hike the Chilkoot?"

"Yes. Merri wanted to do it, and we started planning. It's a fun family opportunity for us to spend time together in a way that's not often available. Hiking the miles is a unique experience for Conor and became a goal for Merri. I wanted to create these memories and support my family. Merri's a brave and determined lady."

"Yup, Mom's a trooper," Conor said.

April was delighted by the pride in Rob and Conor's voices.

Rob said, "The scenery has been out-of-this-world magnificent. The people we've met have been positive and friendly. We'll all have something to celebrate when we reach Bennett."

April lifted her drinking mug aloft. "Here's to the rest of the trail."

Conor whistled. Rob clapped. The trio continued talking about the day's trail and tomorrow's six miles.

When April noticed herself leaning forward, curling in on herself, she knew it was time to return to her tent. "I'm done for. I'm off to bed. Good night. See you tomorrow."

As April stepped away, she could hear the father and son speaking about the Chilkoot. They were making memories they could revisit years from now. Her too. She hugged her arms and squeezed.

In her tent still wearing her hat, April, with her phone in

hand, wiggled into her sleeping bag then zipped it up all the way against the cold air of Deep Lake. She contemplated the fact that her time on the trail was almost done. The night noises of breezes, foliage rustles, and whatever creatures traveled about the area were infrequent and lulling. Sleep was about to engulf her, but before she gave in, April wondered if she'd miss the Chilkoot.

CHAPTER TWENTY-THREE

The next morning April awoke to her hot breath spreading across her upper lip. During sleep, she had pressed her face into the sleeping bag seeking warmth. Peeking out of the bag, the tent's protective rainfly obstructed the morning's weather and mountain view.

April flexed her feet. Today's hike was six miles and mostly downhill. She was ready. That excitement had her rising and shining for the day.

She unzipped her tent and paused. The woody pine scent and scene of dampened evergreens enveloped her senses. This day felt different—slower, more easygoing.

As April walked to the pit toilet, the early daylight pushed blue-green shadows back and lit up the few tents. The camp looked somewhat like a shelf attached to the valley wall.

After retrieving her food from the bear box, she set up her kitchen at last night's community platform. It was oatmeal again. She wrinkled her nose and swallowed big spoonfuls of the rehydrated oats. In two days, she could eat whatever she wanted from the Inn's breakfast table. Her choices wouldn't include oatmeal.

April heard cheerful humming and saw Merri approaching the platform. As her name implied, her smile was almost as wide as her jawline. Merri's 'good morning' played like a rising xylophone scale.

April attempted to emote an equal 'good morning,' but bits of oatmeal had plastered the back of her mouth and garbled the phrase.

"Did you sleep well last night?" Merri asked. "I was out like a light."

April nodded and recalled the family's summit snoring.

"It's a lovely morning. I hope it continues the whole day," Merri said.

"The weather has been good most of the hike. I read stories online about people hiking in days of rain. Plus, the trail is becoming easier. It's mostly downhill except a thousand feet of gradual climb after Lindeman City," April said.

"I think our plan is to have lunch at Lindemann. You're always welcome to hike with us."

Again, April was happy and comforted by Merri's inclusion and graciousness. "Thank you."

She was going to add, "I think I'll hike alone today," but April stopped herself from saying it. Why not join them again? Or start with them and see how the day went.

"I would like to join you," April said.

Merri patted the tops of her thighs. "We have ourselves another hiking party."

"We won't have the big climbs and descends like yesterday," April said.

"Yesterday's Pass descent was unnerving. I had to concentrate so much not to slip going down the mountain that I barely looked up. When I did, the views were breathtaking. I'm excited to get to the end, and a shower, but I keep reminding myself to appreciate these moments," Merri said.

April could feel tears tucked into the corners of her eyes. An "mmm-hmm" was all she could push out. Why was she emotional at this moment?

"I was curious how you learned about the Chilkoot? What made you decide to hike it?" Merri asked.

"Last year, my life was at a crossroads. I wasn't happy. I didn't quite know what to do with myself. I got divorced, then hid at home, camped on my couch in front of the television when I wasn't at work. I saw a show about the Klondike Gold Rush. I was awed by the miners and people who were willing to risk traveling to this wilderness to find gold and adventure. What was I willing to pursue to find my gold?"

Merri nodded. "I've been in a similar place a time or two. Asking those questions: What makes me happy? What do I want to do with my life? What comes next? And all that."

"I mentioned to Rob and Conor that I encountered a guy in a coffee shop with a Chilkoot patch on his backpack. I took it as a sort of sign to consider hiking the Chilkoot."

"When did you decide?" Merri asked.

"That day, but I think I was also playacting. I knew next to nothing about hiking or camping. I started with short day hikes. Then moved to longer mileage and eventually backpacking. My first overnight was scary. I started the night in my tent and finished sleeping in the car."

Merri spread her arms out. "Look at you now."

April agreed. "Look at *us* now. I may not be a miner, but in a sense, I've been mining myself along the way."

"That's beautiful, Merri said.

April heard nearby conversation between Rob and Conor and let her story rest.

Later, when Big Blue was trail-ready, in a practiced, and more natural, upward swing, she placed her pack onto her back. The pack was pounds lighter than when she started at Dyea.

The group started for Bare Loon Lake campground. The never-ending crystal blue sky roofed the Chilkoot boreal forest of needle-rich spruce and pine trees. It had been a couple of days since April had enjoyed significant tree canopy overhead. For the next four and a half hours, the group walked the easier, packed-dirt path. They had the comfortable rhythm of talking and silence found in a group of friends and always the gorgeous mountain scenery. Small flower patches of conical darts of purple arctic lupine and the hanging stars of tangerine-red western columbine appeared along the route.

Reaching the more level landscape of Lindeman City was again like arriving in an abandoned town. The camp's energy and activity paused while it waited for tonight's campers. Beyond the typical amenities was an interpretative tent and history wall detailing the area.

April refueled on handfuls of chewy turkey jerky, broken crackers, salted mixed nuts, and chocolate. The family ate the hiker lunch standard of peanut butter and jelly sandwiches.

She pedaled her feet from one position to another, unable to keep still. It was three miles to Bare Loon. April's trail legs were ready to move.

"I'd like to continue on. I'll see you tonight at Bare Loon," April said.

"Sounds good. Thanks for an enjoyable morning," Merri said.

Rob added, "Have a fun afternoon."

Conor raised a 'see you later' hand gesture.

April stood. "Thanks for letting me hike with you this morning."

"You're always welcome. Take care. We'll see you at Bare Loon," Merri said.

April left Lindemann City. The thought of how she'd not see this section of trail again wedged in. The thought's melancholic underpinning made April rotate and try to memorize the panoramas.

She hiked with an unencumbered stride looking forward and down, steering clear of rocks and roots. Unlike the first day on the Chilkoot, where the tree roofing kept the temperatures cool, this area was warmer. She sipped water every quarter of a mile to prevent dehydration.

The ground became sandier and drier with straggly spruces intermixed. A subtle scent reminiscent of Christmas trees intensified as the day warmed. An hour had passed when she noticed that her mouth was parched. It was her first time on the Chilkoot that April considered modifying her pants into shorts.

The trail climbed and descended into expansive, deep valleys, and dead-end spurs branched off. Previous hikers had created directional cairns. With minimal scouting, April discerned the correct direction. Soon, smooth-rounded granite boulders ranging in size from garbage cans to climbing mounds occupied space with and in between tree groves. Broken off mineral fragments were strewn about. The illusion of the mountain ranges moving further away persisted until several miles separated them and her.

By mid-afternoon, April reached Bare Loon Lake. In an uneven space of dirt and boulder groupings, the pavilion-style picnic cooking shelter appeared to be plopped in the flattest spot. April stepped into the structure. Without unbuckling Big Blue, she leaned into the hip-high walls and admired the picturesque lake rimmed by trees and the mountain range in the distance.

April's attention dove into the beauty. She didn't know how many minutes she'd stayed plugged into the moment. The phrase 'take your breath away' entered her consciousness, easing the amazement that cradled her. Here would be her last night on the Chilkoot.

The spell cast by the scenery and serenity ebbed when a family of three, who April presumed, was a father, mother, and teenage daughter, entered the shelter with welcoming grins and hellos.

"How was your hike today?" the mother asked.

"Good. Warmer than the last few days. I'm glad to be camping here tonight. The lake is beautiful. It's so serene," April said.

"Enjoy the peace because it will all change when the rest of the hikers arrive," the dad said.

"I'll do just that."

They spoke for more minutes sharing their adventures and mishaps on the trail and their lives off. When the conversation slowed, the daughter added, "We went for a swim in the lake."

"The water looks inviting. After setting up my campsite, I'm going to put my feet in," April said.

Thirty minutes later, April's sandals smacked their way to the lake's edge. The day of sweating in her wool socks and shoes had made the skin on her feet moisten like a damp washcloth. Their exposure to air felt refreshing. Trees bordered the knuckles of dirt shoreline and huddles of reed grasses. She found a slanted rock to sit on.

Depending on how the sun rays bounced off, the lake's color was a palette of light and dark blues. Across the water were reflected projections of undulating trees. She could hear birdsong.

April's knees reared up when the bottoms of her feet touched the chilly clear water.

"Oh," slipped out.

Then she plunged her feet into the lake. April knew she'd remember this sweet spot when she was back home.

The view across the lake reminded her of a jar of different colored sand layers. The forest, bright green of winged and pointed trees, was the foundation; above was a wavy, smooth dark green forest growing up the mountainsides; next a gray layer of exposed mountain rock; then the tops coated in a melting whipped cream cloud cover, crowned by a band of light blue sky.

A wafting summer breeze rose up and faded only to repeat minutes later.

April had less than a day left on the trail. It was four miles to Bennett. There she would catch the afternoon train. A night in Skagway, then back to Whitehorse to fly home. Home. What would it feel like after being on the Chilkoot? Was she different? Happier? This trip was going too fast. She needed to slow this all down.

April gulped back a clump of emotion.

Two days ago, she had been crying on the trail because she forgot to set her alarm and had to climb the Golden Stairs later in the day. April had wanted to go home so badly. Now, she wanted to stay longer.

The Chilkoot had imprinted April more than her shoe prints had marked the Chilkoot. She swished her calves and feet through the water.

This trip has meant so much to her. She hiked the Chilkoot. Well, almost.

April knew, without doubt, that her personal landscape was changed. The challenge and experiment of not only the hiking and camping, but also last year's life choices and the resulting experiences, had bloomed her uncertainties, insecurities, and struggles. It had also created space for new places, adventures, and people. She had to problem solve and press on, depending on herself and knowing when to ask others for help in ways that amplified her life for the better. April was more confident, sturdy, and steady. Resuming her everyday life would create opportunities for refining and testing her new personal growth.

But uncertainty snuck in. Would she revert back to some of her old, unhelpful patterns? Maybe. She was human, but April wasn't a carbon copy of who she was before. She would change again as she moved through her life. Whatever occurred, April hoped it included growth, evolution, and happiness.

She heard voices move about the campground. Hikers arrived and began to set up their tents. All these profound realizations and understandings were in her. If April wanted to tunnel more into them, there was plenty of time on the trail tomorrow and beyond. She lifted her knees and shook the water rivulets off her legs. She returned to her tent for rest and not refuge.

When April awoke, she checked her phone. It was supper time. At the pavilion, she cooked her dehydrated mac and cheese chili meal. This time the shelter had at least fifteen people spread about the place. Camp had become a community. To April's surprised pleasure, the Curlies were there.

April joined them. "Hi! I haven't seen you all in a few days. When'd you get to Bare Loon? How's the hiking been?"

"Forty-five minutes ago. The Chilkoot's been good to us, but were tired," Rita said.

Dot chimed in, "It's been an experience."

Claire added, "That my heart loves, and my knees protest."

They all laughed.

"I'll not forget this adventure," April said.

A hiker at another picnic table commented, "I'm glad to be done with that climb up the Pass."

"Happy Camp was aptly named after that day of hiking," another hiker said.

The conversation kept building and rolling as hikers spoke about their literal and figurative high points and missteps. April enjoyed it all, the shared stories, camaraderie, and the anticipation of the finish.

Rob, Merri, and Conor reached Bare Loon and joined the impromptu party. Merri passed around chocolate bars to share, another hiker offered up trail mix with dried bananas and coconut, and Hoodie Hiker contributed a spicy cracker mix. The party volume of conversation rose to the shelter's ceiling and was carried on the evening breeze into the campground.

An invisible clock and a need for rest began to thin out the group. Assorted hikers, including the Curlies, called out good nights and headed for their tents. Rob and Conor wandered off to check out the lake. Merri and April sat across from each other.

Merri asked April, "How'd your afternoon work out?"

"The hiking was fine. The trail markers were confusing at times. How about you all?" April asked.

"The same, plus the heat. This campground is a gem. Couldn't have asked for a better last night on the trail."

"I feel the same way." April paused and then added, "I'm going to miss being out here."

Merri looked around. "It's a special place. I'm glad you decided to do the trip and hike."

"Me too. It was lucky that I saw that television show and met the guy with the Chilkoot patch. I'm a little worried about life when I get home," April said.

"How so?"

"Looking back, the Chilkoot was a bit of a lifeline. I started this adventure because I was miserable and wanted to sort of reinvent myself. I practiced hiking and camping because I needed to learn how, and it filled my free time. I have my job, but what will I do with myself next?"

"Why do you think you'll stop hiking when you go home?"

"I did all that to prepare for the Chilkoot. The Chilkoot is done tomorrow. I don't have another adventure planned."

"April, there's always something on the horizon. I know

you're uncertain and concerned, but what you do is create your next goal, dream. There are so many available to you. You're energetic, healthy, and have resources."

"My first-world problem must sound small and immature," April said.

"Seeking happiness is never small. Sometimes it's the framing we, and other people, use to define and understand that tries to shrink the significance."

"Before, I did what I thought I was supposed to do. In many ways, it served me well. I'm different now. There's more to all this," April said.

"Which will grow and evolve again and again," Merri said.

"I was thinking just that down by the lake earlier. All this time outdoors has given me space to think and stretch."

"One of nature's inherent qualities is its constant invitation for contemplation," Merri said.

"Or miles to hike."

Merri laughed. Her head had a thoughtful tilt and lift. "The jubilation of hiking the Chilkoot will stay with us all the way home. It will diminish in time, but nuggets of it will always be there to be resurrected when you wish. Instead of big leaps of what you could or should do next, let yourself settle back into your life. When your next idea comes, take the first step, then the next."

"Sounds like a hiking metaphor."

"The same process applies," Merri said.

"I can do that. Thank you for the advice and for listening to me."

Merri stood. "I'm glad you shared. I've hiked with you, and I know you'll get where you want to go."

April's hope felt more fortified. "I'm going to turn in. See you tomorrow."

Lying in her tent, April heard the campers settling in and

the trilling call of a loon closeout the day. The position of her tent door allowed a twilight view of the lake. She wanted to gaze for as long as she could before sleep claimed her. It was still warm. This was the first trail night she hadn't had to wear socks to bed.

April felt her life was well. Not perfect, but more grounded than it had been in months. Her body dropped heavier onto her sleeping pad. She knew she wouldn't be able to stay awake much longer. Pushing up on her elbows, she gazed at the shadows enclosing the mountains. In her next breath, April exhaled a thank you.

CHAPTER TWENTY-FOUR

Softened marigold morning sunshine made the waters of Bare Loon Lake shimmer. April lolled in a contented half-awake state. An hour, more or less, may have passed. April wouldn't look at a clock. It was her body's needs that had her exiting the tent.

The dew coating her shoes splashed up and licked her ankles, making her shiver. The scrape of the gravel she walked on blared. She slowed her pace to muffle the audible jarring.

April thought that without the mountains, this area would look similar to several parks back home. Thinking of home seemed out of place in this minute. The idea of dallying here a couple more days felt pleasurable, but her homesickness had a secure tug. She was surprised by her emotional balancing scales.

She chuckled. This had not been her quandary the morning she left Sheep Camp. That misery seemed to have occurred years instead of days and miles ago. Time could be slippery on the trail.

Today, it was four miles to Bennett. There, April would catch the White Pass and Yukon Railway Chilkoot Hiker service train. The short distance and lower elevation would make this the easiest hiking day. The Chilkoot would have an affable finish.

Gurgles and pops sounded from April's stomach as she retrieved her traveling kitchen from its bear box.

"April, good morning," Rob said as April stepped up into the shelter.

The early bird hikers half filled the structure.

"Morning," April said. Then heard the sunny echoes of the greetings from the assorted hikers. Their hands wrapped around portable travel mugs or used camping cutlery to eat oatmeal or pouch breakfasts of rehydrated eggs and bacon.

April caught sniffs of their coffee as she sat at Rob and Merri's table. "How'd you all sleep?"

"I've slept well this entire hike. I rarely sleep so good at home," Merri sighed. "I'm going to miss that."

April ignited her camp stove. In a minute, she poured boiling water into her coffee mug and then added the remaining volume to oatmeal flakes and raisins.

"What time are you leaving camp?" April asked.

"Another couple of hours. There's no rush to get to Bennett. This is a leisure day. You?"

"After eating, I'll pack up and start hiking." April surprised herself. She had time to relax in camp. The nudge to start hiking felt natural.

"The early bird gets the worm, " Rob said.

April laughed. "I'll pass on the worms. I want to meander. Plus, I don't want to be late for the train."

"I don't think a one of us will miss the train. Have you noticed how much talk there's been regarding people's first meal back in Skagway?" Merri said.

"Lots of votes for pizza and burgers," Conor said.

"Ice cream and salads too. Merri, what do you want to eat for your first meal back in Skagway?" Rob asked.

"That seems too far off to decide yet."

April stacked her breakfast things. "I'm going to clean up my dishes and repack. I'll see you at the Bennett train depot."

"You certainly will," Merri smiled.

April smiled back in what she hoped conveyed her fond appreciation of the family's friendship.

After leaving Bare Loon Lake, April attempted to memorize the wilderness around her. This section was similar to yesterday's dry trail. It didn't take long for her to slip into a meditative, contented stride. The memory-making was interrupted by floating, random thoughts of how to repack her dirty clothes in Skagway, work project details, driving to Whitehorse, and other minutiae.

Past mile two, April was thirsty and winded. The trail had become a ribbon of beach sand. Her steps plodded on, and her mind had ecstatic springiness.

After drinking more than half of her water bottle, she studied the landscape. A vehicle would be comfortable driving the width of the trail. From above at this point, the Chilkoot probably appeared as a beige line with green borders that ran to the blue waterhole of Lake Bennett. The remaining section of the trail was very different from the enclosed coastal rainforest of the Dyea trailhead.

April surmised that in less than two hours, barring an emergency, a long resting break, or an unknown trail situation that would tack on extra miles, she'd reach the end. She wanted to throw her arms up in triumph.

Up ahead, there was a cabin on the left. When April was meters away, she noted the buckling roof, planed and time-gouged wall logs, and broken window. The dilapidated box looked abandoned and forgotten. Maybe this was a stampeder's cabin? Or a homesteader? Someone had chosen a wilderness home address far from people and help.

April thought of her house. It had felt lonely after Justin had moved out. There had been a strange mix of relief and sadness. Unspoken fears of 'can I do this on my own' and 'maybe I made the wrong decision' hung like spider webs in the ceiling corners. Divorce grief and failure hadn't sunk into April until she had signed the papers legally, busting up the wedding promises. Months later, a truer healing release had been actualized.

She wasn't sure exactly when it happened, but her house felt like truly her own place somewhere around spring. April knew there would be someone down the road to share her life and home. For now, she enjoyed her space.

Thick branches scraped free of twigs and with seeable gaps in between lined the path. It wasn't long before April saw a strip of light aqua, streaked with white. She presumed that was Lake Bennett. The water divided mountains to the West and East.

Soon, April glimpsed a wood-shingled spire crowned with black metal ornamentation similar to a weathervane. In minutes she came to a building wall of weathered, faded planks in competing directions underneath gabled rooflines. A placard identified it as a Presbyterian church and the only Gold Rush-era building on the trail. April liked the idea that something the gold seekers had built was intact and maintained, along with the leave-where-it-lay living museum of wheels, mining imple-ments, wire, and shoe artifacts that were scattered and exposed on the trail.

She left the church and wound her way down several hills to a gray metal-roofed building with jaunting chimney stacks. April followed the lake's rocky beach to the two-story structure that was flanked by attached smaller buildings and painted farm barn red with white trim. Affixed to the top was a White Pass and Yukon Route circular sign.

The train tracks separated the shores of Lake Bennett and the depot. Multiple doorways were open. April wondered if she should carry her pack in or leave it outside. She saw no one and decided to prop Big Blue outside against the building. April withdrew the plastic bag that contained her 'real' world possessions of money and passport and walked inside to what she guessed was the lobby. A railroad attendant looked clean and fresh in her braided hair, jeans, and black fleece pullover as she pushed a broom across the floor. The employee was absent of trail dirt scuffs and smears.

The attendant stopped sweeping. "Welcome to Bennett. Would you like a cup of hot tea?"

"Thank you. Is there a bathroom I could use?"

The attendant pointed. "On through there."

"I'll be right back."

April found the bathroom. When she saw her reflection, April froze in shock. She wanted to reach for a towel and wipe clean the flattened greasy ponytail of the outdoorsy woman. There was a dirt constellation near her hair and neckline she had missed during this morning's wipe down.

Instead of sticking her feet in the lake, April should have bathed her whole body.

She wetted a paper towel and scrubbed at the dirt. For good measure, April rubbed at her neck, chest, and armpits. There wasn't much she could do for her clothes.

As April walked out of the bathroom, the question of 'how badly do I smell' braked her movement.

She tented her shirt collar and sniffed.

April couldn't smell herself. This can't be. Her nose was blocking for self-preservation.

As she reentered the normal world, this consideration became reestablished on her priorities list.

April had done what she could. The rest would have to wait until she could shower and put on clean clothes. She would be careful not to get too near the tea lady.

Back in the lobby, the attendant said, "Have a seat. Here's the tea. There's sugar in the bowl."

April stepped as close as she dared and stretched her arm to pick up the stout white ceramic mug.

"This is great. Thank you." April moved back and sat in what she hoped was a friendly but safe-smelling distance.

Did you enjoy the Chilkoot?" the tea lady asked.

"I had a fantastic hike. The scenery is incredible. The climb up the Stairs was more of a scramble. Because of time and weather, a few of us had to overnight on top of the Pass. The Pass was my hardest part. Have you hiked the Chilkoot?"

"No. Maybe one day."

"There's something special about being on this trail. Plus, the hikers. Including the historic Klondike Gold Rush stampeders. They were all so bold."

April was babbling. There had been plenty of hikers to talk to on the trail. Why was she nervous with this person? The realization was swift. The shared experience of the Chilkoot required no need to explain and convince others of the joy and merit of the trail. She held the tea below her lips and blew, diverting her mouth in another direction.

The attendant picked up the tea things. "It sounds like you enjoyed your hike. I expect more hikers will be arriving shortly. The train will be here in a little over two hours. The beach and main street parallel each other. If you walk around there, you'll be able to make out the footprints of the Grand Palace and Dawson hotels. Between 1897 and 1899 this was a fully operational gold rush town."

"I'll do that. Can I leave my backpack here?"

"Sure. Outside, to the left, at the far end of the building, there's a sign that says 'Hikers load here.' Leave it there. No one will bother it."

"Thanks. For the tea too," April said.

April walked back to Big Blue and left it where directed. Several backpacks were already there.

She retraced her steps back to the church via the beach area. April saw a couple of hikers entering Bennett and waved to them. Her excitement of arriving in the old mining town was flagging. Maybe it was a combination of completion relief, ground sleeping, and muscle fatigue that was allowing her to slacken into languidness? There was nothing to do or a place April needed to go for the next couple of hours. All she had to do was hand Big Blue to a porter who would load it onto the railcar and board the train. An engineer would drive the train and the hikers back to Skagway.

April was less interested in Bennett's history and more interested in her recent history. She could not pinpoint when her life's dissatisfaction had begun. Maybe it didn't matter when it started but that she recognized it for what it was. April had first looked at the external factors of husband and career. Digging deeper, she recognized her emotional dissatisfaction and boredom. Admitting the boredom felt like an ungrateful problem.

She wanted to be happy. To pretend her needs were unimportant was an exercise in delusion. April had the opportunities to consider and examine what she wanted and needed. It was this appreciative sentiment that she carried weightless and weightier than any backpack.

April would seek out more adventures. That was her gold strike. This hike was over. It was not over for future dreams, hopes, and wishes.

There were other places to explore and other parks available. She was proud of herself. A warm feeling the size of a baseball sat in her stomach. It expanded up towards her shoulders, and down past her hips until phantom lights danced in front of her eyes. She relished the sensations of satisfaction, success, and soothing. Minutes added up. The warmth began to recede. A peacefulness remained.

A train whistle blew across the valley. The train from Skagway was arriving with tourists. The passengers would unload, and they and the hikers would board for their southbound return.

Studying the area mountains, the peaks appeared higher and too distant to touch. The lake water looked turquoise. A soft wind brushed the down hair on April's neck and forearms. It was time to walk back.

She saw backpacks and legs headed to the depot. Near the tracks, tourists ambled around the lake, and hikers sat in a conversation ring. More red, blue, black, and forest green backpacks leaned and laid near the building. The Curlies and other hikers who April had and had not seen at Bare Loon Lake campground or on the Chilkoot Trail waited.

Hoodie Hiker waved and smiled.

April called out, "Hi. When did you arrive?"

"An hour ago," Puffy Vest said.

"Just got here," Rita said. "You?"

"Not too long. I feel like celebrating."

"With a beer would be great," Rita said.

"And a pizza," Hoodie Hiker said.

The surrounding people laughed and voiced more foods for their Skagway return meal choices. Over the next hour, people relaxed, unwound, wandered, used the indoor plumbing, spoke of travel plans, and cheered and clapped for arriving hikers. It was a shared party whose entrance fee was a hike across the Chilkoot.

It was 2:45, and the train departure was soon. April wondered where Rob, Merri, and Conor were.

April asked the Curlies, "Ladies, have you seen Merri, Rob, or Conor yet?

"No. I hope they get here soon," Dot said.

"They'll be here in time. As we were leaving Bare Loon, they said they'd be hiking out shortly after us," Rita affirmed.

"I hope nothing bad has happened," Claire said.

April's inquiry metamorphosed into concern.

"I'll walk up to the trail and see if they are there. The railroad porters will probably want to start loading packs shortly. I know we're supposed to be here to hand over our backpacks, but can one of you make sure mine is loaded onto the train?" April asked.

Rita, exuding the tone of an organized classroom teacher, said, "April, show me which backpack is yours. We'll make sure it gets loaded."

It took April minutes to reach the Gold Rush church. No one was there. Subdued whooshes of wind lifted and waved coniferous, needled limbs.

It was time to say goodbye to the Chilkoot. April closed her eyes and let the emotional winds pull and whirl inside her. A muffled whistle edged near her ears.

In less than a week, this hike and its landscape had contributed to the personal alchemy occurring within April. She knew this trip was important, and the depth of it surprised her. She didn't want to let go. An ache fluttered shallow chest heaves. She pulled long seconds of air into her nostrils.

The intensity slowed like an airplane landing and rolling to the gate. Then everything in April calmed.

Another whistle cracked the shell of her peace.

The train was leaving without her!

April sprung and sprinted past the church and to the depot. She saw no people waiting. The locomotive crept towards Skagway.

CHAPTER TWENTY-FIVE

April ran down the hill after the departing train. She took a sharp right. Her soles skidded and slid. She pivoted and righted herself. A farewell whistle blasted through the mountain valley. Fear jumbled and jangled her nerves.

Should she wave to get their attention? They couldn't see her.

She pistoned her elbows to build momentum. Her rapid inhalations partnered frantic leg pumping and cycling.

April ran past the depot. Grasping at her available options, she shouted. "Stop!"

The likelihood of her catching the train diminished as the distance grew between her and the last railcar. The possibility of being stuck in Bennett waiting for another day's train without Big Blue, coupled with missing her flight home, yapped in her brain and eradicated her previous peace. She refocused her running effort.

Keep going and catch that train.

April noted a curve further down the tracks. Her heart thumped in her ears and competed with her loud breathing. She saw a couple step out onto the caboose's platform. April was torn between waving at them or running. Performing both concurrently would slow her down.

She wanted to yowl, "Don't leave!" The woman of the couple went inside the train car. She reappeared with another person. The additional individual looked potentially railroad-official in a fluorescent green vest.

The train sped up. April watched as the three people became visually smaller.

An elongated screeching sound of metal clamping on metal scraped April's ears. The train began to slow.

Hissing air announced its stop. She heard the quelling rumble of the train's idling engine over her chest heaves.

April lessened to a lurching trot as if she was moving into a windstorm. The slower pace made her aware of the sweat rolling from her armpits down her torso. What wasn't caught in April's shirt corralled at her waistband.

She grasped her side stitch. In a hoarse huff, she let out, "Stop."

Steps from the watching trio, April began walking.

The vested railroad employee wore a lanyard and had a walkie talkie covering her talking mouth. April detected words encased in buzzing and static, but she could not make them out.

Looking up at three pairs of shocked eyes, April wheezed, "Thank you for stopping."

The employee pushed her sunglasses up atop her head and said, "I don't think I've ever seen someone chase after a train like that. You weren't going to stop."

April climbed the three caboose steps. "I had to catch my train."

"Do you have a ticket?" the employee asked with raised eyebrows.

April rubbed her sweaty hands on her gray hiking pants

then unzipped a front-leg pocket for her plastic bag wallet. She handed over her rail pass.

"Great," the now broad-smiling agent said, inspecting the ticket. "All aboard. You look flushed. Maybe you should sit down."

April didn't think she could convey how badly she wanted to do just that. Her adrenaline redirected into a compulsion to throw back her head and spout laughter laced with craziness.

She reigned in her impulse and flashed what she hoped was a sane, pleasant smile. "I'll do that."

The woman of the couple remarked, "Good thing we wanted to step outside and take a picture, or we'd never have seen you."

"Thank you for seeing me."

The train whistle bellowed. April thought she perceived the conductor's irritation in the sound. She yanked open the caboose's door and crossed the threshold.

Several steps inside a younger adult man wearing the railroad's branded polo shirt and a lanyard appraised April. "You the runner?" he asked.

April delivered a wobbly smile. "After trains."

"We've never stopped the train this far from the depot. You must have luck on your side."

"Maybe? Maybe more perseverance? But I'll take the luck. I'm going to sit down."

April shuffled to the nearest open brown leather battered seat, then sank like the fabric of a tent when the last pole is removed. The vibrations of the steel wheels rattled up the train car producing a continuous light jostle. The train's locomotion relieved April.

Whew, she made it.

The other passengers were hikers April didn't recognize. They looked her over. She took deep yoga breaths. The breaths stuttered. April pushed out her stomach to inhale more oxygen. She leaned back and let the relief of sitting on the train take over her body. Her previous adrenaline was gone and replaced by an engulfing droop.

I'm okay. I'm headed to Skagway. I'll be sleeping in a bed tonight. I won't have to set up my tent.

She was disappointed at the last thought. April found her response strange.

Her attention reoriented to the tall side windows and the mountain range beyond. The sunlight shifted, and the glass reflected her image. All her hiking miles had contributed to a deeper summer tan. Her ponytail had loosened during her train chase and now hung about her face in sweaty chunks. Bright red streaks rouged her cheeks.

The train steamed over the tracks and ties laid across the wilderness. Its progression created an illusion of proximity and distance. She saw the ash-gray mountain bellies, the boreal forests of skinny white birch and emerald green spruce that planted and spread themselves into the valleys and up the mountain's flanks, and the paralleled rivers that moved closer and receded. It had a hypnotic effect on her.

April was disheveled and worn-out, but also elated. The exuberance shot down her neural tracks like a bullet train. She sat up straighter.

This euphoria was the opposite of the emotional tolls the prior months' sluggish discontentment had accompanied.

April heard her name then turned to the walkway and saw Rita, Merri, and Rob standing next to her seat.

"We're glad to see you," Rita said.

Merri followed with a furrowed forehead. "We are so sorry. We thought you had boarded the train. If we had known you hadn't, we'd have asked the conductor to wait and have gone looking for you."

An undercoat of humor tinted April's next statement. "We'd have been looking for each other."

"We'd have found each other," Rob laughed.

"I'm here now."

Merri pointed at a railcar window and the landscape beyond. "It's ending too fast. In no time we'll be at the Fraser stop. A train employee announced we'll be stopping so the Canadian Border agents can check our passports. April, do you have your passport?"

"Yes," April patted the zippered pocket on her upper thigh. "I had taken my wallet and passport with me."

"Oh good," Merri breathed out. "The porters will be passing out boxed lunches. We have an extra bottle of water if you're thirsty."

"I am. Thank you," April said.

Rob left to retrieve the water. After a little more discussion of April's race to catch the train, everyone settled into the ride's rhythmic sway and rumble. They watched the land they had hiked transform into a story of memories.

At the Fraser, British Columbia customs checkpoint, April hesitated at the top step of the train car. An irrational fear that she wouldn't be let back on bubbled up inside her.

They'll let her back on.

She stuck close to the Curlies, Merri, Rob, Conor, and the other hikers as they lined up at a square wood building painted burnt red with a white and black Fraser sign.

While they stood in line, Rita said, "When we get to Skagway, I want a shower followed by a burger and beer."

"In the bathroom?" Rob teased.

"Pizza would suit me," Merri said.

"I want ice cream," Claire said.

April considered what she wanted. All the food suggestions

sounded delicious. Then it occurred to her that if she didn't plan, she'd be eating alone.

To the group at large, April asked, "Does anyone want to meet up for supper?"

Dot nodded and said, "I'd like that. One more night together would be lovely. It will be strange not to see you all tomorrow."

April's heart rippled at Dot's sweet sentiment.

Rita jumped into organizing. "How many of us will there be? Size may drive our restaurant choices."

Merri began pointing. "Myself, Rob, Conor, April, and you three ladies.

"Us too?" Hoodie Hiker asked and pointed to Puffy Vest, and two of their friends.

"That makes us eleven. There's that Klondike-themed restaurant down on the main drag. They'd have room. I imagine their menu will have something for everyone," Merri said.

"We have ourselves a party!" Rita cheered.

"Let's meet there at 6," Claire said.

During the conversation, the customs line continued to move. When it was April's turn, she handed over her passport. She was again dismayed by the missing 'why are you here' question. April wanted to share the glee and glory of her Chilkoot experience. Her letdown was shoved away when the customs agent used a soda pop-sized silver date stamp. The device thunked and retracted. Inked in black on the center of the page was an irregular shaped pentagon. The words FRASER, BC arched over an outlined image of Klondike Gold Rush stampeders hiking up the Stairs.

She savored the picture. A hiker behind her tapped her shoulder. April moved on and returned to the train.

The second time she boarded, April noted the two railcars for hikers. At the time of her online ticket purchase, instructions stated that specific cars were reserved for hikers. Then it had amused her. Now she had sympathetic understanding for those passengers whose sense of smell had not been Chilkoot Trail inoculated.

Back on the train, most hikers relaxed in the loud solitude of the train noise, watched the mountain scenery, blinked at the daylight after exiting the tunnels, and leaned towards the windows for a better view of the occasional cliff drops.

April overheated in the enclosed, sunshine bright space. She sought the caboose platform for fresh air. The velocity of the wind pulled and whipped her hair. Her hands wrapped around the cold metal of the handrail. Looking back, April could see how the tracks adapted to the terrain. At times, they had a roomy bed of land; more often, they squatted on the bases of the mountains, and a few times, they appeared to cling to narrow bowling alley sized-strips as cliffs or ravines dropped off.

Leaning over the side rail, April looked south to Skagway and sea level. The closer they came, the less snow was in the ranges. The mountain slopes were colored summer green by clumps of free-range brush, bushes, and trees that covered and obscured gray rock piles. Further down the line was a wide, deep-cut canyon with a dividing white-water river at the bottom. An open-sided trestle bridge spanned what April guessed was a quarter-mile long open space. She was glad she didn't have to cross on foot.

When the rolling train began to reduce speed, April reen-tered the caboose. As they pulled into Skagway, a large group of tourists gathered to watch the disembarking passengers. April and the other hikers shuffled off the train. The sliding door of the baggage car boomed open. A porter began passing down backpacks.

April saw Big Blue and went to claim it. In a graceful, second-nature arm swing, she had it on her back. Turning around, April saw tourists watching and taking photos. She looked for Merri or Rob. When she found Merri on the other side of the crowd, she waved. After making eye contact, April held up her hands with six fingers pointing upward, indicating that she'd see them that evening. Merri nodded and waved goodbye.

April started for the Inn. Moving through the tourists, she drifted into the thin parade of black, blue, red, and green backpacks heading downtown. The attention of the curious watchers made April walk with an arch in her back and head up.

At the Inn, April paused before entering. Scouting around the property, she located a dumpster at the back. With relish, April flung her traveling trash bag into the bin. She wouldn't miss that.

In the Inn, the front desk was empty. April went to the kitchen. Jasper, her Chilkoot drop-off driver, wore a chef's white smock and stood in front of a table laden with multiple bowls of different sizes and colors.

"Hello," April called out.

"Hi. Welcome back. How was your hike?" Jasper asked as he used a whisk to mix a bowl's ingredients.

"Excellent," April said.

"Good to hear. Let me get your room key," Jasper said as he wiped his hands on a green and white kitchen towel.

With the room key in hand, April climbed the stairs and eased down the hallway, making sure not to scuff the walls or hit any of the framed landscape and wildlife pictures with Big Blue. When she unlocked and opened her room, she paused. The afternoon sunshine streamed through the window, making the area a cheerful yellow-bright. To minimize tracking dirt, April removed her hiking shoes at the doorway and then set them on a tourist magazine. The bed looked comfortable and soft. She would not have to get down to crawl into it.

April should text her parents and Lauren. Let them know she finished the Chilkoot and was back in Skagway.

April picked up her phone, but she didn't want to send the text just yet. Shower first.

It was then it occurred to April that her clean clothes were in the trunk of the rental car. She unpacked her camp sandals and went outside. On the street, April noticed the noise: vehicles, people, overhead aircraft, doors closing, and the other everyday urban sounds. There was nothing out of the ordinary, but she was jarred by it. The train noise had been louder. April suspected it was the accumulation of it all that had created a sensory overload inside her.

After retrieving her clothes from the sedan's trunk, she ambled back to her room. She turned the plastic bag upside down and dumped its contents onto the bed: clean beige shorts, a light blue t-shirt, and underwear. There was no high performance, wicking function, or temperature protection needed. This was another sign of returning to her normal life.

Inside the shared bathroom down the hall, the showerhead rained heated water. April looked down at her nakedness. She was surprised to see black and blue bruising around her hip bones that appeared to stick out a bit more.

April made a big lather with the shampoo and rubbed it into her greasy hair. During her first soaping, dirty water ran down her legs, pooling around her feet before flowing down the drain. She had to wash herself a second time before the water ran clear.

Clean and wrapped in a white bath towel, April stood in the middle of the bathroom. Being back in Skagway and bathing were the next steps into reentry. When April looked in the mirror, she cocked her head. The reflection was her. And something new. She watched herself comb her hair and brush her teeth. April inventoried her features and searched for what had changed. Her face, other than her tan, was the same. The way she held her carriage was different. There was a thriving calmness.

Back in her room April opened the window. A brush of a breeze entered. She texted her parents and Lauren that she was safely in Skagway. April decided to take a small nap before dinner. She muted her phone. April wanted to keep the outer world at bay a little longer. She laid spread-eagle on the mattress. Her body dropped into the softness of the sheets and bed. Her thoughts were untroubled and laid back. She enjoyed the benign floral smell of the bathroom soap mixing with her skin. April was content.

CHAPTER TWENTY-SIX

April woke, not knowing where she was. Above, the ceiling was painted white instead of green tent fabric. She sat up and looked around her rented room. On the floor were a crumpled pair of dirty khaki hiking pants, a green short-sleeved wicking shirt, a balled-up pair of socks next to her camp stove, a silver insulated mug lying on its side, bear spray, and a plastic bag with two snack bars. Big Blue slumped against the half-wall of light-yellow painted wainscoting. More dirty clothes waterfalled from the unzipped and unbuckled compartments.

She turned off her 5:30 phone alarm. It was time to start for the restaurant.

April's camp sandals thudded as she walked across the sidewalk boards. A few people lingered as the town shifted into unhurried tranquility. Farther down the street, April could see groups of tourists waiting at the dock to board their cruise ships.

Entering the restaurant, April recoiled at the hanging lights, neon signs, multiple televisions, and customers' voices. It felt too much.

Welcome back to the real world, thought April.

The walls were decorated with battered mining pans, two-handle saws, wagon wheels, and other scrounged period artifacts.

At a long table in the middle, she spotted Rob, Conor, Merri, the Curlies, and assorted Chilkoot hikers. April knew it was them, but each person looked unfamiliar dressed in their non-hiking clothes. Most everyone wore jeans and t-shirts. Absent were brimmed outdoor hats with chin straps, hiking pants, and loaded backpacks.

Rita waved. April walked over to the laughing and talking group.

"Hi, April. Ready to eat a meal, you don't have to prepare yourself?" Rita asked.

Rob poured April a glass from a plastic pitcher. "Or filter water?"

"Definitely. No pasta or soup this evening," April said.

"And no oatmeal for breakfast tomorrow," Claire said and wrinkled her nose.

Cheers of agreement rushed to respond. A couple of people raised beer glasses.

"I think this hiking adventure is one of my top 10 favorite experiences," Dot said.

Puffy Vest, minus her vest, wearing jeans and a red and white striped long-sleeved shirt, said, "It's in my top 10 too. When I was showering, I didn't get all the dirt off the first time. I had to scrub myself twice."

April laughed. "Me too."

A server appeared and took Claire and Hoodie Hiker's salad orders, followed by several pizzas, a steak, and many hamburgers with fries. April salivated for her burger.

"I didn't think I could get tired of trail mix, but it happened," Conor said.

"I won't be reaching for a protein bar anytime soon," Claire added and then took a sip of her cocktail.

"We ate ramen each night, but since I'm still in college, my ramen days will continue," Hoodie Hiker said.

More food banter continued at the table.

Merri turned to April. "How does it feel to be back in civilization?"

"Easy enough to merge back in, but kind of strange too. This restaurant feels loud. There are too many lights, too much stuff, and too many people. The noise of the train didn't annoy me as much. Of course, I wanted badly to be on it. How about you?" April asked.

"I can relate. I enjoyed not having to answer telephone calls, check email, and pay attention to the world for a few days. It was heavenly. Disconnecting from all that made connecting to nature and the trail a fuller experience."

"I agree. For those days, I only needed to hike, to camp, make a home for the night, and do it again the next day. There was a simplicity to it."

"Yes. Funny, we worked hard to get to the end, and now we're missing it."

"Aside from trail food," April quirked.

Merri let out a full-throated laugh. "Aside from trail food."

The kitchen prepared food arrived. First bites were followed by several happy moans and ahh's let loose. More minutes of chewing limited talking.

Dot restarted the conversation when she asked, "Remember getting up early to climb the Stairs?"

"That was the toughest day," Claire commented.

Rita rested her hand on her forehead. "I was relieved to reach Happy Camp and set up our tent."

"Myself, Merri, Rob, and Conor camped at the warming shelter on the Pass after the Stairs," April said.

"You all spent the night on top of the Pass!" Rita exclaimed.

"By the time we made it up the Stairs, and over the summit,

questionable weather was moving in. The Warden suggested we camp at the top and resume hiking in the morning."

Merri lowered her fork. "It was an extraordinary experience."

"How wonderful!" Dot rushed out.

"That is very cool," Hoodie Hiker added.

Merri reclined back in her chair. "It was. We left the mountain top early the next morning. The snow was firm and solid for us when we descended the Pass. There was so much snow on the trail in those next miles."

"Yes, and hardly any mosquitos," Puffy Vest said.

Rita raised her beer glass. "Here, here, to small mercies."

The remember whens, how abouts, what did you thinks, and did you sees rolled and skipped through the meal as they finished their entrees and feasted on chocolate cake, cheesecake, and ice cream sundaes with whipped cream.

When the food was eaten, the hikers quieted. April sensed tiredness, but also a peaceful thoughtfulness. No one had to race away to store food and cooking accessories into the bear lockers, filter water, turn in early, or hike a few more miles to get to camp. They all stayed, making the last fading minutes of the Chilkoot hold them a while longer.

Yawns interrupted chatting about travel arrangements. A couple of people leaned back in their chairs. The Curlies stood up first and then the younger people. Hugs and earnest 'take care' farewells were exchanged. April, Merri, Rob, and Conor remained at the table.

Rob finished his beer and said, "I guess it's time to head back to the hotel."

Merri nodded. "I guess."

"Thank you for a last evening together before we all go home. I know how lucky I am to have met and hiked the Chilkoot with you," April said.

"We feel the same," Merri said, then stood and handed April a piece of paper. "This is our contact information. Let's stay in touch."

"I'd like that."

Merri hugged April. "I'm looking forward to it. You take care."

Rob, and even Conor, hugged April goodbye. Together they walked out of the restaurant. The family went one direction and April another direction. April reached into her pocket and rubbed the addressed paper between her fingers. She pulled out the sheet to look. In elegant cursive was Merri and Rob's address. April learned her new friends' last name was Taro.

Tonight was bittersweet. She'd miss the Chilkoot and the friends she had made. They all hiked the trail, but for many varied reasons: a wilderness adventure, a family trip, a bucket list wish, to walk a historical path, and more. As April strolled back to the Inn, she considered her reasons.

She wanted something new. She wanted adventure. In a way, she tested herself and finished a little more transformed.

April regarded the mountains that rimmed and nestled Skagway. They seemed so close. The midnight sun kept the gray peaks, patches of high elevation snow, and the forested slopes viewable even in the later evening.

Back in her room, she texted her parents and Lauren telling them she was back in Skagway, and her Chilkoot hike was a success. In less than five minutes, her telephone rang. It was her parents.

Her Dad reeled off his excited questions. "Hi honey, how are you? Was it fun? Did you see any bears? Did anyone get hurt."

April waited a few seconds to make sure her dad had stopped speaking. "It was fun. No bears. I know of no injuries except for scrapes. I'm exhausted."

"Honey, it's Mom. You rest up. We'll catch up when you're home."

There was a reconfirmation of return flight details. They exchanged goodnights and I love yous before disconnecting.

Lying in bed, April stared up into the closed window blinds darkened room. The precious Chilkoot bubble was popped. April decided what vacation time was left, she was going to savor.

April woke to blue-tinted yellow daylight pushing into the warm room. The bed felt luxurious. She didn't want to get up. Today she would drive back to the Whitehorse airport and take a late afternoon flight home. April was refreshed and ready.

There were few vehicles on the highway back to White-horse. April left the radio off. She rolled the window down some. The solitary drive invited her into a fluid contemplation as well as the opportunity to take in the landscape one last time. The day was bright and the visibility clear. Cloud sheets were tacked high in the atmosphere. The mountains wore aprons of green with dusky rock upper halves. Some had, and others did not, snow-peaked caps.

She felt relaxed. Her muscle soreness made her sit heavy in the driver's seat. April reveled in her body. The successful hike, beautiful scenery, and the novelty of her trip were swirling pleasure throughout her. There was happiness, sweetness, capability, a tiny teaspoon of leaving sadness, and curiosity. Now that her big hike was over, she wondered what came next? What else was in her future? What did she want to explore?

How would she know what to choose? On the Chilkoot, the day of the Stairs, there had been a false summit and a true summit. Would she know how to discern the false summits? She may not be able to know which of her life's metaphorical summits were false, but she would keep going forward.

The rental car drop-off, customs gate, and flight boarding

were stress-free. April exhaled a private sigh as the jet taxied down the runway and was grateful it carried her home.

April arrived back in-state on Tuesday morning a little after 10:00. Her parents waved as she walked through the security doors into the airport baggage claim.

"Hi, honey! How are you? How was your hike?" her Mom asked as she hugged April tight.

Her Dad's arms encircled both the women. "Good to see you in one piece. Can't wait to hear your stories."

"The hike was fantastic. The only bears I saw were on post-cards and videos. I'm exhausted."

"Let's get you home. We picked up some groceries for you to get you restarted," her Dad said.

At home, her parents helped carry luggage and groceries into the house. They made a plan for family dinner on Sunday and to hear about April's trip before each giving her a quick goodbye hug. Her home was still and a little stuffy from being closed up for the week. She could set down the Chilkoot Trail challenge and Big Blue. April missed both.

CHAPTER TWENTY-SEVEN

April texted Lauren that she was home. In seconds, Lauren wrote back, saying she would telephone that evening.

Her jetlag demanded a nap. She left a packed Big Blue in the kitchen and went to her couch. When April woke, she stayed prone. Far-off noises of lawnmowers, infrequent traffic, and birdsong passed through the house's windows and walls. She and the neighborhood relaxed in the summer twilight.

Disinterested in cooking, April made a turkey sandwich for supper. While chewing, she wandered around her kitchen and circled the empty table. April was rested yet jittery. She needed to move. To walk. Her body was used to the hours of daily exercise and now demanded it.

Under April's hiking shoes, which she had dug out of Big Blue, the concrete sidewalks were smooth and obstacle-free. The air was a mix of hot pockets and warm shadows. She had gone two miles when Lauren called and asked in breezy excitement, "So, how was your hike?"

"Beautiful. Fun. More than I expected and realized it could be."

"That's good. Right? Tell me everything. Do not leave out anything."

"Even the part about me crying on the trail?"

"Especially that. Did you hurt yourself?" Lauren's words flew out.

April shook her head even though no one could see her. "I'm fine. In fact, I'm out for an evening walk as we speak."

"Didn't you walk enough miles last week?"

My body wants to move," April said.

"If you say so. Start from the beginning."

April walked along straight lines of street lights and told her Chilkoot story. "I picked up my rental car in Whitehorse and headed to Skagway. I was nervous. Excited. Unsure. It was like driving in a beautiful postcard. As I drove further into the mountains, a thick fog settled in. Visibility was next to nothing. I couldn't stop in case someone was behind me, but I didn't want to go too fast because it was hard to see. I wondered what I had gotten myself into."

"Not the best of starts," Lauren agreed.

"Looking back, it sounds like a good metaphor for the experience. I had a planned route, but there were surprises in my future."

Lauren chuckled. "Isn't that the truth about life in general?"

A dog barked in a yard as April passed. "Fair point. After passing the U.S. border stop, the fog cleared. I could see these immense mountain ranges. Once in Skagway, I found my inn, purchased last-minute supplies, then checked in at the National Park Service for my orientation class and to get my trail permit." April characterized the Victorian-themed inn and the mountains and ocean that hugged the refreshed Klondike mining town.

"The next day, the inn shuttle driver dropped me off at the trailhead. I was the only one there." April described the coastal rainforest of tall trees, bogs, and the open-sided boardwalks and grid-rail bridges.

"Did you see any animals?" Lauren asked.

April had to think. "I saw squirrels and birds. No bears."

"Just as well," Lauren said.

April could hear silverware banging against each other and then a dishwasher door shutting. "As the elevation built, the land became dryer and filled with evergreens. On my second night, I camped at Sheep Camp. The park ranger recommended leaving around 4 a.m. the next day because of the snow on top of Chilkoot Pass. The hikers would have an easier time traversing the snowfields in the earlier morning when it was firm. I forgot to set my alarm. I don't know if it was nerves or self-sabotage."

Lauren interrupted, "Or just a mistake."

"I woke up late and panicked. I almost quit and returned to the start. That was the hardest and longest day. I cried as I hiked to the Scales. I was miserable. I think I spent more time looking at my feet than I did the scenery around me, which was magnificent when I looked up. After the Scales comes the Stairs. The Stairs is a stacked boulder wall up a mountain. With my backpack on, I climbed, crawled, and scooted my way up."

"That sounds hard and a little scary," Lauren said.

"Funny thing, I was upset about how my day began, so I wasn't fully cognizant of my efforts. I just did what I had to do to get to the top. While working my way up, I met my friends, the Taros—Merri, Rob, and their teenage son, Conor. Together, we crossed over the Pass and into Canada."

"What was it like?" Lauren asked.

"You can see for miles. A combination of bad weather moving in and the time of day prompted the Canadian warden to suggest we spend the night. I slept on a mountaintop."

"That's amazing!" Lauren exclaimed. "What happened next?"

"The low clouds created a socked-in darkness. A wind blew, but we were safe and snug in this shelter that was more like a garden shed with windows. I laid in my sleeping bag, upset at myself for screwing up."

Lauren interrupted. "If you hadn't overslept, you wouldn't have had that experience."

"True. I woke up the next day feeling like a real adventurer and was ready to hike down the other side of the Pass. We had to do this shuffle walk where each step your heels make a small shelf in the snow to anchor and avoid sliding and tumbling down the mountain. There's a lake at the bottom. I had this crazy fear I was going to roll down and crash in. The color of the water was an incredible icy turquoise."

April had circumnavigated herself back to her house. She sat on the bottom step of her front porch. The street and porch lights blended with the darkness. No one was in sight.

"How many days did you have left on the Chilkoot?" Lauren asked.

"Three more. The next handful of miles were mostly snowfields, with occasional wild grass sections where the snow had melted, plus rock piles and streams, and a few trees. Near Happy Camp, which was the campground I had planned to stay at, the land changed again. There are more trees and vegetation because of the lower elevation. That night my new friends and I camped at Deep Lake. The next day, the trail began a steady descent. We camped at Bare Loon Lake," April said.

"Were there loons?"

"Yes. The lake shimmers blues and oranges as the sun moves. Mountains all around. That night we had a party where we passed around snacks and stories. I positioned my tent such that my door faced the lake. It was magical. I heard a loon as I laid in my tent falling asleep."

"That sounds wonderful. All your trail challenges were done, and you were onto better times."

April laughed. "Until I almost missed my train back to Skagway."

"What?!" Lauren hooted.

"On the last day, I hiked the few miles to Bennett and waited to catch my train. I didn't see the Taros. I walked back to the trail to look for them and didn't pay close attention to time. The train whistle announced its leaving. I had to race to catch it. I ran after it like a wild woman. A couple saw me and notified a railroad employee."

Lauren gasped, then burst into laughter. When her friend's guffaws slowed, and she was able to speak, Lauren said, "You've got to be kidding me. You chased down a train and stopped it. That's like something in a movie."

"Everything happened so fast. I dawdled too long at the old church. Thank goodness the train whistle was loud and carried through that valley, or I'd still be there."

"It sounds like you had fun. I'm glad you had support on the Chilkoot," Lauren said.

"Hiking the Chilkoot was exciting and a little scary. I saw incredible mountains and scenery. The people I met on the trail were fantastic. I hope I get to see several of them again."

"I hope so too. Your trip was a combination of solo traveling and community. What's your next adventure?"

"I don't know. Should I be worried that I don't know?"

"No. Something will turn up. It always does."

"You're right. I'm slipping into my old habit of second-guessing myself," April said.

"But, you caught yourself and stopped."

"I did. Thank you for supporting me."

"April, of course I would. I'm very proud of you."

Tears welled in April's eyes. "Thank you."

"You're welcome. It's getting late. Let's grab brunch this weekend or next."

"I'd like that. And Lauren, thanks again."

April returned to work on Wednesday. The drive there was relaxed and annoyance free. After setting her messenger bag on her desk, she walked to Kari's cubicle.

"Good morning, Kari," April said.

"You're back! How was your trip?"

"More memorable than I could have imagined. The trail was an adventure and the scenery beautiful. I met fantastic people. How are you?"

"I'm so happy that your trip was wonderful. I'm well. The team project has sped up and been added to. I suspect the boss will make you hit the ground running. I took care of last week's reports so you won't have to worry about them."

April was touched by Kari's actions to lessen April's workload. "I appreciate that. Thanks."

"You're welcome. I have to finish an analysis of the temporary contractors needed. Do you have time for a lunchtime walk? I would love to hear more about your trip."

April knew her eyes had rounded in surprise. "Sure."

"Okay, let's meet at the front doors at 12:15."

Kari was accurate in that the department project's speed and needs had more than doubled. Her boss Judith asked for status updates and immediate coordination with other team members. April foresaw several long work weeks in August and into the fall.

Her morning was taken over by email reading and report analysis. By lunch, April's revved focus was unaware of the time. When she looked at her computer clock, it read 12:20.

Dashing from her cubicle to the front of the building, she saw Kari waiting.

"Sorry to keep you. I was lost in work".

"I can relate," Kari said.

"It feels good to be outside." The August sunshine tried to wither with its bright heat. April wished she had remembered to grab her sunglasses. They began walking across the parking lot over to the city sidewalk bordered by trees thick with the summer's green leaves.

"Tell me about the Chilkoot. What was it like?"

April surprised herself when she admitted, "I was scared and nervous at the beginning."

"Really? You don't appear to be intimidated by much at work. Going off to hike the Chilkoot takes courage. Such a trip would scare me," Kari said.

April told Kari the almost exact retelling that she had told Lauren, ending with the dramatic train chase.

Kari gasped. "You stopped a moving train?!"

"I did, and I hiked the Chilkoot." April felt pride at her words and trip.

"How did you learn about the existence of the Chilkoot?"

"I was unhappy a year ago. I thought if I divorced Justin, that would make it all better. It didn't. My happiness is my responsibility. After my divorce, I spent depressive hours on my couch watching television. I saw a documentary about the Klondike Gold Rush. Something was invigorating about people willing to travel thousands of miles and risk their lives so they could find their gold strike, or at least have an adventure. That drew me in."

Kari stopped walking, and with her mouth agape, stared at April. "A television show inspired you? I knew you had divorced, but not the other stuff."

April grinned and laughed. "Considering it from that point, it does sound kind of crazy. And also inspired."

"I wonder what your next adventure will be like?"

"Me too," April said. This time her words were filled with assurance.

CHAPTER TWENTY-EIGHT

A couple of months had passed since April had finished the Chilkoot. Her work-life balance was heavier on the work side of the scale. She found herself becoming annoyed more often. She missed being outside. Evening walks and weekend hikes had been replaced with walking breaks at the office.

On her first day back to work, April had changed her computer background from the fantasy beach picture to a photograph of Bare Loon Lake she had taken. She looked more often and longer at the image attempting to offset the developing burnout of double-digit hour workdays and Saturday mornings.

A hurried, scheduled second project launch frenzy arrived at the beginning of October. The leaves in her neighborhood were changing to burnt orange, bright red, dusky maroon, and a yellow reminiscent of curry powder. April felt blue on an early Tuesday evening.

Her work project was slowing down. She felt good, and there was a contentment in her home. She missed the Chilkoot. She missed Merri, Rob, Conor, and the Curlies. She missed nature.

That's it. She needed to go hiking. Maybe weekend camping.

April knew the winding-down camping season would have an availability of campsites. A web search located a state park an hour and a half away. She made a reservation for the upcoming weekend. On Thursday night, she'd pack her gear and car like old times.

On packing night, she had a joyful half-skip to her walk as she moved about her spare bedroom. The closet in this room had become her hiking and camping storage. She grinned in the happiness of gathering her camp stove, sleeping bag, tent, a newly purchased fuel can, and the other gear on her list into a pile on the new bed she purchased to replace the one Justin had taken with him.

April scanned the closet to make sure she hadn't forgotten anything. Big Blue hung limp from a hanger at the back. April stared at the blue nylon that, without any stuffing, had collapsed in on itself. Big Blue had done its job. One day it would be readied for another adventure.

On Friday, a flaw in the project kept April at the office until 6:30. When she could, April left her cubicle and hurried to her car. Her gear was stored in the trunk. The lateness of the day missed rush hour traffic. The time of season brought earlier sunsets.

It was dark when April arrived at the state park. Her car headlights passed over a closed park entrance booth. She had anticipated some reduction in park amenities and had taken screenshots of the park map the day before. Using the pictures saved on her phone, April located the campground.

Her campsite was in the middle. Two recreational vehicles parked on opposite sides of the campground. The swath of the headlights showed a picnic table, firepit, and flattened dirt ground to pitch her tent.

April's late arrival and site setup reminded her of the first overnight camping weekend last spring. She exited her car and stood in the darkness. It felt exhilarating to breathe the chilled air. She listened to the silence.

This is where I want to be, April thought.

Opening the trunk and then her daypack, she found her headlamp. Slipping the strap around her head created a jutting out appendage. The light swayed, bounced, and spotlighted the immediate area in front of her feet.

April erected the tent and furnished it with her sleeping bag, pad, and bedroom pillow in ten minutes. The pillow was an extravagance of comfort, but April didn't have anything to explain, or prove, to anyone.

Another special treat was the firewood she had purchased at the store in addition to her camp fuel. April knew she could learn how to cook over the campfire but had decided that would be for another night. As quick as the tent was to set up, getting the logs lit was a different matter. Yesterday's newspaper procured from her work break room ignited and burned out. The logs didn't catch the flame. Exasperation flamed in April.

She had her camp stove. A campfire was unnecessary. But the desire for one overrode her irritation.

April needed something to intensify the burn and catch the logs on fire.

She had once overheard that potato chips worked in a pinch as a firestarter. The oil on the chips was the ignitor. She didn't have any chips, but maybe she had something similar in her pack or car. In her vehicle console next to an old pair of sunglasses were a handful of coins, restaurant napkins, tampons, and pens. Buried was a travel size bottle of bug spray.

She guessed that spraying the wood might not produce enough of a burst. If she doused paper, maybe it would provide a stronger accelerant. Taking the napkins and a tampon, she went back to the firepit.

April soaked an unwrapped tampon and several napkins with bug spray. She set her new firestarter in the center of the log triangle. When the match flame touched the enhanced paper, quick combustion flared up. April reared back. The blue and orange flames sparked with gold and spread across the papers, then a log, and then another log. As the fire built stronger and higher, yellow, red, and soft pink flames merged and weakened the blue colors. The wood cracked and popped. Smoke tendrils floated up. The ash became soft sand on the bottom of the firepit.

April set a camp chair near, but back enough for safety. Next, she boiled water in her camp stove for noodles. When the food was ready, she sat back in the camp chair and ate by firelight. It was peaceful.

Contented pleasantness, like wrapping one's hands around the first cup of coffee in the morning, settled into her bones. A dreamy, out-of-order review played in her brain. No memory held long. When the internal show ceased, April sat mesmerized by the fire.

When her eyelids fluttered, she knew it was time for bed. The ease of the evening stayed with her as she extinguished the campfire, put her food in the car, and removed her hiking shoes before crawling into her tent. Her recently laundered sleeping bag seemed puffier. There was no smell of earth or sweat.

Around her tent, the land was encased by the serene night. What animals moved about did so without being observed or encountered. April reviewed the different trails and paths she could explore tomorrow. Wherever she walked, she'd use her insight, skills, and hiked miles to guide her.

THE END

Thanks for joining April on and off the trails!

If you enjoyed *Hiking In*, I would appreciate a short review
where you purchased the book, on your local library's website,
or tell a friend.

Want to hear the soundtrack of April's adventures? I assembled
a Spotify playlist called Hiking In.

Plus, I've created a collage of several of the Minnesota state and
regional parks that inspired April's practice hiking and
camping. In the novel, I took some creative license with the
trails and parks.
www.billijolink.com/books/hiking-in/parks

Interested in updates and some extras? Please, sign up for my
newsletter at www.billijolink.com and find me on social media.

Mistakes happen. If you discovered an error in the novel, please
email me through my website. www.billijolink.com

AUTHOR NOTES

In July 2012, I hiked the Chilkoot Trail. I knew while on the trail that someday, I would write a story that included the Chilkoot. In *Hiking In*, I attempted to describe some of the landscapes I saw and experienced.

The following is my post-Chilkoot Facebook post.
July 24, 2012
"Just got back from hiking the Chilkoot Trail--it was a lot like summer camp. Many adventures, met really fun people & came back w/ a backpack full of dirty clothes."

The 'fear I pack' for is starvation. It's smart to pack extra, but sometimes that is too much and becomes a burden. During my Chilkoot, hikers would leave food behind in bear lockers. I suspect the overpacking of food was also not knowing how hungry a person will be on the trail.

I still have my backcountry blue backpack, but it's not named 'Big Blue.' My mom owns a suitcase my sister and I call 'Big Blue.' I repurposed the nickname.

I wore hiking boots on the Chilkoot, which I have kept and am unable to discard. Though, now I wear trail runners while hiking.

I did sleep on top of Chilkoot Pass and I caught my train back to Skagway! It was an extraordinary adventure.

Acknowledgments

Thanks to the early readers of *Hiking In*: Sarah, Elisabeth, & Carrie!
I fondly recall the people I met on the Chilkoot Trail. I hope they're out enjoying the 'trails' when they can.

ABOUT THE AUTHOR

I'm a Midwestern author who writes comfort reads that uplift, an explorer of hiking trails and neighborhoods, a library power-user, a fanatic sunglasses wearer, a card sender, a daily meditator, and will only own hardy houseplants.

I enjoy caramel rolls with coffee, the sound of gravel while running under red and gold-leafed Fall trees, Masterpiece Theater on Sunday night, loon calls as evening settles in at the lake, Rainer cherries, and reveling in my loved one's fireworks laughter.

I've nested in North Dakota near prairie and pasture that waves and shimmies in the wind.

ALSO BY BILLIJO LINK

I'm switching gears with the release of a 1930's historical novel called *Leaving Ordinary*. The first chapter is included.

Leaving Ordinary

(Publication Date: Fall 2020)

In 1926, Louise Miller was not interested in remaining on her family's Minnesota farm after graduation. At a dance, she meets the Midwest Musicale's violin player Leo Zint. After a "postcards and promises" courtship, Leo turns up and asks her to marry him and his bohemian band life. Music and adventure swing until Leo changes his tune and settles them in Bonetrail, North Dakota, which echoes the small town Louise left behind. As their new farm life rhythms begin, an economic and ecological disaster plows America into the Great Depression. Louise will discover if the grit inside her is stronger than the land blowing away around her.

CHAPTER 1

1999

Today Louise would visit the land. This trip would return her to a past she brushed against almost daily. It could happen when she filled the blue speckled enamel roasting pan used to make years of meals, dusted a color photograph of the farm framed by wheat fields and grass pastures, or heard violin music. The moments could generate cheer or reflection, and, at times, land emotional wallops.

The stretched doleful coos of mourning doves voiced her melancholy. Louise's knee hooked the bedsheet as she rolled away from the North Dakota summer sunrise that spread from between the white pull blind and the window frame.

She told herself to stop being so mopey.

Get up. You can't get out of this.

The hem of her lace-trimmed blue nightgown dropped low as she left her bed. She raised the blind seeking the hush-filled planned and pruned senior community's landscaping. Dwarf shrubs squatted in oblong beds of pea gravel or rusted brown mulch surrounded by a brochure-ready lawn.

Louise thought it was all tidy and dull.

Why can't there be more flowers around this place?

Turning from the view, Louise questioned if there was an easier way to go back. She gripped the dresser top, and her 89-year-old knees lowered her like an antique, overworked elevator. She tugged the heavy bottom drawer an inch at a time as wood scraped wood. The smell of mothballs stung the air.

I haven't looked at his violin in years. What if seeing it makes the missing hurt more?

Louise saw the travel-worn violin case. Her mind wanted to fast swing away, but her heart locked on and looked. When Louise moved into her apartment five years ago, she placed Leo's violin in the drawer of the oak dresser. Storing away the instrument had quieted memories, but their magnetic pull had not lessened: a life created by two when now there was one. Her age-spotted hand caressed the case's cracked and wounded leather. Her thumb stroked the handle.

"I miss you."

Louise let the instrument be and moved aside newer photo albums with the plastic pockets until she saw the ebony scrapbook with the ragged gilt edging. The book had the heft of longevity built into it. Louise hoisted this scrapbook and herself and went to the kitchen.

I'll make coffee first.

She brewed strong, tongue-burning coffee like all the gallons she had made before. Louise settled in at the small kitchen table that her children had given her when she'd moved into the apartment. The newer dining set wasn't as sturdy as her old farm table, but it fit the space. Taking a few sips, she steadied herself before reaching for the memory book.

This is silly. Nothing in there is going to bite me.

The coarse, ebony sheets crackled as she pulled apart and turned pages of old-timey black-and-white photographs bonded into place by paper corner brackets. One picture showed the farm's wooden windmill that creaked and swayed in the gusty prairie winds. Another, their first automobile: a third-hand used Ford truck. Family and friends grew up and grew old in the flip of pages. Grainfields and vegetable gardens in different stages of growth and seasons were kept static. This stop-and-go chronicling continued until she came to a photograph that was years out of order.

Framed by scalloped white borders, the photo showed a young couple sitting outside on uneven wooden high-back chairs next to a white clapboard house.

Louise recalled that house party. She had been eighteen, and Leo was nineteen. They'd been married a short time.

Leo's brash smile tight-lipped a cigarette. He held a violin. Leo rarely turned down an opportunity to play. Louise, next to him, smiled softly and posed in proper posture. She was not wearing a hat. Mother said ladies were supposed to wear hats outdoors. Louise never did like wearing one.

She stilled. The music was faint, but she could hear it nonetheless. It was no song in its entirety but instead a high-spirited compilation of chords, melodies, and crescendos.

She whispered, "I want the music."

Sometimes when Louise was washing her few dishes, she fantasized she could hear Leo playing. Foolishness, she knew. There was the radio or television, but she ached for him and his music. When Leo held his violin and gripped his bow, it was as if the dirt on his palms disappeared, and his musician's heart came out to play. Back on the farm, on the silent evenings when there was no music, its absence was so loud it reverberated all over the house. A person could reach out and touch the missing.

———

1926

Wheatville's town hall doors were propped open in wide welcome. Late April evening breezes attempted to cool the steamy makeshift dance hall of that western Minnesota farm town's Annual Fireman's Dance.

The salt and pepper mustached band leader's voice boomed. "Folks, welcome! We are the Midwest Musicale Extravaganza. We hope you have a grand time. Boys, let's begin."

Like a train leaving the depot, the Musicale's quartet eased, then chugged until they picked up steam and raced along the rails. Rotating on and off the dance floor were ladies wearing short-sleeved cotton dresses whose mid-calf hemlines floated and snapped as men wearing their Sunday button-up-best trousers or bib overalls spun them in polkas and waltzes amongst a fragrant fracas of rose and lily perfumes, sweat, and rolled tobacco smoke.

Sixteen-year-old Louise looked good-girl charming in her homemade flowered red and blue voile dress. Her below-the-knee hem showcased her legs, stepping and whirling across the tongue-and-groove oak floorboards. She shined from her short bobbed brown hair, held back by a green apple brain-binder headband, to her black patent leather shoes.

Her eyes were drawn to the fiddle player, not much older than herself, and his slicked-back hair. The musician's talent pushed and pulled jubilant notes across his instrument, revving up the crowd.

The fiddler's pant cuffs hung above his ankles, making his slim five-foot ten frame appear taller. The black wool fabric matched the snug suit coat gaping and straining its button threads. Early into the music show, the musician removed his coat and rolled back his shirtsleeves, displaying muscled fore-arms and a torso outline. The man's suit didn't fit, but it didn't display "farmer." The verve of his music and rascal smile kept her sneaking looks. She wished he'd ask her to dance.

He held his back straight, then tilted back, and then leaned into the rhythm's vigor. His left foot planted firm. The right foot tapped the beat. The violin player grinned at the horn player, who threw a smirk to the drummer, and the drummer beamed at the crowd as the band showed off their up and down swings of tempo and musical swagger.

At nine o'clock, the bandleader stood up from his piano and called a break and announced that the Homemakers Club was serving a meal. Wives, widows, and daughters hurried to organized positions at long food tables offering home-baked bread and cooked-to-a-blush ham. Similar to the upright pipes of a church organ, the famished and tipsy partygoers lined up to choose homegrown lettuce and cabbage salads, coffee, and water. For something stronger, a person sidestepped Prohibition and located Jacob Swansen's automobile.

Several matrons shooed back residents so the musicians could fill their plates first. Louise's insides fluttered when she saw the violin player approach her dessert table. Smiling, Louise asked, "What would you like?"

The musician's mouth corners hooked high, and then his gaze moved over the tall chocolate and vanilla cakes, juicy apple and sour cream raisin pies, and flat, brown-speckled Norwegian lefse. "Ahh...how about some of everything."

"Was that your approach at the other tables?" Louise asked nodding at the two plates he carried laden with golden fried chicken, sliced bread, sour pickles, and sharp white onion-seasoned chunky potato salad.

"Hard to pass up food like this. Plus, I don't want to offend any of the ladies."

She filled a third plate for the musician. "That's smart, and a potential bellyache."

It was then Louise noticed he was staring at her. The hall was overheated, but the added recognition of the man's interest made Louise want to fan herself with a plate. She must have been distracted for too long because he raised the plates in his hands.

She glanced down, up, and stopped at his grin. Their shared laughter skipped with nervousness.

Louise asked, "Would you like me to carry this to where you're sitting?"

"Please. Ladies first."

Louise scanned the hall. "There's the band," and moved towards the table.

The musician stretched his step to walk alongside her. "My name is Leo Zint. A pleasure to make your acquaintance. You are?"

Her keen hazel eyes noticed his sparking brown ones. "My name is Louise Miller."

"Are you enjoying the evening?"

"Yes. The music and dancing have been wonderful." She noticed him stand straighter.

"Are there any songs you would like us to play?"

Delighted, Louise said, "I like what I've heard so far. Keep doing that."

They reached the seated band members. The horn player, who appeared a few years older than Leo and wore his suit like a city slicker, pulled out the chair next to him. "Miss, this seat is for you."

Louise raised an eyebrow. "Isn't that for Mr. Zint?" Good manners dictated she address Leo formally, but Louise already thought of him as Leo.

The musician laughed. "He can find another seat. I'm Erik..."

Leo interrupted, "Don't pay him any mind. He can't help

himself when a pretty girl is around."

"Is that so?" Louise said.

"You're welcome to join us."

"I'm Colson, the bandleader, singer, and all-around musician. Nice to meet you. Erik is our horn player. Karl here is our drummer. Of the four of us, he's the loudest musician and talks the least."

Karl's quick head nod bounced with shyness, and the rest of the Musicale chuckled.

"I'm Louise Miller. I've been enjoying the music."

"You're my kind of gal," Erik said.

Louise heard Leo say under his breath, "Not tonight."

She set Leo's plate down. "I have to return to my table. It was nice meeting you all. Enjoy the food."

Louise could feel Leo watching her stroll back to the desserts. She added a frisky swish to her glide. Her rash behavior made her hands twitch. To calm herself, she rearranged platters of desserts. Throughout the meal, Louise peeked at Leo. The boisterous band ate, laughed, and invited anyone who strayed near to join their party.

When the musicians returned to their instruments, the cooled-off townspeople reassembled on the dance floor. Soon enough, the dancers wore damp clothing and high spirits, including Louise. When she looked in Leo's direction, she flashed him flirting smiles, and he reciprocated.

Colson yelled, "Last song!"

The rambunctious finale rocked the revelers who clapped and hooted their appreciation. The Musicale began packing their instruments, and the town hall cleanup followed. As Louise wiped a table, she saw Leo amble towards her.

"Did you like the rest of the show?" Leo asked.

"I did. Most everyone stayed until the end."

"I like hearing that. Tonight's crowd had a good time. When

you're standing on stage, you get to see what the audience likes and doesn't. People-watching makes the music better. Helps too if there's trouble brewing."

Louise held the rag in her hands and tugged at the ends. "You sounded good to me. Have you been playing long?"

"I bought my violin when I was thirteen. You have the long, pretty fingers of a piano player."

Louise looked down at her hands. On one hand she spread out her fingers. "Thank you. Does the Musicale leave today, or will you stay around for a couple of days?"

"We'll sleep for a few hours and then head to the next gig."

"It must be exciting to go places and play for audiences. See something other than the hind end of a cow."

Leo let loose a fast laugh. "Playing music is more fun than plowing a field. I started with the Musicale when I was fourteen. The band gave me a job and a suit that was too big for my bones. That was three years ago, and now there's more of me, and my suit still doesn't fit."

Louise giggled. "Maybe you could find someone to sew you a new suit?" and then, with a searching tone, asked, "Do you like life with the Musicale?"

"I can't imagine doing anything else." Leo cupped his hand on the back of his neck. "We're headed out. Could I...write you?"

Louise swallowed so she wouldn't stutter on her next words. "I'd like that."

She hoped Leo's request was more than a traveling man's empty flirtation.

Leaving Ordinary
(Publication Date: Fall 2020)